A LADY'S FIRST SCANDAL

MERRY FARMER

A LADY'S FIRST SCANDAL

Copyright ©2019 by Merry Farmer

Cover design by Erin Dameron-Hill (the miracle-worker)

ASIN: B07RFHH36J

Paperback ISBN: 9781074002732

Click here for a complete list of other works by Merry Farmer.

If you'd like to be the first to learn about when the next books in the series come out and more, please sign up for my newsletter here: http://eepurl.com/RQ-KX

❀ Created with Vellum

CHAPTER 1

LONDON – MAY, 1885

*L*ady Cecelia Campbell couldn't remember the last time she'd been so excited. She could barely stand still as she and her family waited at the edge of Regent's Park for the doors of the barracks to open. Every small movement from the barracks caused her heart to leap into her throat. Her head swam with anticipation. Tears even stung the back of her eyes when she thought about how long she'd waited for this day to come. But at last, it was here. Rupert was home.

"Calm down, my dear," Lady Katya Campbell, Rupert's mother and Cece's father's wife, said, resting a hand on Cece's arm. "If you don't remember to breathe, you'll swoon."

"I think she's going to swoon anyhow," Natalia

Marlowe, Rupert's younger sister, giggled, stepping closer and holding out her arms as if she would catch Cece mid-faint.

"Swooning is so antiquated," Bianca Marlowe said in a lofty voice. She couldn't hide her own enthusiasm, though. Rupert was her brother, after all, and she loved him almost as dearly as Cece did.

"I think swooning is lovely," Natalia said with a romantic sigh. In a more practical voice, she added, "I just wish I had someone to swoon over."

"You will soon enough," Katya told her. "Too soon, if you're like your sister." She eyed Bianca disapprovingly.

Bianca merely grinned up at the brilliant sunlight. The entire family was well aware of her attachment to a certain Chief Inspector of Scotland Yard, a Mr. Jack Craig, who was not only miles below Bianca in social standing, he was also older and far more experienced than was good for her.

Cece's thoughts about the Bianca and Mr. Craig situation vanished in a heartbeat as the barracks door opened. Her heart sank a moment later when a single man in civilian dress walked out, shutting the door behind him.

"Oh, when are they going to let them out?" Natalia fretted, biting her lip with a frown. The expression emphasized the distinct resemblance she bore to Cece's father, Lord Malcolm Campbell, who stood with them, frequently glancing at his watch.

"The army has any number of procedures and ceremonies before releasing soldiers from active duty," he grumbled. "It took all day when they let us go after the Crimean Campaign, and most of us were injured."

There was a good reason Natalia looked more like Cece's father than anyone in society was willing to ask about. Cece's father had married Rupert, Bianca, and Natalia's mother four years earlier, but they had secretly been lovers for decades. When the truth about Natalia's paternity had come out, Cece had been shocked, but not particularly surprised. And since the entire muddle of sharing a half-sister with the man she intended to marry made Cece's and everyone else's head hurt, they rarely spoke of it.

Because Cece *did* intend to marry Rupert Marlowe. The understanding had been in place for years, since before Rupert joined the army and ran off to practically the other side of the world without her consent. And part of her was still furious that he'd enlisted without consulting her. The conversation four years ago still rang in her head. She'd been expecting a formal proposal. She'd gotten a typically male speech about duty and country. And a week later, Rupert was gone.

She'd worried about him journeying so far south. She'd fretted over every report coming out of Cape Colony. She'd been in agony when war had broken out in 1881 and she'd heard nothing from Rupert for six months. She'd sent prayers and money and linens for bandages when she'd heard he'd been wounded in action by the Boers, then wept in relief for days when he finally wrote to tell her he would make a full recovery. Then she'd been so angry she'd thrown a vase across the room and shattered it when he wrote to say he was staying on in South Africa, even though the war had ended.

But all of that was behind her now. At last, Rupert was home.

Once again, the door to the barracks opened. Once again, Cece's heart lifted. She clutched her chest in anticipation only to be disappointed yet again. Another civilian stepped out into the street and went about his business.

"It's positively aggravating, isn't it?"

Cece started, her back snapping so straight that she was dizzy for a moment as Lady Tavistock spoke beside her. She hadn't noticed the regal young woman approach, and she certainly never would have imagined someone as admirable and powerful as Lady Tavistock would even speak to her.

"It is, my lady," Cece said, hoping her voice didn't squeak.

Lady Tavistock smiled at her with a look of friendship that warmed Cece down to her toes. She wore a fashionable walking dress in a shade of purple that indicated she was at the end of the prescribed mourning period for her husband. Lord Richard Tavistock's death two years earlier had been the talk of the town. He'd left behind an heir—indeed, the four-year-old Marquess of Tavistock clung to his mother's skirts as they watched the barracks—but it was well known that Lady Tavistock managed the vast wealth of her late husband's estate as expertly as any man could. Which was likely why the poor woman was reputed to receive at least three offers of marriage every week.

But more importantly, Lady Tavistock was renowned as the leader of the influential May Flowers, a group of women who not only involved themselves in politics, but were also rumored to control the actions of Parliament from behind the scenes.

"I take it you're waiting for your beloved?" Lady Tavistock asked.

Cece blinked, astounded that such an important woman would know that about her. "Yes, my lady," she said. "Lord Rupert Marlowe, the Earl of Stanhope." She instantly felt embarrassed about throwing Rupert's title into play, as if she were bragging.

But Lady Tavistock continued to smile as though they were friends. "I'm here waiting for my brother, Freddy," she said.

Cece drew in a breath as she made the connection in her mind. "Yes, Rupert has written frequently about the Earl of Herrington. They've become close friends."

Lady Tavistock hummed in affirmation. "Freddy has mentioned Lord Stanhope several times in his letters." She let out a breath, facing the barracks. "I'm so glad he's home. I've missed him so. Although he has little to come home to. Our father ruined the estate, and—" She pressed her lips together and shook her head. It wasn't civil to speak of such things, but everyone was widely aware that the former Earl of Herrington had bankrupted his estate and left his son with nothing more than a title. If not for Lady Tavistock's brilliant marriage to one of Lord Herrington's school friends, she would have been in exceptionally dire straits just as her brother was.

Panic welled up in Cece as Lady Tavistock remained silent, her expression sorrowful. She did the only thing she could think to do on short notice by blurting, "I was quite impressed with the speech you gave outside of the Palace of Westminster last week. Irish Home Rule is an issue I feel quite passionately about."

"Do you?" Bianca asked behind Cece.

A jolt of embarrassment hit Cece. She hadn't realized Bianca was listening. There was no telling what the wild young woman might do.

"Yes," Cece said, reluctantly shifting her stance to include Bianca in the conversation. That meant including Natalia and Lady Katya as well by default. "Gladstone is perfectly right when he says that it is long past time to create an Irish Parliament and give them a measure of control over their own destinies."

Lady Tavistock's smile returned tenfold. "I couldn't agree more," she said. "Though the opinion is not a popular one at the moment."

"A fact I find confusing and ridiculous," Cece went on. "Particularly considering British administration of Ireland has resulted in ruination for so many of its population."

"Don't say that so loudly," Natalia gasped, glancing

around them as though the disapproval of a nation was about to rain down on them.

"Why not, if it's true?" Lady Tavistock said. "We women have been told to be silent in matters of politics and importance for far too long. It's well past time we make our voice heard."

Lady Katya laughed. "I couldn't agree more. You young ones are lucky that you're able to speak as much as you can. In my day, things were very different."

"Times are changing," Lady Tavistock said with a shrug. "It's imperative that we change with them."

"I agree," Cece said. "And if we don't take charge of the change ourselves, it may never happen."

Lady Tavistock smiled approvingly at her.

Bianca, on the other hand, laughed. "I never expected to hear such radical views from you, Cece," she said.

"Oh?" Lady Tavistock asked. "And why not?"

Cece felt her cheeks go pink, especially when Bianca grinned and said, "Cece is as traditional as they come. She plans to devote her life to domestic duties as my brother's wife. She never expresses her opinions about things, even though we all know she has them."

"That's not true," Cece said in a quiet voice, staring hard at Bianca and hoping her outspoken friend would know when to be silent.

Of course, where Bianca was concerned, silence was too much to ask. "You should hear the way she scolds me for being too bold," she told Lady Tavistock with a conspiratorial look. "Cece is forever correcting my deportment and my opinions. She constantly tells me I should take care to be more deferential to gentlemen and to wait until I am spoken to before speaking."

"That's because you are a ridiculous flirt," Natalia said, both defending Cece and mortifying her at the same time. "You're going to ruin your reputation if you continue to pretend you're a man in social situations."

"I most certainly do not pretend I'm a man," Bianca said, one eyebrow arched.

Cece's face burned hotter. Bianca behaved more like a celebrated, renaissance, Venetian courtesan than anything else, expressing her opinions openly and flirting scandalously. As far as she was concerned, Cece had every reason to constantly correct her friend.

Fortunately, rather than being scandalized, Lady Tavistock laughed. "I always approve of women who speak their mind," she said. She hugged her son tighter to her side and said, "And I am teaching Ricky to appreciate them as well. You like Lady Bianca, don't you?"

The young Marquess of Tavistock nodded, blushing and giggling as Bianca wiggled her fingers at him in a wave, then hid his face in his mother's skirts.

Cece was on the verge of saying more when the door to the barracks opened yet again. Only this time, instead of a single man slipping out in civilian dress, the entire, wide door was thrown open and a veritable sea of men in red coats poured out.

She gasped, forgetting the embarrassment Bianca had caused her, forgetting Lady Tavistock's kind notice, forgetting everything but the fact that Rupert was home and would be in her arms at any moment. Her heart raced so hard she could hear her pulse in her ears as she stood on her tip-toes, searching desperately for Rupert among the men leaving the barracks.

At last, she spotted him, and tears sprang to her eyes. He looked older, slightly more careworn, but fitter and even more handsome than the last time she'd seen him. The red of his uniform coat suited him splendidly. He'd grown a moustache that conformed to the latest style—which she wasn't sure she liked—and his cheeks were rosy and full of health. And when he glanced across the street and found her in the crowd, his whole countenance lit up.

But instead of rushing to her, arms open, he turned back, saying something to one of the men behind him. That man stepped up to Rupert's side as they crossed the street. When Rupert pointed at Cece, the other man waved.

"Look, Ricky," Lady Tavistock said, lifting her son into her arms in a rare show of maternal affection for someone as highly-ranked. "There's your Uncle Freddy."

The boy waved back as Cece's heart fluttered uncertainly in her chest. Rupert still wasn't running to her. Instead, he turned to a red-haired gentleman on his other side and said something. The two of them laughed.

When the group of three finally made it across the street to where the families of the returning soldiers were waiting in the park, Cece was beside herself with uncertainty instead of joy.

"Hello, Mother," Rupert said, heading straight to Lady Katya and catching her in an enormous hug. "You look as beautiful as ever."

"Flattery will get you everywhere," Lady Katya laughed, hugging him back.

When Rupert broke away from her, he turned to scoop Bianca and Natalia into his arms at the same time. "Look at the two of you. What happened to the naughty children I left behind?"

"We're naughty women now," Bianca said in a saucy voice.

To her other side, Lord Herrington had stepped up to give his sister and nephew a strong, affectionate hug. "You've no idea how much I've missed you, Henny," he said in a voice filled with emotion.

"And I you," Lady Tavistock replied, blinking back tears.

Cece could see more unspoken depth to their greeting than she needed to be part of, so she turned away. She clasped her hands in front of her to keep from flinging herself into Rupert's arms when he broke away from his sisters. At any moment, he would open his arms wide and greet her the way she'd dreamed of for four, long years.

Instead, he stepped back to the red-haired man's side and said, "Well, O'Shea? What do you think of this splendid family of mine?"

Cece's jaw dropped and her heart sank. It was unclear to her whether Rupert included her in his family at all.

"They're splendid," O'Shea said. Cece blinked. He had to be Lord Fergus O'Shea, the Irishman Rupert had written about so often, the one who had saved his life in the Transvaal.

At last, Rupert turned to face her, glowing with affection. "And this, my friend, is the most glorious flower in all of England." His voice softened and deepened as he beamed at Cece. "This is the one and only Lady Cecelia Campbell."

Cece's smile returned, and her heart overflowed with affection. At last, Rupert stepped forward and swept her into his arms. Cece was helpless to do anything but hug him back with everything she had as she burst into tears.

"I've missed you so," she sobbed against his neck. He smelled of a different kind of soap than he'd used before departing for the army, but the essence of him was still there and as familiar to her as her own skin.

Rupert squeezed her tight, resting his head against hers. "I would kiss you like you've never been kissed before if there weren't so many people watching," he whispered against her ear.

"I don't care," Cece said, shaking with relief to have him home.

But instead of taking her up on her implied offer, he let go of her and stepped back. A moment after that, he turned to Lord Herrington.

"Lord, it's good to be home, isn't it?" he asked with a laugh.

"I'll say," Lord Herrington agreed. He stood taller and glanced around. "Is this our entire welcoming committee?"

"Who were you expecting to see?" Lord O'Shea asked in his Irish accent. "The queen herself?"

Rupert laughed and slapped Lord Herrington playfully on the back. "He's probably looking for a wealthy widow to bolster his fortunes, now that he's no longer on the army payroll."

"He already has a wealthy widow to support him," Lady Tavistock said, ostensibly teasing, but with seriousness in her eyes.

"No man wants to be supported by his sister," Rupert said, nudging Lord Herrington's arm.

"As much as he loves her," Lord Herrington added, moving back to Lady Tavistock's side and kissing her cheek.

Cece's smile faltered. It was ridiculous for her to think that Rupert would have eyes only for her upon his return, but she hadn't expected him to fall instantly into joking with his friends. Not when they'd been apart for so long. Not when she'd agonized day and night while waiting for his return.

Her heart pinched with indignation when Rupert clapped his hands together and asked Lady Katya, "Shall we all head home now? I'm famished, and I just know that Mrs. Phillpotts has something delicious waiting for me."

"Mrs. Phillpotts retired two years ago," Lady Katya said. "But Mrs. Morris has been cooking for days." She gestured to a pair of carriages waiting at the far end of the street then took Lord Malcolm's arm to start toward them.

"I hope there's room for Fergus and Freddy," Rupert started after her.

Cece's stomach tightened. He hadn't offered her his arm.

"I'm off to Tavistock House with my sister," Lord Herrington announced. "But I'll drop by for a visit in the morning."

He and Lady Tavistock nodded their goodbyes. Lady Tavistock sent a particularly sympathetic look to Cece.

The rest of them, including Lord O'Shea, marched on toward their waiting carriages. As if as an afterthought, Rupert finally held back and offered Cece his arm. But instead of whispering sweet words to her as she'd dreamed he would once he was home, he called ahead to Lady Katya, saying, "Are we all at Campbell House or Marlowe House at the moment?"

"Marlowe House," Natalia answered for him, rushing to take Rupert's other arm. "It's bigger."

Cece was seized by the sudden, irrational urge to throttle Natalia for laying claim to Rupert. Guilt eclipsed her anger, though. Natalia had missed her brother as much as she had. Still, the whole thing hadn't been the homecoming she'd dreamed of.

"Then there's room for Fergus," Rupert said as they walked. "O'Shea needs a place to stay."

"There's plenty of room," Lady Katya called back.

"Just as long as you don't forget where your loyalties lie," Lord Malcolm added. He narrowed his eyes at Rupert, then turned a protective look on Cece.

Cece wasn't sure whether she was touched and grateful that her father was apparently as aware of Rupert's less than enthusiastic greeting toward her or embarrassed that he was singling Rupert out for it in public. Either way, she wasn't certain Rupert even noticed.

"The advantage of having a complicated family situation is that it gives one a variety of homes to choose from," he told Lord O'Shea as they reached the carriages. He handed Cece into one while continuing to talk to his friend. "They're only two blocks away, though, so it's jolly convenient."

"Are you getting in?" Bianca asked once she, Natalia, and Cece were seated.

Rupert peeked into the carriage, then said, "No, there's not enough room. Fergus and I will find our own way home. We'll see you there."

Without ceremony, he shut the carriage door.

Cece wilted with disappointment. It was as though she'd waited for the delivery of a treasure for years, only to find that it was fool's gold.

CHAPTER 2

*I*t was bliss to be home. After the roughness of four years of army life, Rupert reveled in every pleasant scent that filled his family's London townhome, every soft cushion that caressed his backside as he lounged for the first time in what felt like forever, every crumb of shortbread his mother's new cook had prepared for him, every drop of sweetened tea, every ribald laugh and snort from his impish sisters, every ray of sunlight peeking through the curtains—in short, everything.

"This tops military rations any day," he said to Fergus as he bit into the last of the lemon tarts. The burst of citrus pinched his face with deliciousness, a luxury he'd forgotten how much he loved.

"It certainly does," Fergus answered with a sigh of contentment as he rested back in his seat. "I don't think I could eat another bite."

"Oh, but supper is only an hour away," Natalia said.

She sat on the sofa beside him, perched on the edge, glancing between him and Fergus with bright eyes. "Tell us again about the battle where you were shot."

"Natalia," their mother scolded. "He's already told the story once and he wrote to you about it years ago. I'm sure he doesn't want to relive it now."

"On the contrary," Rupert said. He finished the lemon tart, swallowed with a groan of satisfaction, then leaned forward as though on the stage. "It was shortly after I arrived in the Transvaal. The Boers had been mercilessly ambushing British supplies for weeks. Mail convoys were particularly vulnerable. So General Colley decided to escort a particularly sensitive mail convoy personally, so as to keep our supply lines open. I was one of the men chosen to accompany him."

"And you nearly died," Natalia gasped, clutching his arm.

"I nearly did," Rupert answered gravely. The events of that day felt like they were a lifetime ago, like they'd happened to someone else, and yet, the horror of the whole thing remained with him. "We were ambushed, like so many other convoys. The Boers, damn them, were excellent marksmen. Half our complement was killed. I was shot in the leg myself. I was only spared death because Fergus here threw me out of the way of another shot and dragged me to safety. He took a bullet in his arm for his efforts."

"And I'd do it again if called to," Fergus said, saluting Rupert with his teacup.

"We limped back to safety, and I spent the better part of the rest of the conflict convalescing," Rupert went on. "But our position in South Africa has always been under threat, from the Boers and the natives."

He glanced to Cece to see what she thought of his dashing tales of adventure and daring. He expected to find her on the edge of her seat, like Natalia, stars in her eyes. But instead, her posture was slightly slumped, and instead of watching him like a lover should, she stared morosely at her still-full teacup. Her mouth was pulled tight and there was a certain hardness to her jaw.

He couldn't imagine what was wrong with her. Was she ill? He did the only thing he could think of to bolster her.

"I was lucky to recover from those wounds as quickly as I did," he said, watching her as he spoke. "I was doubly lucky to meet Freddy, that is, Lord Herrington, in the field hospital. You're friends with his sister, Cecelia, are you not?"

Cece glanced up somewhat belatedly. She blinked, her mouth remaining tight, then said, "I admire Lady Tavistock and the political work she does immensely, but no, I do not think she counts me as one of her friends."

"But you were standing side-by-side this afternoon," Rupert argued.

Lines formed between Cece's eyebrows and her jaw tensed further. "Physical proximity does not define the closeness of a relationship. You of all people should know that." She punctuated her remark by sipping her tea. Her lips twitched into a grimace, and a moment later she set her teacup aside, then muttered, "Although perhaps it does."

Rupert frowned, at a complete loss. Clearly, she meant something by her words, but he couldn't see what it was for the life of him.

Once again, he fell back on what he knew. "Africa was a baptism by fire, certainly. We were all lucky that the conflict was short-lived. The bulk of our duties after the peace was signed were mostly guarding British interests and subduing the local population." He paused, studying Cece's expression to see if his words were allaying the fears he assumed she had, then said, "So really, there was no need for you to worry."

Instead of relaxing in relief, Cece's posture stiffened, and if he didn't know better, the look she shot him was one of indignation. But she kept her mouth firmly shut.

"There was that one time we caught that German chap trying to make off with supplies," Fergus said with a smirk.

"And he wasn't even a Boer," Rupert laughed, gladder than he could express that his friend had saved him from the unfathomable censure of the one person who should have been most overjoyed by his return. "None of us expected the bloke to have that revolver with him," he went on, launching into the story of the German scavenger who had tried to use them all for shooting practice just so he could make off with a sack of bread and cheese.

Unfortunately for him, Cece's inexplicable attitude didn't improve, even when he and Fergus switched into stories of the mischief they'd all gotten into during their free time. He was particularly careful to emphasize that he hadn't engaged in any inappropriate behavior where women were concerned, even though the majority of his fellow officers had indulged whenever a bit of skirt presented itself, English, Boer, or native. He'd remained loyal and true to Cece through it all, writing to her whenever temptation reared its ugly head and dreaming only of her.

Which was why her coldness now was a complete mystery to him.

It was a relief when Mr. Stewart announced that supper was ready. Rupert leapt to his feet, anxious to get away from the awkwardness that had descended over the room.

But when he began to approach Cece to escort her into the dining room, she stepped out of his way, marching toward her father—who had wandered into the parlor along with Mr. Stewart—and taking his arm without so much as a second glance for Rupert. Dread pooled in his stomach.

It didn't lessen at all when his mother swept up to his side and took his arm without him offering. Especially when she led him into the hall in the opposite direction from the dining room.

Rupert decided to nip the whole problem in the bud

by asking his mother, "What the devil is going on with Cece? Is she ill?"

His stomach sank further when his mother raised one of her severe eyebrows at him. "My dear boy," she began in her most foreboding tone, "I did not raise you to be an ass, so kindly stop being one."

Rupert gaped, an indignant sound bursting from him. "I'm not being an ass, Mother. Cece has turned into a cold fish. One would think that after four years apart she'd be clinging to my side and sighing with joy."

His mother's disapproving eyebrow arched higher. Then she shook her head. Rupert knew he was deep in the soup. "That dear girl has waited four years for you," she said in a tone that made it clear whose side she was on. "She remained loyal to you. She declined invitations that she should have accepted because a letter arrived from you. She refused to dance when asked for years because she didn't want so much as a whisper of a rumor to reach your ears. She studied military dispatches and any news of South Africa religiously so that she would be aware of what you were facing."

Rupert's heart swelled at the revelations. It also pinched with helpless confusion. "That's all wonderful," he said. "So why is she so clearly displeased with me?"

"Because you're ignoring her, you dolt." His mother smacked his arm hard enough for Rupert to wince. "Because you're spewing on about war stories and telling her she wasted her time worrying."

"I didn't say—"

"Because you're giving more of your attention to Lord Fergus O'Shea than you are to her," his mother went on.

"Fergus is my guest," Rupert argued. "I have a duty to make him feel at home, especially after what he's been through." He leaned closer to his mother and said, "His own family barely speaks to him. His father sent him a curt letter when his mother died and nothing else. And the man saved my life. Besides, the bond of brothers in arms is almost stronger than that of brothers by blood. I'm not sure if you'd understand."

"Is he more important than the woman you profess to love?" his mother asked.

Rupert opened his mouth, but no sound came out. He dropped his shoulders and shook his head. "I didn't want to say this because you're my mother, but I was hoping that my true reunion with Cece could happen in private, where we won't be disturbed or questioned." He fixed her with a significant look that he never would have dared use except under extreme circumstances.

To his surprise, his mother laughed. "If you think you'll be spreading honey on your toast any time soon, then you know even less about women than I thought you did."

She tugged him on, proceeding to the dining room at last.

"Believe me, Mother. I know about women," he said. "Your friends saw to that years ago."

His mother only laughed harder.

Dinner ended up being a far more frustrating affair than Rupert ever would have imagined for his first, grand meal at home. The conversation that danced around the table was lively and interesting, but led mostly by his sisters—who had grown far too bold for comfort in his absence. Lord Malcolm chatted mostly with Fergus about the situation in Ireland, although Fergus wasn't as up to date as Malcolm was, having been away from his homeland for so long. Rupert tried his best to engage Cece in conversation, but she had taken up a place at her father's right hand, which was across the table and two places down from him.

He wasn't truly able to get a word in edgewise with her until after supper, after the ladies had retired to their sitting room and the gentlemen for cigars and brandy, and when most of them were on the verge of giving up and going to bed for the night. It was only then that he was able to catch Cece's hand as she attempted to exit the parlor and to lead her down the hall to his mother's library. He considered it a good sign that she came with him willingly and that he didn't have to scoop her over his shoulder and carry her down the hall.

"Cece," he said, filling the single word with every emotion that had been locked inside of him for the past four years. "Thank God we're alone at last."

He drew Cece into his arms and slanted his head to kiss her. She let out a sigh and sagged against him, parting her lips and letting him drink her in. It was so good to kiss her again, the way he'd dreamed of for so long, that he closed his eyes and threw his whole heart into it. She tasted as sweet as nectar, and her body felt like heaven against his. She'd filled out in the most delectable way in four years' time, and it took a monumental effort of will not to caress her curves.

"I've wanted to kiss you like that for so long," he breathed at last, resting his forehead against hers. "How I've missed you."

"And I missed you," she said in a small voice, glancing longingly into his eyes. "So very much. You cannot imagine."

"I can," he said. "I can imagine the way you've held yourself back from social engagements, the way you must have sat by the window, pining and waiting for a letter from me, the way you must have dreamed of the blessed day when you will become my wife."

To his vast surprised, she jerked out of his arms, staring fire at him. "Is that what you imagined?" she asked, her voice sharp with pique.

Rupert blinked. He could practically hear the zip of sniper bullets. His stomach certainly dropped the way it had in the ambush. "Isn't that what it was like for you?" he asked uncertainly. It was what his own mother had told him, after all.

Cece planted her hands on her hips. "Do you think that I simply sat by, waiting for your return so that I could do nothing more than be your countess and bear your heirs?"

He blinked again, feeling heat rise up his neck even

as his heart pounded against his ribs in fear. Yes, fear. He'd never seen Cece so upset before, and at a time when she should be over the moon. "Yes?" he answered hesitantly. "Isn't that what you've always wanted? Isn't that what we used to talk about before I enlisted?"

"Before you enlisted," she huffed in a tone that was almost mocking. "An action, might I remind you, that you took without my consent, without consulting me."

"I had to serve my country," he explained. "It was my duty."

"And what about your duty to the woman you love?"

Her question caught him completely off-guard. His mouth flapped as he scrambled to think of an answer. "Perhaps you don't understand," he said. "As Earl of Stanhope, it is my duty to uphold the laws and interests of the empire. How can I be expected to do that if I haven't served? We both know that I am unusually young for so much responsibility."

"And that excuses you from showing the woman you profess to want to marry an adequate amount of respect?" Her voice reached a high squeak that made him wince. "I've missed you, Rupert," she went on with passion, taking a step closer to him. "I've dreamed of this day, of our reunion, for four long years. And you repay me by giving your friend, a man who has been right there with you every day for almost your entire absence, more attention than you give to me?"

At last, Rupert thought he understood the nature of the problem. His mother had been right about the cause of Cece's upset. He smiled, relaxing his stance and resting his hand on Cece's cheek. "I understand, sweetheart. It's only natural for a woman to want to spend time with the man she loves. But Fergus is my guest. He's like a brother to me, the brother I never had. I have a responsibility toward him. Certainly, you must see that. Once you've had a good night's sleep, you'll see that I'm doing the right thing by making him feel at home. After all, the two of us will have our whole lives together."

He leaned in to kiss her, but she pulled back so fast he lost his balance.

"I thought you were a decent man," she said, her chest heaving with emotion. "I thought you were sensitive and romantic, but you're just as much of a cad as the blackguards in Parliament who kicked and screamed and fought against the act my father fought so hard to pass ensuring the rights of married women."

"I supported that act with my whole heart," Rupert insisted, anger rising over his confusion. "I would have voted for it if I'd been in the country at the time."

"Precisely," Cece snapped. "If you were so keen to serve your country, you should have stayed at home and taken up your seat in the House of Lords rather than abandoning everyone who cares about you and everything that needed your attention to nearly get yourself killed playing soldier."

Rupert was so alarmed by her outburst that he blurted, "Calm down," before thinking better of it.

"I will calm down when I'm ready to," she fired back.

"I will calm down when you understand how wretchedly you've treated me."

"I love you," he nearly shouted in indignation. "I've never loved anyone else. I've never so much as kissed anyone since we met and fell in love."

"Are we in love?" she asked, her chin tilted up, crossing her arms.

"Of course, we are," he growled. He blew out a breath and shook his head, rubbing a hand over his face. "Why don't you go to bed now," he went on. "It's been an eventful day for both of us, and I dare say we're both exhausted. Everything will look better in the morning."

"Will it?" Her brow arched in frightening imitation of his mother when she had her nose out of joint.

"I'm certain it will, dearest," he said, trying his best to placate her.

He stepped closer to her, opening his arms to hug her. She dodged out of the way, her arms still crossed, marching toward the door.

As she reached the doorway, she turned back to him with the superiority of an empress and said, "I hate that moustache, you know. It doesn't suit you." She then swept out of the room as though she'd won the argument.

Rupert would have run after her to make things right. Maybe. More likely, he would have stood where he was and shouted every one of the colorful obscenities he'd learned in the army. He didn't have a chance to do either. Before he could move from his spot, Lord Malcolm stepped into the doorway Cece had just stormed through.

His brow was knit in a scowl that made lesser men piss their trousers. Rupert's insides turned to jelly at the fury in his would-be father-in-law's eyes.

"She's right, you know," Lord Malcolm said in a voice that reminded Rupert not only that Lord Malcolm had served in the army and seen action himself, but that he'd killed men when called on to do so. "That moustache makes you look like a cunt."

Without another word, Lord Malcolm walked on, leaving Rupert with the feeling he'd been thoroughly dismissed. He sagged, breathing out the frustration his conversation with Cece had left him with. And he'd thought the war had ended three years ago. Something told him it had only just begun.

CHAPTER 3

*C*ece had been beside herself with excitement about the ball to welcome the returning soldiers home before her disappointing reunion with Rupert, but by the time she climbed the steps to Spencer House, where the ball was being held, with the combined mass of her family and her mother's friends, her heart was heavy and her enthusiasm dampened.

"I know that things have been...difficult between us these last few days," Rupert said in a quiet voice as he escorted her down the long hall toward the gaily decorated ballroom, "but tonight is supposed to be joyous, festive. What would it take for me to coax your beautiful smile back into existence?"

Cece turned to him with a look of utter indignation. "Whether or not I smile is none of your concern," she said through a clenched jaw. Her arm felt as brittle as glass tucked into his.

Rupert sighed, deflating. "I'm sorry, Cece. I don't know what I'm doing wrong. You weren't like this when I left for South Africa."

It took every ounce of her willpower not to launch into a tirade and to tell him that she wouldn't have been the woman she was now if he had never joined the army in the first place. The last few days had taught her that no good was to be had from pointing out what he would never understand.

They joined the queue of guests waiting to be announced as they entered the ballroom. Cece had half a mind to step back to her father's side and to be announced with him instead of Rupert, but her father was busy whispering something—probably entirely inappropriate for the public sphere—into Lady Katya's ear. She would have hung back to enter with Bianca and Natalia, but they were already waving to gentlemen they shouldn't have been and making too-loud comments about who they hoped to dance with. Cece was stuck with Rupert.

And it wasn't as though she wanted to disassociate herself from him. She loved Rupert dearly, in spite of his boorish behavior since returning home. They'd had sweet moments in the past few days along with the rough ones, it was just that—

"Oh, look. Reese is here," he said mere moments after they had been announced and paid their respects to Lord and Lady Spencer. "It's been years since I saw him. Looks like Freddy's already talking his ear off." He turned to glance past the cluster of their families to where Lord O'Shea brought up the rear of their pack. "Fergus, I have to introduce you to an old friend, Lord Maurice Howsden. You don't mind, dearest, do you?" Rupert sought out her permission almost as an afterthought.

In spite of the sour taste in Cece's mouth over yet another abandonment, she sighed and said, "Go along."

"Thank you, my angel." Rupert squeezed her hand before letting her go and ushering Lord O'Shea across the room to his friends.

Several of the aristocratic guests cast suspicious looks at Lord O'Shea's bright, ginger hair as they left, but the uneasiness that filled Cece's stomach at their blatant show of prejudice was nothing to the hollow sensation of being on her own once more.

"Don't mind my brother," Bianca said, sweeping up behind Cece, taking her arm, and carrying her a few yards to the side, where a group of young, available women had claimed a spot from which to survey the ballroom and show off their gowns. "He continues to be stuck in a regimental mindset. Given time, he'll return to the ranks of the civilized."

"Are we civilized?" Natalia asked in a jovial voice as the three of them found a spot from which to view the increasingly active ballroom.

"I should say not," an unkind voice muttered behind them.

It was followed by a chorus of titters, but when Cece

glanced over her shoulder with a frown to rival any her father could produce, every one of the young ladies nearby wore placid, innocent faces. She shook her head and ignored the comment, turning to face forward.

"I understand his loyalty to his friends," she said, brushing an imaginary piece of lint from her kid gloves. "But I would have thought his loyalty to the woman he loves would count for something as well."

"Of course he loves you," Bianca said, too loud once again. Cece winced at the implication she believed Rupert had fallen out of love during his time away. "Men in love are horribly obvious."

"And you would know?" the mean voice behind them asked.

It was Bianca's turn to glance over her shoulder with a sharp look. "As a matter of fact, Claudia Denbigh, I would. Which is more than you can say, you sour old cow."

Cece winced.

Lady Claudia gasped in offense. "How dare you address me in such a manner?"

Bianca turned to face her fully, crossing her arms. "Which part of my statement offends you more? The fact that I, the daughter of an earl and step-daughter of a marquess, would address you by your given name or the fact that, after three seasons, you have not had so much as a sniff from any gentleman of worth?"

Cece would have groaned aloud if it wouldn't have

drawn even more attention to Bianca's reckless lack of respect for all propriety. Then again, Bianca had long since torn up the rulebook of social etiquette and thrown the pieces into the fire of her own boldness.

Lady Claudia's back stiffened. "I would rather go without a beau than debase myself for a man born in the gutter who has barely risen to the depths of the middle class."

A victorious grin spread across Bianca's lips. "That's because you do not have the first clue what you're missing."

Cece gulped and pressed a hand to her stomach. It was bad enough that most of London knew Bianca was particular friends with Mr. Jack Craig—who was merely a policeman in their eyes and who, it was rumored, had been born in a brothel—for Bianca to even imply that her association with Mr. Craig had resulted in anything less than absolute, virginal innocence was tantamount to social suicide. As far as Cece knew, nothing untoward had actually happened between Bianca and Mr. Craig, but that hardly mattered.

Particularly not when Lady Claudia raked Cece with a disapproving look and sniffed. "No wonder Lord Stanhope has cast you aside. You have the stench of scandal about you."

"Cece is the least scandalous person I know." Natalia rushed to her defense. "She is far gooder than all of us." She paused, tilting her head to the side. "Is gooder a word? Well, it should be a word."

"Ignorance and debauchery," Lady Claudia said, her chin tilted up. The friends that flanked her sides imitated her posture. "I have no doubt that, by the time the season is finished, the finer part of society will not lower themselves to even look at you, let alone consider you part of their social circle." She directed her remarks at Cece rather than Bianca, which came as a bitter surprise. "And as for Lord Stanhope...." A sly grin tugged at the corners of Lady Claudia's mouth as she glanced across the room to where Rupert stood, chatting with his friends. "I've no doubt he will be on the marriage market again within weeks."

Cece had never hated anyone in her life, but the fire that burned in her gut at Lady Claudia's comment was the closest she felt she could come. She suddenly understood the level of freedom Bianca must have felt in having no qualms about expressing her true feelings boldly. It was torture to try to maintain a blank expression in the face of such an insult.

She was saved from any more humiliation by none other than Lady Tavistock approaching their tense group.

"Ah, Lady Cecelia," Lady Tavistock said, smiling directly at Cece and stopping by her side. "How lovely to see you this evening."

"Lady Tavistock." Cece nodded formally to her, heat flooding her cheeks. The last thing she needed was for the confrontation and humiliation to be witnessed by someone she admired so much.

But instead of making things worse, Lady Tavistock

laughed gently and said, "You must call me Henrietta, since we are friends." She glanced pointedly at Lady Claudia.

Lady Claudia's cheeks flooded with color and her jaw clenched tight. "I would not be so quick to associate yourself with someone so notorious," she hissed.

"Lady Cecelia is far from notorious," Henrietta said in as pleasant a voice as if they were talking about the blooms in their garden.

At that thought, Cece took notice of the white iris pinned to both Henrietta's and Lady Claudia's bodices. She sent a furtive look between the two women. She'd forgotten that Lady Claudia was a May Flower as well.

The confrontation was stopped before it could escalate as Henrietta hooked her hand under Cece's elbow and said, "My dear, you must come meet Mr. Langley. I'm sure he'd be terribly interested in your thoughts about Irish Home Rule."

Cece wasn't sure if it was a real invitation or if there was such a man as Mr. Langley, but she was so grateful for the excuse to get away not just from Lady Claudia, but from Bianca and Natalia as well that she walked eagerly with Henrietta halfway across the ballroom before letting out a breath of relief.

"Thank you so much for rescuing me, my lady," she said once they were away, pressing a hand to her flaming cheek.

"Henrietta," Henrietta corrected her. "I was earnest in my wish for you to call me by a familiar name. And I'm earnest in my desire to introduce you to Mr. Langley. He is a rising star in the House of Commons, but I think he needs a bit of a push to come around to Gladstone's views on the essential nature of Irish Home Rule. Ah, Mr. Langley."

They reached a group of older men who were already deep in discussion. Henrietta introduced Cece, then launched into her own views of the topic at hand. Cece held her own as best she could, but it was just her luck that the political discussion Henrietta had drawn her into was directly adjacent to Rupert and his friends. Remembering the finer points of the argument in favor of setting up an Irish Parliament and allowing it to govern the day-to-day aspects of Irish life was next to impossible with the focal point of all her emotions within earshot.

Still, she tried her best to keep Rupert out of her thoughts.

"I believe the issue is one of sovereignty," she said in response to Mr. Langley's question about why a nation that was so close in proximity to England would need their own parliament. "That and the fact that England has done such a poor job administrating Ireland. The Irish people have suffered so."

"They have indeed," Henrietta agreed. "Not just in the famine of the eighteen-forties. The tragedies of the last decade could have been avoided if only the Irish had been able to govern and respond to their own crisis."

"Your compassion serves you well, Lady Tavistock,"

Mr. Langley said with a smile. "It is a shame you cannot run for a seat in Parliament yourself."

"Believe me, sir, I have had the same thought on a number of occasions," Henrietta said with a smile.

"It's a wonder you do not remarry, my lady," Mr. Barr, one of the other gentlemen in the conversation, said. "You could have more influence with a like-minded husband."

"I could have a great many other things that I do not wish for as well," Henrietta answered.

Cece marveled at how smooth and witty the reply was, particularly as she considered the implied disapproval of Henrietta's single state rude. And yet, she, too, wondered why someone so beautiful and clever, not to mention wealthy and influential, was content to remain a widow. Perhaps she didn't need a husband. Perhaps she had a string of lovers, like Lady Katya had when she was widowed. The idea of a woman being free to take a lover captivated and excited Cece.

"I would wager Lady Tavistock remains in her current state because she has yet to meet a man strong enough to tempt her out of it," Rupert said, turning from his conversation to hers, as if he could hear her thoughts. "Fortunately, that is not true of all beautiful young ladies." He smiled fondly at Cece.

Cece's nerves bristled. How could Rupert compliment her and make her feel so small at the same time?

"The problem with the Irish governing themselves is that so few of them are capable," Mr. Thomas, the third man in the original conversation steered the whole thing back the topic at hand. As much as she disagreed with the man's stance, Cece was beyond grateful to him for drawing attention away from her.

"It's ridiculous to say the Irish are incompetent," Rupert said, pulling focus back to himself. "Why, Lord O'Shea here would be a prime contender for Irish Prime Minister." He shifted his stance enough to physically draw Lord O'Shea, Lord Howsden, and Lord Herrington into the conversation.

Cece had nothing against Rupert's friends in and of themselves, but she could have screamed at the way that, once again, Rupert had turned to them instead of remaining content with what he had. As a result, the men would inevitably take over the conversation, relegating the ladies to passive observers, in spite of their intelligence and grasp of the situation.

"You think you're up to the task of governance?" Mr. Thomas said, raking Lord O'Shea with a narrow-eyed glance.

"I wouldn't presume," Lord O'Shea said, looking as though he wanted to back out of the confrontation.

The orchestra struck the opening notes of a waltz. Cece thanked God for the opportunity to end what was swiftly turning into an embarrassing confrontation. She turned to Rupert, resting a hand on his arm, and whispered, "I would like to dance."

Rupert patted her hand, but remained focused on Mr. Thomas. "In a moment. Are you saying, sir, that my friend, who has served in Her Majesty's Army for the past six years, and served with distinction, I might add, and who has obtained the rank of Lieutenant, would be unable to handle the reins of government?"

"Rupert," Cece whispered sharply.

"*He* may be able to," Mr. Thomas said. "But it is a well-known fact that the Irish are inferior in almost every way."

Dread dropped into Cece's stomach like a brick thrown in a murky pond. She drew her hand away from Rupert as he tensed, ready for battle.

She was ready to turn and beat a speedy retreat to avoid what was sure to turn into a bloodbath when Lord Howsden leaned close to her and asked in a calm voice, "Would you care to dance, Lady Cecelia?"

It wasn't the rescue she'd hoped for, but Cece wasn't about to turn down the offer. "Yes, please, Lord Howsden."

She didn't know whether she wanted to sigh in relief or sob as Lord Howsden took her arm, led her out to the center of the dance floor, then took her into his arms for the waltz. She barely knew the man, but at that moment, he was her hero.

They danced in silence for a minute or so. Only when Cece began to notice the pointed stares and clusters of old women whispering behind their hands as they watched did she begin to feel nervous.

"Forgive me," Lord Howsden said. "I didn't mean to cause comment by dancing with you. It's just that I haven't asked any woman to dance in more than five years."

"Oh," Cece said, blinking and feeling even more self-conscious. "I should thank you even more then."

"I could see your distress at the conversation and, as a gentleman, I had to act," he went on.

"And I suppose it doesn't help the gossip that I have rarely danced myself in Rupert's absence," she said.

Lord Howsden smiled. "Good heavens. What have we done?"

It dawned on Cece that she liked Lord Howsden, in spite of him being one of Rupert's friends and thus the cause of his neglect. All she knew about the man was that he had been married for long enough to produce an heir before his wife died of a fever, that he was a moderate voice in the House of Lords, and that his brother had scandalized everyone by marrying an American woman and moving to Wyoming Territory. He was as handsome as any man, with refined features, broad shoulders, and an air of intelligence about him. Everything about him was as far from the aggressive, military mien Rupert and the other returning soldiers had. And he danced like a dream.

She would have liked to spend more time in the genteel man's company, but as soon as their dance was over and Lord Howsden escorted her back to where the political conversation was still going on, one look at Rupert told her that would be impossible.

"What do you think you're doing?" Rupert asked in a

tense, quiet voice once Lord Howsden let her go. He cupped her elbow and led her to the side so they could speak undisturbed.

Cece blinked at him. "I was dancing," she said, astounded by the force of his objection, ire rising within her. "Seeing as you didn't want to."

"I never said I didn't want to, only to wait," he snapped.

"To wait?" Cece gaped at him, growing hot. "You have the audacity to ask me to wait?"

"I was in the middle of a conversation."

"A conversation of little importance," she said, standing taller. "I have waited for four years, Rupert. After all that, a woman grows tired of waiting."

Fire filled Rupert's eyes, enough to make Cece nervous. Without another word, he slipped her arm through his and marched into the heart of the ballroom.

She expected him to stop in the midst of the couples that were forming for the next dance, but instead, he continued to march, all the way to the far end of the room where the orchestra was tuning for the next song. Without so much as a by your leave, he let go of Cece's arm and stepped up onto the small dais where the conductor stood.

"You're tired of waiting?" he told her as those nearest to the orchestra dropped their conversations to turn and look at him. "Fine. You won't have to wait anymore. Ladies and gentlemen," he called out in a loud voice.

A cold sweat broke out on Cece's back, and her irritation mingled with alarm. She turned, eyes wide, toward the ballroom. There must have been two hundred people in attendance that night at least, and all of them were turning to stare at her.

"Ladies and gentlemen," Rupert repeated, clapping his hands together for extra notice. "I trust you are all enjoying your evening," he said as soon as he had the entire room's attention. "I'm sure I speak on behalf of all us soldiers when I say it is good to be home."

Cries of, "Hear, hear!" rang out around the room, as well as a spattering of applause.

But Rupert didn't stop there.

"This is an especially happy day for me as well, for I have been blessed with something I have longed for these past four years. I am exceptionally pleased this evening to announce my engagement to the beautiful and loyal Lady Cecelia Campbell."

He gestured toward her.

The room broke into applause.

Cece's heart dropped to her feet. But even as it did, the rage that had been smoldering within her boiled over.

"No," she shouted. She stepped up onto the dais with Rupert, standing toe-to-toe with him and glaring at him with the heat of a thousand suns. "No," she shouted again, even louder. "How dare you make such a presumption? How dare you stand up here and announce something so personal without consulting with me first? Can you do nothing without treating me as a mere afterthought?"

It wasn't until she was halfway through her angry questions that she realized the rest of the room had gone dead silent. Two hundred startled, confused faces stared back at them, mouths hanging open, hands poised as if they weren't sure whether to celebrate or call for a constable.

That didn't stop Cece or her fury.

"How arrogant must you be to simply assume that I have been idling here the whole time you have been gone, that I want nothing more for my life than to be your wife? I deserve a great deal more than that." Her voice grew so loud that she was certain she could hear it ringing in the rafters. "I demand passion and excitement. I want more than to be an ornament on your arm. You have failed to see me as more than an accessory in your life and I will not stand for it another day. I want more than that."

She jerked to face the stunned crowd, finding Henrietta's face in the sea of awed and uncomfortable guests.

"I want to be like Lady Tavistock," she declared, pointing toward her new friend. "I want to have a voice— a voice in politics, a voice in my family, a voice in my own life. I want to stand up for causes I believe in, like she does, and not to be treated as a pet. I want to be like Lady Katya, with a string of lovers, if I so choose. I want to be a modern woman. I am through with being second in importance to your friends, and I am through with you."

She whipped back to face Rupert, adding, "And I don't care how fashionable it is, that moustache looks dreadful on you—like, like an emaciated hedgehog trying to crawl up your nose."

Rupert's face had gone pale, and he stood there, wide-eyed with shock. Cece had no sympathy for him, though. None at all. She fixed him with one, final, furious glare, then stepped down from the dais and shoved her way through the scandalized guests toward the door.

When she was nearly there, she burst into tears. The orchestra had struck up the next dance and conversations had resumed, but she felt as though her life as she knew it had ended as certainly as if she'd fired a cannon into it.

The one, shining moment of grace in the whole, embarrassing debacle was when her father appeared seemingly of nowhere and wrapped her protectively in his arms.

"There, there," he said, hugging her close.

Cece spotted Lady Katya, Bianca, and Natalia hurrying toward her out of the corner of her eye, but all she really wanted was her papa.

"I'm proud of you," he said, his Scottish brogue thicker than usual. "I want to wring your neck for making such a public spectacle," he went on, "but I'm proud of you for speaking up."

"Yes," Bianca said. "If only more women would do the same."

"Hush," Lady Katya warned her in a more serious voice than usual. "We should leave."

Cece nodded, pushing gently away from her father and wiping her eyes on the back of her gloves. She knew exactly why Lady Katya was in such a hurry to shepherd them out of the room. Bianca may have approved of her shocking display, but Cece was smart enough to know that she had, in all likelihood, just destroyed any chance she had of being accepted into polite society for the rest of her life.

CHAPTER 4

$\mathcal{C}$ece's head throbbed when she awoke the next morning. It reminded her of the time, several Christmases ago, when she'd accidentally imbibed too much wine and had been utterly miserable in the morning. The difference this time was that her soul ached with regret as well as her head and her body.

Still, she managed to drag herself out of bed and dress with the help of Gemma, the upstairs maid on whom fell the unfortunate task of helping her, Bianca, and Natalia with bathing and dressing. Gemma was judiciously silent as she buttoned the back of Cece's morning gown, but Cece had no doubt that the sober maid had heard the entire story of the scandal she'd caused at the ball.

Her feet were like lead as she left her room and headed downstairs to breakfast. Not that her stomach felt up to the task of digestion. She dreaded running into Rupert in the hall and flinched at every creak of the floorboards and every opened door. She'd embarrassed him as much as she'd embarrassed herself, perhaps more so. His pride had to have been sorely wounded by her public outburst. Not that he didn't deserve it. But in the cool light of day, her heart withered more over the ass she'd made of herself and him than because of her anger.

Her family was all gathered around the breakfast table, Bianca and Natalia chattering away as her father read *The Times* and Lady Katya *The Daily Telegraph*. Because, of course, Lady Katya would never stoop to reading one of the journals designed specifically for women. Rupert was not there, though, and neither was Lord O'Shea.

As soon as she appeared in the doorway, Bianca spotted her. She cut short her conversation with Natalia and jumped to her feet, rushing to put her arm around Cece.

"Come in, dearest," she said as though speaking to a child or an elderly aunt. "Sit down and fortify yourself."

"I'll fix a plate for you," Natalia added, leaping up and charging toward the sideboard to load a plate with eggs and meat and all the things Cece knew she wouldn't be able to stomach.

"I'll pour you some tea." Bianca continued to fuss over her as she pushed Cece into her usual place by her father's side at the head of the table. "You poor thing," she added with a sigh.

"I am not a poor thing," Cece said quietly, head bowed. "I am an embarrassment."

All at once, Bianca, Natalia, and even Lady Katya burst into protest.

"Of course, you're not," Lady Katya told her soothingly.

"We all make mistakes," Natalia agreed, though Cece was convinced she was too young to have had a chance to do more than step on a gentleman's foot while dancing.

"I've done far worse," Bianca added.

"You made an ass of yourself," her father said without glancing up from *The Times*. Everyone at the table went silent, staring disapprovingly at him. He glanced up and around at the ladies. "Well, she did," he said, then shrugged. "But you're beautiful and you're intelligent, and when beautiful, intelligent women put on a show in public, it only makes them more alluring." He finished by sending a look across the table to Lady Katya that was entirely inappropriate for so early in the morning.

Lady Katya blushed and returned the look with one that reminded them all that age was not a barrier to passion.

It was not, however, the sentiment Cece wanted to see expressed in that moment.

She drew in a sullen breath as Bianca set a full cup of sweet, milky tea in front of her and Natalia slid a plate heaping with food into her place. "Where is Rupert?" she asked, reaching for the tea.

Another, awkward silence followed. Cece's heart sank even before Lady Katya cleared her throat and said, "It was decided, after you went to bed last night, that perhaps Rupert would be better off residing at Campbell House for the moment."

Cece lowered her teacup without taking a sip. She swallowed the urge to weep, but managed to say, "We are fortunate to have two townhouses at our disposal."

"Yes, we are," her father said, turning a page in his paper. "But if he drinks my scotch or smokes any of my cigars, I'll hang him from the banister in the hall and have Mrs. Mellon beat him with a carpet-beater."

Cece managed a weak smile for her father's joke. At least, she thought it was a joke. Her father had a bit of a reputation for ruthlessness. It didn't matter either way. Rupert was gone and she'd driven him away. He'd deserved it, but she could have found a more dignified way to bring him to his senses.

"Think of it this way," Bianca started once she'd resumed her seat.

"No." Cece sat straighter, holding up a warning hand. "Please. I cannot bear to talk about this anymore. Please just let me eat my breakfast in silence."

A heavy pause followed before Bianca let out the breath she'd taken for whatever speech she'd wanted to make. Cece reached for her teacup, staring at her over-laden plate and bolstering herself to take just a few bites.

The table was silent for two minutes before Bianca and Natalia resumed their previous conversation—something about how abominable Lady Claudia and her friends had behaved and how Natalia had pulled off a coup by convincing Lord Eakins to dance with her.

Things were beginning to feel almost settled and Cece's appetite had just begun to return when Mr. Stewart appeared in the breakfast room doorway with a letter on a silver salver. Cece only sent him a cursory look, until he cleared his throat and said, "Lady Cecelia, this letter has just come for you."

Instantly, Cece's fledgling appetite vanished and her stomach turned sour. The letter could only be from Rupert. He had likely written to her at length, scolding her for her behavior. She was both mortified and furious at the thought. What right had he to censure her when he was the one who had interrupted the ball, drawn attention to the both of them, and humiliated her with his shocking and entirely inappropriate assumptions?

But when Mr. Stewart brought her the letter, a whiff of rose tickled her nose. Not only that, the envelope he presented was a subtle shade of pink. Cece took it from him with a frown and a brief thank you.

A chill of absolute dread shook her at the sight of the embossed initials in one corner of the envelope, HH.

Natalia—who had leaned over her shoulder to get a look as soon as the envelope was in Cece's hands— exclaimed, "Good Lord. It's from Lady Tavistock."

Heat flooded Cece's face. Even more so when she opened the letter and read its brief contents. *"Dear Cecelia. Please call on me at your soonest possible convenience this morning on a matter of great importance. Yours, Henrietta."*

Cece tucked the letter back into the envelope with a gulp, pressing the whole thing to her stomach.

"Why does Lady Tavistock want you to call on her?" Natalia asked. It didn't surprise Cece one bit that she'd read the private correspondence.

"No doubt to give me a thorough dressing down for dragging her into my personal troubles," Cece said in a rather sick voice. She stood, pushing back her chair. "I'd better go right away and get it over with."

"Do you want me to come with you?" Bianca asked with a little too much enthusiasm, rising from her place across the table.

"No." Cece shook her head. "The condemned always go the gallows alone."

"I'm certain everything will be fine," Lady Katya said as Cece rounded her end of the table. "Henrietta Hopewell has always been a sensible woman."

Cece could only reply with a nod as she stepped into the hall. Mr. Stewart had heard the entire conversation and offered to have the carriage prepared before Cece could reach the stairs. She plodded up to her room to change into something suitable for visiting, and by the time she plodded down again, the carriage was waiting.

Only a few minutes later, she arrived at Tavistock House and was escorted to Henrietta's fashionably-decorated morning parlor. Cece had resolved to take her punishment as a lady. She kept her chin up and her shoulders square, but she couldn't bring herself to manage even a slight smile. She was utterly unprepared when Henrietta smiled fondly and rose from her settee as she entered the room.

"Ah, Cecelia. How lovely to see you," she said, crossing the room to take Cece's hands and to kiss her cheek like a friend. "How are you holding up?" she asked with what appeared to be genuine concern and sympathy.

Cece's jaw went slack, and for a moment all she could do was stare at Henrietta, still half expecting to get a tongue lashing. "I'm...." She hesitated, but the well of emotion that suddenly bubbled up inside of her was too much to resist. "I'm shattered," she said with a burst of regret. "I'm so terribly sorry for embarrassing you the way I did last night. It was utterly unforgivable. I let my frustration get the better of me, and now I've caused a scandal that is affecting so many people."

Henrietta continued to surprise her by responding with a light laugh and, "You're new to causing a scandal, aren't you?" She met her eyes with a mischievous glint.

Cece could only stare back at her in shock. "You don't hate me for it?"

"Heavens, no," Henrietta said, drawing Cece deeper into the room and gesturing for her to sit. "In fact, the passion of your speech and the way you stood up for yourself so boldly are exactly the qualities we need to further our cause. And I wouldn't mind having a string of lovers myself."

Cece perched on the edge of the chair she'd been offered as though she would be asked to jump up and leave at any moment. She blinked at Henrietta's words, too many thoughts jostling in her head. She latched on to the one that seemed safest. "I don't understand. *Our* cause?"

Henrietta's smile turned triumphant. "The May Flowers, of course. I suspected before, but now I am certain. You would be the perfect addition to our ranks."

Every other surprise Cece had had until that point was dwarfed by the shock of what she could barely comprehend Henrietta was asking. "Are you...are you saying you would like me to join the May Flowers?" she squeaked.

"That is exactly what I'm saying." Henrietta turned to the elaborate arrangement of lilies, tulips, and cherry blossom beside her. She took a small pair of scissors from behind the vase, clipped one of the pink tulips, and handed it to Cece. "It's pink tulips this week," she said. "We change weekly. A bouquet will be sent to you early each Monday morning with the week's flower, although you're welcome to procure your own if those begin to fade." She put her scissors down and brought out a long pin from behind the vase. As she handed that to Cece as well, she went on. "We wear our flowers above our hearts, bloom up. I don't need to tell you that the flower of the week is to remain a closely-guarded secret until such a time as we are seen in public. To avoid imitators, of course."

Cece was too astounded to pin the tulip to her bodice on her own. Henrietta must have seen her hesitation. She stood and took the tulip from her, doing the pinning herself.

"I need all the help I can get speaking up for the causes that matter within the group," she went on. "I regret to say that there have been divergent opinions about several issues within the May Flowers in the last few years, as there have been in the Liberal Party. And not all of our members consider themselves Liberals. I am in particular need of help with Irish Home Rule, and since you explained the issue so cleverly to Mr. Langley last night, I knew I could count on you."

"But I'm no expert," Cece said, finding her voice again at last as Henrietta resumed her seat. "I only know what I have heard my father and Lady Katya discussing and what I have read in the newspapers."

"Ah, but already you know more than most women, and I dare say most men in London," Henrietta said. "I can see you have an inquisitive nature, and that is what matters most. We have a rally in St. James's Park next week, but that gives us plenty of time to research the relevant issues and to come up with a strategy for your speech."

"My speech?" Cece's voice rose to an impossible treble. She blew out a breath and shook her head. "I can't imagine you want me giving any sort of speech after the one I unwittingly gave last night. Everyone who means anything witnessed my horrible behavior. Why would they take a word I say seriously?"

"Because you stood out," Henrietta explained.

"Because you spoke aloud thoughts that most women are condemned to keep locked inside of them. Do you know how many women wish they could express the things you did last night? How many ache to have a chance to tell the men in their lives, the men who neglect and belittle them, just what they think?"

Cece closed her mouth, pressing her lips into a line, before saying, "It was not my intention to speak for those who cannot speak."

"Perhaps not last night, but wouldn't you love to be their voice going forward?"

The question hit its mark and sank deep into Cece's heart, finding a wellspring of determination underneath her shame and regret. Once tapped, that spring flooded her with a world of new emotions.

"Yes," she said, bursting into a smile. "Yes, I would like to be that voice."

"Perfect," Henrietta said, a wicked grin settling on her lips. "Now, let's talk about those lovers we would like to have."

Rupert stomped from one end of the study in Campbell House to the other, his footfalls heavy and his brow knit in a dark scowl. His head throbbed after barely sleeping a wink the night before. It didn't matter how vast and comfortable Campbell House was, it wasn't his home. The expansive bed wasn't his own. Most annoyingly of all, Cece wasn't there with him.

"It's damnably unfair," he said, crossing back through the gauntlet of sofas that faced each other in the center of the room.

"Life is never fair," Reese said with a sullen look, his arms crossed.

"You can say that again," Freddy agreed from the other side of the same sofa.

His two friends exchanged a quick look before dragging their eyes away from each other and following the course of Rupert's pacing.

"What isn't fair about it?" Fergus asked from the other sofa. Unlike Reese and Freddy, he seemed perfectly at ease, stretched out across the sofa with a cup of coffee in one hand. "You're the one who put your foot in it last night."

Rupert stopped just past the sofas and turned to glare at him. "*I* put my foot in it?" he demanded, incredulous. "Cecelia was the one who broke off our engagement in front of hundreds of people in the most humiliating way possible."

Fergus's mouth twitched and his green eyes danced with Irish mirth. "Were the two of you actually engaged to begin with? From the way I understand it, the promise between you was only ever implied."

Heat rose up Rupert's neck and he resumed pacing. He only got as far as Malcolm's desk before turning back and marching to the sofas to defend himself. "So what if there wasn't a formally stated engagement. Cece knows that we were meant for each other. We've had an understanding for years. It was outrageous of her to contradict me the way she did."

His statement was met by silence from his friends. Silence and averted looks. Not one of them was willing to look him in the eye, nod, and agree with him. Instead, they peeked nervously at each other, appearing almost embarrassed.

"I am right to be furious, aren't I?" he asked, his certainty slipping.

Reese cleared his throat. Freddy chewed his nails. Fergus chuckled and shook his head.

"Come on, gents," Rupert said. "Tell me I am the wronged party here."

At last, slowly, reluctantly, his friends glanced in his direction.

"You could have handled the situation differently," Reese said.

"After all, there really isn't a formal engagement between the two of you, only an informal understanding," Freddy agreed.

"You pushed her into it," Fergus said, far more direct. "What was the poor woman supposed to do but assert herself? You dragged her up there and more or less announced to a crowd that you were the master and she the submissive female."

A cold slither of guilt curled its way through Rupert's gut. "But I am the master," he said. "The man is always the master of the house. It's always been that way and it always will be that way."

Fergus laughed, sitting straighter. "You know who you sound like? My father."

"What does your father have to do with anything?" Rupert grumbled, moving to the table where the coffee service was set up, although he really needed something stronger.

"My father is merciless," Fergus said with surprising passion. "You should see the way he treats his tenants. They're poor farmers, in a vulnerable position. Famine wiped out their father's generation, and famine hit them all again in seventy-eight. But how did he handle it? Did he give them assistance and feed their starving children? Did he loosen the burdens on them and give so much as a thought to their plight? No. He idled away his time on his English estate, demanding more than they were capable of, and setting that bastard, Connolly, as overseer until every one of them was bled dry."

"What does Irish politics have to do with Rupert's female problems?" Reese asked, clearing his throat.

"It's the same thing," Fergus went on, his passion towering. "We have been placed in a position of power, and we abuse it. At home and abroad."

"I'm not abusing a position of power where Cece is concerned," Rupert argued. "I love her and she loves me."

"And how do you show it?" Freddy asked, his voice far quieter and softer than Fergus's.

"I...." Rupert's mouth hung open. Come to think of it, what had he done to show Cece how much he loved her since returning home?

"Expressing love is the most difficult challenge any of us men face," Reese said in a circumspect voice, staring at a spot on the carpet. "The feeling is so nebulous to begin with. How does one let their beloved know that the sun doesn't truly rise until they enter the room? That it sets far too early when they leave and stay away? How does one convey the feeling that their heart is not truly alive within them except when they can be with their beloved? Especially when those feelings have been so inadequately expressed before."

Silence followed Reese's emotional speech.

At last, Freddy said, "That was beautiful."

Reese glanced to him, but turned quickly away, his face red.

Rupert resumed his pacing, telling himself he hadn't seen what he knew full well was right in front of his face where his friends were concerned. He had bigger things to worry about.

"So what if I did make a hash of things?" he asked in a reticent voice, stroking his moustache—the feature Cece abhorred so much. "What if it was my fault?"

"It was your fault," Fergus said, leaning back against the sofa once more. "Make no mistake about it."

"So what do I do about it?" he asked, turning to his friends and extending his arms as though appealing for answers.

"The same thing we did after being defeated by the Boers," Fergus said with a shrug. "You retreat, which you've already done by moving here. You regroup your forces, which you're doing, both by entertaining us and by conversing about the mess you made. And finally, you plan a new strategy and course of attack."

"Are you suggesting I start over where Cece is concerned?" Rupert asked, both dreading the prospect of erasing the last five years of their relationship and wooing her all over again and knowing it was what he had to do.

"It seems fairly obvious," Freddy said. "First you have to apologize for what you put her through."

"What *I* put *her* through?" Rupert's brow flew up.

"Then you have to show her that you truly do love her and that what you want more than anything is to make her happy," Fergus went on, ignoring his incredulity.

"Spend time with her," Reese suggested. "That's the best way I know of to express how much you care. Do the things she wants to do."

"How do I know what women like to do?" Rupert asked in a huff.

"I'm beginning to understand why Lady Cecelia was so upset," Freddy said with a teasing grin.

Rupert frowned at him, but he knew what Freddy meant. He knew what all of his friends meant. He was being a prick, letting his pride get in the way of his good sense. But he'd spent years fighting for what he believed was right and noble, fancying himself a hero, nearly dying in the process. It was a rude homecoming not to be congratulated for his efforts, even if it was arrogant of him to expect nothing but praise for a job well done.

At last, he let out a breath and flopped onto the sofa beside Fergus.

"Fine," he said. "I'll start over. I'll pay more attention to Cece. If she'll see me. I'll try to find out what things she likes, and, heaven help me, I'll do them. But if I end up sitting beside a fire, holding yarn on my hands while she winds it into a ball, not one of you has the right to laugh at me for it."

"We won't need to," Fergus said. "We're already laughing at you for being a stubborn stick-in-the-mud."

"You might actually find that you like the same things she does," Reese said.

"You won't know until you try," Freddy said, summing everything up succinctly.

"I guess not," Rupert said. Though it was vastly uncomfortable to set out into the uncharted waters of the feminine world.

CHAPTER 5

St. James's Park felt far cooler than Cece thought it should for early May when she arrived at the rally several days later. Grey clouds skittered across the sky, matching the gusts of winds that blew at Cece's sturdy, caramel-colored walking dress. She'd had no idea what one wore to a rally about Irish Home Rule in St. James's Park, but since a bouquet of cream-colored orchids had arrived at her house that morning, signaling a change in decoration for the May Flowers, Cece had dressed to match.

"There are so many people here," she commented to Henrietta shortly after arriving and glancing around at the increasing crowd.

"Yes, isn't it marvelous?" Henrietta said with an excited smile. "It shows that people care about the Irish and about the issues that face them."

"Or that they believe those of us defending them are

ridiculous and they want to see our downfall," Cece replied in a barely-audible voice.

There were quite a few fashionably-dressed women with orchids pinned to their bodices, which indicated she wasn't alone with Henrietta in the cause. Not all of them looked pleased, though. Several glanced up at the cloudy sky, murmuring to their friends about rain. Some eyed the growing crowd of middle-class men who had come to observe the debate with wary looks. And a few studied Cece with disapproval.

One of those was Lady Claudia Denbigh.

"I thought we had decided the entire group must approve of any new members," she said, gripping the handle of her elaborate, French parasol so hard Cece was surprised the ivory didn't crumble in her hands. With the sun behind clouds, there was no reason for the woman to carry the thing except to show off how terribly expensive it was.

Henrietta's smile didn't diminish by a hair as she greeted Lady Claudia. "I felt as though we could make an exception," she said with a simple gesture, as though it were obvious. "Lady Cecelia has shown herself to be a powerful voice in London society."

Lady Claudia barked an ugly laugh. "Lady Cecelia has shown herself to be a scandalous harridan." She sniffed and looked down her nose at Cece.

Cece gulped, scrambling to find a way to handle the situation with the sort of grace Henrietta displayed. She settled on smiling and saying, "You look quite lovely today, Lady Claudia. And what a beautiful parasol."

Lady Claudia's face pinched, as though she had no idea what to do with a compliment when she'd expected confrontation. "Thank you," she said with a superior air, giving her parasol a twirl. "My brother, Charles, the Earl of Basingstoke, gave it to me. It cost five pounds. But then, Charles always was generous. I'm his favorite sister, you know. And his Irish estates have been so profitable since he hired that new man, Johnson or Jameson or something like that, to manage them for him." She fixed Cece with a smile as if daring her to top that.

Cece kept her smile in place and said, "You're so very fortunate."

She was spared having to make further conversation with Lady Claudia as a well-dressed man who didn't quite look like an aristocrat stepped up onto a small dais and announced in a booming voice, "Ladies and gentlemen, can I have your attention please?"

"This is it," Henrietta whispered, resting a hand on Cece's arm. Her eyes glowed with excitement as she watched the man on the dais. "That's Mr. Henry Shaw. He's a close friend of Charles Stewart Parnell himself."

"What is the Irish Question?" Mr. Shaw asked as his increasing audience quieted. "Is it the question of whether our Irish neighbors should govern themselves?"

A few voices in the crowd shouted, "No!" They were largely ignored as everyone continued to focus on Mr. Shaw.

"Is it a response to the dreadful situation in Ireland in the last decade, in the forties, and now? Is it a pesky annoyance that takes up Parliament's time with endless filibusters?"

"Yes!" someone in the crowd shouted and was met with a round of laughter.

"No," Mr. Shaw went on. "The Irish Question is the defining moment of morality in the British Empire. It is the kernel at the heart of our duty toward our subjects. It is the single most important issue that faces this nation today."

"It's a bloody nuisance," someone else yelled. They were met by cheers of agreement.

Mr. Shaw continued to ignore them. "Today, we will hear from representatives of the core of British morality. For who better to guide our consciences and show us the way than the women which form the backbone of everything we are?"

His question was met by a combination of derisive snorts and cheers of approval that made Cece's blood feel as though it were rushing through her in a cold panic. That feeling only intensified when Mr. Shaw went on.

He glanced briefly at a paper in his hand, then announced. "Our first speaker this morning will be a new voice of reason and sensibility, Lady Cecelia Campbell." He gestured toward Henrietta, who pointed subtly to Cece.

Cece's heart shuddered within her as a smattering of

applause broke out in the crowd. Her mouth dropped open as she glanced to Henrietta with wide eyes.

"Go on," Henrietta encouraged her, hooking a hand under her elbow and escorting her forward. "You have so much to say."

"I can't say it," Cece whispered tightly. "I'm not prepared. I haven't written a speech or anything."

"You don't need a written speech," Henrietta assured her. "All you need is to speak your mind. You're only expected to say a few words to warm the crowd up for Mr. Dillon."

Cece had heard the name Dillon before, but her mind was scattered into too many pieces for her to match the name to how she had heard of him. Henrietta ushered her up to the dais, and when they reached it, Mr. Shaw offered a hand and helped her to step up.

The moment Cece stared out at a sea of faces from the dais—some curious, some hostile, some leering—her throat squeezed so tight that she didn't think she could whisper a prayer, let alone speak out in favor of Irish Home Rule. Up until the disastrous ball the week before, she'd never so much as stood in front of a group larger than her family and close friends to sing or recite. The task Henrietta had pushed her into was daunting, to say the least.

"What do you think of the Irish being granted the ability to govern themselves, Lady Cecelia?" Mr. Shaw asked, prompting her to say something.

"I—" The single word came out as a croak. Prickles

broke out down her back, and her hands went completely numb.

But then she saw him. Rupert was standing at the far edge of the crowd, Lord O'Shea by his side. He wore a look of surprise that bordered on disbelief. And it rankled.

Cece let her shoulders drop as she let out a breath. How dare Rupert just stand there, waiting for her to fail. Did he think her incapable of speaking to a crowd? Did he, like too many of the other men arrayed in front of her, think that a woman's opinion meant nothing? Did they think that women had no opinions at all? Her father hadn't raised her to be a weak and simpering mouse. She was the daughter of Lord Malcolm Campbell, and she would behave accordingly.

"Thank you, Mr. Shaw," she began in a loud, clear voice, turning to nod at Mr. Shaw. "You are quite right when you say that the Irish Question is at the very heart of our nation at this moment. And I will answer the questions you posed."

She turned toward the audience, glancing across the expectant faces staring back at her. She caught sight of Henrietta's encouraging smile out of the corner of her eye and Rupert's dazed look of shock.

"It is absolutely essential that Ireland be given control of its domestic politics," she said, her confidence rising. It was a revelation to have so many people, so many men, listening to her. "On the one hand, as great as our nation is, we have been woefully inadequate in our reactions and responses to crises so close to our own shores. If we cannot respond with speed and efficiency to our closest colony, how can we effectively administrate the rest of our empire? On the other hand, who knows the needs and concerns of the Irish people better than they do?"

"The Irish are incompetent," a middle-class man shouted from the crowd. "They're illiterate animals without the mental faculties to govern a potato, much less a nation."

On instinct alone, Cece answered, "And you know this from personal experience of speaking to every Irishman?" A few chuckles followed before she went on with, "If the men are as incompetent as you believe them to be, perhaps we should allow Ireland to be governed by its women."

An even louder chorus of laughter rose from the crowd. It wasn't entirely mocking either. Quite a few of the men listening to her appeared to like what she was saying. It filled Cece with a sense of power, a sense of possibility. It made her feel as though she truly did have a voice. Now all she had to do was use it.

Rupert stared at Cece as she handled the heckler far more deftly than most men he'd seen give speeches in the House of Lords. His heart thrummed in his chest as she went on.

"Home Rule is a solid concept," she continued, her voice strong and clear. He could see her relax into her speech with each new idea she spun. "It has worked brilliantly with Canada, for example. The Canadian people were granted self-rule in eighteen sixty-seven, and for nearly twenty years now, they have continued to be productive, efficient, and forward-thinking."

"They're not Irish," another heckler bellowed from the fringes of the crowd.

Cece turned to him and blinked as casually as if he'd attempted to sell her rotten apples in the street. "On the contrary," she said. "I believe a great many Canadians emigrated from Ireland in the last few decades. Or does your ridiculous belief in the inferiority of the Irish mind spring from an insistence that there is something in Irish waters which addles the brain."

"It's called whiskey," the man shouted. He was greeted by rude laughter from his friends.

"Well, if whiskey is what makes men weak of mind and incapable of self-governance, I can think of quite a few Englishmen who should be removed from their positions of authority at once."

An even larger burst of laughter and applause met Cece's words.

Rupert wasn't sure if it was the response she was getting, the confidence that glowed from her, or the brief, superior smile she flashed suddenly in his direction, but his reaction was complete and encompassing. His heart wasn't the only thing that throbbed at the scene playing out in front of him. His trousers were suddenly tight.

This was a side of Cece that he'd never seen before, and it was magnificent.

"I do not believe the commonly-held assumption that if Ireland were to be granted its own parliament, the entire empire would collapse," Cece went on. "Though I know that is the backbone of the argument against Home Rule. What I believe is that—"

"Lord Stanhope, you must put a stop to this horrific display at once."

Rupert's attention was shattered and his state of growing arousal doused as thoroughly as if he'd been thrown into an icy pond. Lady Claudia Denbigh was standing right next to him. The ridiculously ornate parasol she carried came close to poking his eye out as he turned to her.

"I beg your pardon?" he asked, irritation flaring.

Lady Claudia stared up at him with a look of superiority and interest. "You must stop this, my lord."

"Stop what, Lady Claudia?" Rupert asked.

"That." Lady Claudia threw her hand out at Cece, who was continuing to speak with a vigor that lit her face and made her blue eyes sparkle. "Lady Cecelia is your would-be bride, is she not? You and you alone have the power to halt her ridiculous show this instant, and you should exercise that power."

Rupert chuckled, sending a fond look Cece's way. "Lady Cecelia has made it quite clear that I have no power over her whatsoever," he said.

"Then your engagement is not final?" Lady Claudia asked.

"Not at present," he said, suddenly wishing it weren't so. He would have given anything to lay claim to the magnificence he was witnessing. A new part of him wished he had the right to sweep Cece into his arms to express just how intimately her newfound boldness ignited him.

"So you and Lady Cecelia are not together?" Lady Claudia asked.

Rupert almost spoke his thoughts aloud, but at the last moment, he realized just how pointed Lady Claudia's question was. The cat was actually fishing for cream. He faced her again with what he hoped was a mysterious grin. "I honestly couldn't say, my lady," he answered.

Beside him, Fergus snorted.

Lady Claudia burst into a mercenary smile. "What a curious development," she said. Her smile hardened, and she went on to say, "So do you plan to put an end to Lady Cecelia's embarrassing display?"

Applause broke out before Rupert could answer. He turned back to the dais just as Mr. Shaw was shaking Cece's hand and helping her step down and return to Lady Tavistock's side.

"It looks as though my intervention will not be needed," he said. "Lady Cecelia has come to her senses on her own."

Lady Claudia pursed her lips, looking thoroughly displeased that Rupert didn't have the opportunity to cause another scene. She opened her mouth to say something else, but Rupert had no interest in it.

"Excuse me, my lady," he said, nodding slightly, then marched past her toward where Cece and Lady Tavistock were moving to the edge of the crowd.

He dodged his way through several men who had given their attention to the next speaker—an Irish laborer who instantly launched into a tirade about the abuses working class Irishmen were facing—his eyes fixed on Cece. She noticed him well before he reached her and already had her arms crossed when he made it to her side.

"Well done," he said anyhow, smiling and brimming with arousal at his proximity to her.

Cece blinked, her defensive stare softening. "I would have thought you would disapprove," she said.

"He most certainly does disapprove."

Rupert winced at Lady Claudia's statement from directly behind him. He pivoted to see that she had followed him closely. Fergus had followed as well and stood a few feet behind, looking as though he were watching a particularly entertaining circus act.

Fergus might have been on to something. The air between Cece and Lady Claudia crackled with tension. Clearly, there was no love lost between the women. Rupert handled it the only way he knew how.

"Lady Tavistock," he said with a generous nod. "Have you been introduced to my friend, Lord Fergus O'Shea?"

"I don't believe I have been," Lady Tavistock said

with a knowing grin, taking a half step forward and extending her hand, both as a greeting for Fergus and to serve as a physical barrier between Cece and Lady Claudia.

"The pleasure is all mine, my lady," Fergus said, taking Lady Tavistock's hand and bowing over it. From his bow, he glanced up at her with the sort of rakish grin that ladies loved. Indeed, Lady Tavistock's cheeks went pink at the cheeky look.

"I shall be lodging a formal complaint about this, you know," Lady Claudia broke the silence that followed in a peevish voice.

Lady Tavistock withdrew her hand from Fergus's and turned to her with a brief flash of annoyance before assuming a neutral look. "A complaint?" she asked, managing to sound far more mature than Lady Claudia. "What sort of complaint, my dear?"

Lady Claudia's jaw went hard. "About her." She inclined her head toward Cece. "At no point has our position on the Irish Question been discussed."

"The May Flowers is a political organization," Lady Tavistock said with a slight shrug. "We make our voices heard about the issues that matter the most to this country."

"We do," Lady Claudia agreed. "But only on the proper side of arguments."

"You do not believe in Irish Home Rule?" Cece asked.

Lady Claudia looked at her as though she'd suggested

she believed in rolling back protections on child laborers. "I most certainly do not, and neither should the May Flowers." She stared at Lady Tavistock once more. "It is an outrage that you should set someone to speak on our behalf who holds such counterproductive points of view."

"I support Irish Home Rule," Lady Tavistock said, as if giving a reminder.

"Well, I do not," Lady Claudia snapped. "The Unionist viewpoint is the only one that decent people should hold. And if you persist in flouting your radical views in public, believe me, there will be consequences for the May Flowers as a whole."

Lady Tavistock looked as though she would quell the whole argument, but Lady Claudia didn't give her a chance. She tilted her chin up and whipped around, smacking Fergus with the side of her parasol as she did, before marching away.

"Well," Lady Tavistock said. The single syllable summed everything up as well as could be expected.

Rupert shook his head, glad that he wasn't a woman or subject to the furies of a woman scorned. Although, in fact, he was. He turned back to Cece, determined to launch his plan to woo her back to his side.

But before he could so much as smile at her, she looked him up and down and said, "If you will excuse me, Lord Stanhope, I really must be getting home now." She turned and walked away without so much as a "by your leave", leaving Rupert stunned in her wake.

CHAPTER 6

*C*ece bristled with energy, good and bad, inside and out. Standing on the dais, addressing a crowd of mostly men about an issue of such importance had been thrilling. The first few seconds had been terrifying, but after that, it felt as though her heart had latched onto what she believed and had spoken for her. She didn't know how she'd maintained a façade of confidence, how she'd answered the men who heckled her, and how she'd delivered her argument without shattering into dust with nerves.

Those nerves got the better of her as soon as she was out of the limelight and back by Henrietta's side. That was when she began to tremble at the audacity of what she'd done. So much so that she wondered if the thrill she'd experienced as the center of attention and the crash that followed was what opium-eaters experienced in the throes of their addiction.

That was the moment when Rupert rushed up to her, flushed with a sort of excitement that left her trembling for other reasons entirely. He'd never looked at her with that particular kind of admiration before. It was a hidden blessing that the odious Lady Claudia barged into their group, commandeering the conversation before Cece was called on to speak rationally. It gave her time to settle herself.

She still hadn't recovered fully by the time Lady Claudia marched off, which was why it had been absolutely necessary for her to remove herself from the situation. But as she reached the edge of Pall Mall and began striding in the general direction of Mayfair, her hand pressed to her stomach in an attempt to diffuse the butterflies, guilt assailed her. She shouldn't have run off on Henrietta the way she had. It was rude to abandon the rally before it was finished. She had never been so inconsiderate before. What on earth had changed her?

Her answer came in the form of Rupert chasing after her, calling, "Hold up. You shouldn't walk all that way alone. I'll escort you."

Instantly, Cece stopped and turned to Rupert with pursed lips and a stern frown. Her expression was a mask to her true, much more tumultuous feelings, though. A dozen emotions hit her at once at the sight of Rupert jogging to catch up with her—indignation that he was ordering her around once again, relief that she wouldn't have to walk the whole way to Mayfair by herself, and a far more tempting emotion that heated her blood and made her heart race, but that she didn't want to name.

"I'm perfectly capable of walking home alone," she told him, fighting to maintain her newfound dignity in the face of years-old desires.

"I suspect you're capable of doing a great many things that I have never dreamed of," Rupert said, out of breath, as he reached her side.

They continued along in silence, passing several prominent houses and clubs before cutting across Green Park. The longer they walked, the stronger the butterflies in her stomach grew.

At last, she stopped, turned to Rupert, and demanded, "Why are you staring at me without making conversation?"

Rupert blinked in surprise, an entirely too fetching grin lighting his expression. "My apologies," he said. "I was lost in my own thoughts, transported by the wonders I have seen this morning."

"What wonders?" she asked, eyeing him suspiciously and walking on at a slower pace. She told herself the decrease in speed was to preserve her energy, but a mischievous part of her wanted to extend the walk home as long as possible. It was the first time she and Rupert had had any extensive length of time alone together since his return.

"The wonder of seeing something I have never seen before," he said with a casual shrug.

She sent him a sharp, sideways look, as if warning him not to toy with her.

He caught her look and his cheeks reddened. "I didn't know you were such a capable public speaker," he said.

"My speech at the ball welcoming the soldiers home the other night didn't alert you to my skill?" she said with wry teasing, though inwardly her gut twisted with embarrassment.

Rupert laughed. "Let's just say I was too astounded by the content of your speech the other night to appreciate the skill with which it was delivered."

The heat of embarrassment permeated every part of Cece. At least, she thought it was embarrassment. It was the kind of heat that tickled and pulsed, and it seemed to grow hotter with every sidelong look at Rupert she stole.

"You've changed quite a bit in my absence," Rupert said after another uncomfortable silence.

"As I have been telling you for days," Cece said in a flat voice.

"No, but you have," Rupert went on as though she'd denied it. He studied her for a few more seconds as they crossed out of Green Park and into to the lattice of streets lined with the townhomes of England's highest and brightest. "I think I like these changes."

Cece blew out an impatient breath as they paused at an intersection to let a carriage pass. "Whatever changes you may see, I can assure you, they weren't undertaken for your enjoyment."

"No, of course not," he said, then continued to study her as though she were a dazzling curiosity imported from foreign shores.

"If I have changed at all, it is to suit myself," she said, unable to stand the renewed silence. It had never been so difficult to carry on a conversation with Rupert before he entered the army. But then, if she were honest with herself, they had never really had anything serious to talk about all those years ago.

"I should count myself lucky, then," Rupert said as they walked on. "The changes you've made for yourself show great promise of benefitting me as well."

"It was unintentional, I can assure you." Speaking to him in such a high-handed, stilted way was beginning to make her heart hurt, so she looked for a way to shift the conversation. "You abandoned your friend, Lord O'Shea, in St. James's Park, you know."

"Fergus won't mind," Rupert said with a casual laugh. "Not when he has someone as delightful as Lady Tavistock to entertain him."

A jolt of jealousy nearly stopped Cece in her tracks. Did Rupert find Henrietta to be delightful? She forced herself to dismiss the notion.

"Besides," Rupert went on, helping her efforts. "You are far more important to me than Fergus."

They reached another intersection where they had to wait for a passing carriage. She arched one eyebrow at him. "That is a far different tune than you were singing the other day," she said, a little sharper than she intended to. The goal was to not give in to jealousy, after all.

Rupert smiled at her, swaying close enough to brush the back of his fingers along her forearm in a wickedly flirtatious gesture. "I have been made to see the error of my ways."

Cece's heart thumped hard against her chest as the carriage passed and they crossed the street. Marlowe House was half a block ahead, and they couldn't reach it soon enough. In all the time she had known him, Rupert had always been kind to her. He'd been sweet and attentive before he left, and emotional in the letters he'd written from South Africa. But he had always maintained a respectful air. Now, however, he stood a little closer than was appropriate, smiled with a little too much fondness, and gazed at her with a look that hinted he was interested in far more than the mildness of her temperament or her goodness.

She wasn't the only one who had changed in the past four years. As prim and proper as a major part of her was, a new, pulsing part of her was tantalized by what felt like decidedly carnal interest on his part. But, so help her, if that sort of interest had sprung up simply because she had boldly spoken her mind and without continued admiration for her more wholesome attributes, she would slap him straight back to Africa.

"I have friends now as well," she said as they neared home. "Whether you've seen the error of your ways or not, I know the value of maintaining relationships with others."

"You must school me in these matters then," he said as they climbed the steps of Marlowe House and pulled the bell chain.

Mr. Stewart answered the door before Cece could come up with a suitably withering reply, before she was able to decide how she wanted to reply to such overt flirting. She stepped into the house and removed her hat while her blood pumped wildly through her. It could be an absolute treat to flirt in the most wicked way possible with Rupert. She wasn't the same doe-eyed schoolgirl she'd been when she met him, after all. Having Bianca as a friend had educated her in shocking ways. On the other hand, she would be devastated if Rupert turned out to be as much of a cad and a rake as any bounder running around London looking for a good time.

Ironically, it was Bianca who saved her from having to decide what kind of woman she wanted to be around Rupert.

"Cece! Rupert! You're home." She rushed down the hall before Cece had shrugged out of her coat—which Rupert smoothly helped her remove without being asked. "You'll never guess," she went on, her eyes as bright as a child with a new toy.

"We never will," Rupert told her in a teasing tone.

"Of course, *you* never would," she snapped back in true, younger sister style. She took a breath, assuming a more mature and commanding air. "Mama has decided to host a ball."

"Mama?" Rupert gaped. "Hosting a ball?"

"Yes." Bianca's shoulders dropped. "And why should that be such an unusual occurrence?"

"Mama hates hosting large events," Rupert said, removing his own coat and handing it to Mr. Stewart. "She's more of a private supper and musicale hostess."

Bianca snorted. "That only goes to show what you know. She's been entertaining like mad since marrying Lord Malcolm. I think she likes to remind people that she married her Prince Charming in the end. It's why she's hosting the ball at Campbell House."

Rupert frowned, which Cece found curious. At least until he said, "Campbell House is my residence right now. And Mama wants to host a ball there?"

"She's obviously up to something," Bianca said, gesturing for the two of them to follow her down the hall and into the library once their outerwear was taken care of. "And if you ask me, it has everything to do with getting the two of you well and truly engaged. But I plan to use the event for my own purposes, of course. I am Mama's daughter, after all." They reached the library and she turned the corner, sending them a mischievous glance over her shoulder as she did.

Cece hesitated before entering the room, biting her lip. Bianca had brushed across the idea with lightning speed, but it was clear to her that Rupert had heard the important bit as well as she had. Lady Katya must be hosting the ball in an effort to push the two of them together.

"I dislike being pushed around," she told Rupert in a quiet voice.

"As do I," he grumbled in return, then marched ahead into the library.

It was a surprising moment of camaraderie that shifted Cece's internal balance yet again as they entered the library, the kind of moment that made her want to explore the vagaries of free love, like she'd proclaimed at the miserable ball. At the rate she was going, she probably would find herself formally engaged to Rupert by the end of the week.

"I didn't expect to see you back home so early," Cece's father said, rising from the sofa he'd been sharing with Lady Katya. He set the book he'd been reading aside and crossed to greet Cece with a kiss on her cheek. "I was under the impression political rallies lasted far longer than an hour and a half."

"Lady Tavistock asked me to speak," Cece said, sending her father a look that reflected the way she'd felt as Henrietta pushed her toward the dais.

Her father burst into a proud smile. "And how did it go?"

"Brilliantly," Rupert answered.

"Oh?" Lady Katya put her book aside and rose as well. "You were well-received?"

"She was the highlight of the entire rally," Rupert

said, smiling with as much pride as her father—something she found as unnerving as it was flattering.

"I was the first one to speak," she said, downplaying the intensity of the moment. "And I was so dizzy from being the center of attention by the time I stepped down that I had to excuse myself from the crowd."

"Understandable," Lady Katya said, walking up to Cece's father's side and slipping her arm around his waist. "I remember the first time I spoke at a political meeting. I was so exhilarated I couldn't sleep that night."

"That wasn't the only reason you couldn't sleep that night," Cece's father added in a purring voice.

Sharp embarrassment flared through Cece. She looked away, but that only turned her toward Rupert. Rupert was watching her with a scintillating smile that sent the same sort of restless energy through her that her father and Lady Katya's display had.

"What is this about a ball?" she asked, her voice pitched far higher because of her discomfort.

Lady Katya broke away from her father as she said, "I've decided to host a ball next week at Campbell House."

"That's what I told her," Bianca said, sitting on the sofa beside Natalia, who was deeply absorbed in a book.

"Any special occasion?" Cece asked.

Lady Katya smiled mysteriously, glancing from Cece to Rupert. "To celebrate Rupert's return, of course."

"You don't need to host an entire ball on my behalf, Mama," Rupert said.

Whether it was the nagging sensation that she was being manipulated or the restless energy that drew her toward Rupert in ways she wasn't sure she was ready for, Cece indulged her impulse to be contrary. "It sounds like the perfect occasion to deepen my ties with the May Flowers. You wouldn't mind if I invited them, would you?"

"Of course not," Lady Katya said with genuine enthusiasm. "I would never say no to turning an ordinary celebration into a political event."

"Looks like my apple hasn't fallen far from the tree," Cece's father said, moving to kiss her on the cheek once more. "I'll send word to Alex and Peter to get our gang together again."

"Basil and Elaine are going to be in town next week as well," Lady Katya said, following Cece's father out of the room. "I can't wait to see the looks on the faces of London's high and mighty when Elaine shows up to a ball in Grecian dress, as pregnant as she is."

"I should write up a list of my friends for Mama to invite as well," Bianca said, rising as quickly as she'd sat. She cleared her throat and kicked Natalia's ankle.

"Ow," Natalia protested, frowning up at her sister. "What was that for? I'm in the middle of the best part." She held up her book.

"Perhaps you could read it somewhere else," Bianca suggested. "Or help me with my list."

"I'm quite content where I—ow!"

Bianca kicked Natalia's shin a second time, then

cleared her throat and nodded toward Cece and Rupert. Only then did Natalia seem to understand.

She gasped and shot to her feet. "I should read this elsewhere," she said, then marched straight for the door.

Bianca followed, and, as had become her particular signature moment, just before turning the corner, she glanced over her shoulder and said, "Don't go getting into trouble while left alone." She popped around the corner, leaving nothing but her mischievous laugh in her wake.

Cece sighed and shook her head. "Really," she said. "You would never know that Bianca is twenty-three now. She still acts like—oh!"

Before she could finish her sentence, Rupert swept her into his arms, closing her in the sort of intimate embrace she had dreamed of while he was away. He molded her body to his, exciting her from head to toe.

"I have been given to understand that Bianca will never truly grow up," he said in a rich, low voice.

Cece couldn't stop herself from resting her arms over his shoulders and reveling in the heat and firmness of his body. He'd become deliciously fit in his time as a soldier. It felt good, it felt right, and she wanted more.

"Your sister is a scandal waiting to happen," she said, surprised at how thin her voice sounded.

Rupert stared at her lips with a flash of undisguised desire in his eyes. "You really were magnificent up there this morning," he said, each breath bringing them closer together. "I'm ashamed that I didn't suspect you had it in you. I'm ashamed that I didn't suspect a great many things about you. I should have been paying closer attention."

"You should have," Cece agreed, intoxicated by the way he held her and the shocking lack of distance between their mouths.

"On my honor, I will pay much, much closer attention to you going forward," he said, then underscored his promise by slanting his mouth over hers.

The kiss shouldn't have come as such a surprise. She was in Rupert's arms, after all, and he was clearly in a state of arousal. Indeed, it wasn't the press of lips to lips that startled her. It was the way he savored her with frank appreciation. It was the way his tongue teased her into parting her lips for him and allowing him to plunder her. It was the fervor in the way he held her, their bodies fitting so perfectly together. It was no chaste kiss filled with noble promise, it was a declaration of wicked intent.

She sighed and threaded her fingers through his hair, captivated by the new territory they were exploring. Sensation rippled through her, bringing to life a spark that turned into a throb deep in her core. It didn't matter how frustrated she was with Rupert, she wanted more of what he was giving her. Even if it meant her ruin.

He seemed to hear her unspoken request and heeded it by brushing a hand up her side to cradle her breast. She gasped at the sensation, then shivered as his thumb rubbed across her swiftly-tightening nipple. Rupert never would have dared to touch her that way before. She couldn't make out whether that meant he thought more of her or less.

At last, he shifted as if he planned to deepen their kiss, but the bristles of his moustache prickled against her tender skin. It was exactly the sort of return to reality she needed. She jerked back, sucking in a breath, and glared at him.

"How dare you?" she whispered, yanking free of his arms. "Do you think you can take such liberties with me in my own home?"

"It's our home," he said, cheeks pink, lips red, and eyes glazed with passion.

"Remember yourself, Rupert," she told him, adding, "And kindly dispose of that ridiculous moustache." She pressed a hand to her beating heart. Her breasts continued to feel heavy and in dire need of being caressed. But to stay and indulge in those desires would have been a disaster.

She shook her head and marched past Rupert, then broke into a run when she reached the hall. She didn't stop until she reached her room and shut the door behind her. As she leaned heavily against it, breathing fast, she squeezed her eyes closed. The last thing she needed was for Rupert to have such a powerful, tempting weapon to use against her. She had only one hope of defense. She would have to learn to use the same seductive sensuality to her own advantage instead of being swallowed up in it.

CHAPTER 7

*I*t was a blessing that Campbell House was so close to Marlowe House. It meant that Rupert could retreat to a space of his own—a space Fergus was making himself quite at home in, much to Rupert's delight—to rest and regroup, strategize and plan campaigns, and then sally forth right around the corner every morning to continue his siege of Cece's heart.

"Can I fetch you a sausage roll?" he asked Cece as he got up from the Marlowe House breakfast table to refill his plate. He desperately hoped she would take the saucy look he sent her along with his request as the ribald suggestion it was intended to be. After their kiss the other day, he'd been able to think of little else but how delicious the parts of her that seldom saw the light of day would taste.

But Cece answered, "I'm quite content with what I

have," stabbing her eggs with vigor while meeting his grin with a narrow-eyed look of challenge.

"Suit yourself," he said, carrying his plate to the sideboard. "But few things are as satisfying as a particularly thick and meaty sausage roll."

"Honestly," his mother said, shaking her head. She glanced across the table to Lord Malcolm as she bit the end off of her own sausage roll.

Lord Malcolm's face and neck reddened and he cleared his throat. "This family is ridiculous," he said in a rough voice, reaching for his coffee and taking a long swig.

"I suspect we would be banned from all polite interaction with society if anyone were to see us now," Bianca said with a look of glee that hinted she might enjoy the excitement of being a pariah.

"Yes," Natalia agreed, the only one at the table with a modicum of innocence left. "Who in their right mind has sausage rolls for breakfast. They're meant for luncheon, or so Cook tells me."

The rest of the table went silent. Rupert's mother and Lord Malcolm exchanged another, teasing look. Bianca pressed her lips together and looked discreetly down at her plate, as though trying not to laugh at her sister. Cece reached for a scone and slathered it with cream and jam, but as soon as Rupert returned to the table with his second round of breakfast delights, her hands became unsteady.

"Do you need help spreading your cream?" Rupert asked, barely able to suppress a laugh.

His mother snorted in offense. Lord Malcolm glared at him. Bianca burst into a fit of giggles just as she took a sip of tea, resulting in a loud coughing fit.

"What?" Natalia asked, blinking. "I thought it was a rather nice offer."

"Oh, it was," Rupert said, twitching one eyebrow at Cece.

Cece huffed and practically threw her scone and knife down. The knife clattered against the edge of the plate as she pushed her chair back and stood. "I've had enough of you," she told him. "Have you no shame? And in front of your family?"

"Clearly you don't know my family that well," he fired back.

Cece growled in annoyance and pushed her chair back, shifting her mass of skirts to get away from the table.

"Did I miss something?" Natalia asked. "I thought Rupert was being nice." She sighed. "I hate feeling left out."

"In this situation, dear," their mother said, "it's best not to know the undertones of the conversation. We may be an unusual family, but there are limits." She fixed Rupert with a tight stare.

"There are no limits in love," Rupert argued.

His argument had little chance of being heard the way he wanted it to, however. Cece tilted her chin up and marched out of the room. Rupert grabbed the last sausage roll from his plate and bit into it as he stood, intent on following her.

"You're worse than a puppy following the butcher," Bianca told him, still coughing from her tea mishap.

"I beg your pardon?" Rupert asked, pausing behind Natalia's chair in his pursuit of Cece to frown at her.

"You have a house of your own now," Bianca pointed out, cleared her throat, then went on. "And yet, you're always over here, looking for a way to get under Cece's skirts. One would think the army taught you nothing about honor and decorum. You returned far more of a bounder than when you left."

"She is right, you know," Natalia added, twisting in her chair to stare up at him with frank eyes.

"I wouldn't have to be a bounder if the rules of the game hadn't changed while I was away," he told his sisters, then glanced to his mother. "Haven't you always told us we must adjust our tactics in dealing with others to present our case in a way that will be best received?"

"Are you saying the best way to win my daughter's hand is to seduce her until she has no choice?" Lord Malcolm asked from the head of the table in a voice that sent ice through Rupert's veins.

All at once, his rakish act seemed like as much of a folly as General Colley sending them to escort that blasted mail caravan in Africa, and just as likely to result in high casualties.

"Forgive me, my lord." He bowed formally to Lord Malcolm. "I was just having a bit of fun."

Lord Malcolm grunted. "See that you do not have too much fun." He followed his statement by cracking his knuckles. Malcolm Campbell might have been in his mid-fifties, but Rupert had no doubt his stepfather could still kill a man before he knew what happened.

Rupert bowed to him again then rushed out of the breakfast room as fast as he could. He headed straight to the library, knowing full well Cece liked to read after breakfast. Sure enough, he found her seated in her father's chair near the fire, glaring at the latest work by the American, Mark Twain, *Huckleberry Finn*. Her eyes weren't moving in the natural pattern of one reading, however, which brought a cheeky grin to Rupert's lips.

"I've come to apologize," he announced as he strode into the room.

Without looking up from her book, she said, "I doubt you know what to apologize for."

Undeterred, Rupert crossed to her chair and crouched by her side, resting on one knee and looking over her arm at the page she was supposedly reading. "Huckleberry Finn is quite the little scamp, isn't he?" He glanced up at her with heaps of mock innocence in his eyes.

Cece peeked sideways at him, then sighed heavily and slapped her book shut. "What do you want from me, Rupert?"

A surprise twist of earnestness pinched at Rupert's

heart. "I want you to fall in love with me all over again. I want the book of our lives to have a happily ever after. I want you to gaze upon me with the same fondness and adoration that you used to."

She twisted to face him, pressing back into the corner of her chair as she did, and sent him a look of challenge. "Is that all you want?"

He lowered his other knee to kneel beside her chair, clasping his hands together and propping his elbows on the arm of the chair, as if praying in a confessional. "Tell me what I must do to see that sparkling light of love in your eyes again, my darling, my one, true love."

Cece pursed her lips, her expression sour, but her eyes lit with amusement and with provocation. "If you want someone to adore you unconditionally, acquire a kitten," she said in a flat voice.

Rupert's grin widened and his heart beat faster. If he had known years before that sparring with Cece was so much fun, he might never have joined the army and left. "Are you saying I should find a pussy to pet?"

Cece huffed in indignation. "Really, Rupert. Where has this newfound love of vulgarity come from? It suits you about as much as that horrid thing on your face."

"Then it suits me well," he said, brushing his fingers over his moustache with a cocky smile.

"No, it does not." Cece stared hard at him.

"You know," he said, trying a different tack and resting his chin on his hand, his arm still propped on the chair, "if you were my wife, you could order me to shave off this offending facial decoration. You could order me to do quite a few things to please you."

Cece laughed dismissively. "And what makes you think that a woman has any more power as a wife than she does on her own?"

"Well, the law your father and his friends passed several years ago, for one."

Cece shook her head. "Laws change things on paper but not in hearts."

"Then change my heart, dearest one," he said, reaching for her hand and pulling it to rest on his chest. "Fill me with your love, and I'll fill you with my—"

"A letter has come for you, Lady Cecelia," Mr. Stewart announced from the doorway. It was probably for the best, as Rupert would surely have earned himself a slap if he'd finished his sentence.

"Thank you, Mr. Stewart." Cece rose from her chair, tugging her hand away from Rupert and sending him an imperious look before fetching the letter from the butler.

Rupert pushed himself to his feet, straightening his jacket, then wandered across the room to Cece as she read her letter. "What does it say?" he asked when he saw all trace of teasing fall from her expression, to be replaced by a worried look.

"Henrietta requires my presence at her house as soon as possible," she said without bothering to push him away. "It seems there is a crisis within the May Flowers that needs to be addressed with all haste."

"Will you go?" Rupert asked.

She glanced up at him. "Of course, I'll go," she said. "I'll go immediately." She turned and started out of the room.

Rupert followed her. "I'll accompany you."

She stopped in the hall and turned to him with an impatient breath. "I'm not a child that needs a nanny to escort her three streets over and around the corner."

"Perhaps you're the nanny who needs to take this child out for a walk, then," he suggested with a rakish wink.

She shook her head and continued on. "Really, Rupert. You'd think you had more interesting things to do, now that your service to the nation is over."

"It's not technically over," he said, catching up with her. "I am merely no longer on active duty. Should the crown wish to recall me to service, it could do so for several more years yet."

"I've never wanted trouble in the colonies so much as I do now," Cece muttered as they reached the front hall and she sent a passing maid for her coat and hat.

"You don't mean that," Rupert said, coming to a stop far too close to her than was proper.

She glanced warily up at him, her gaze resting on his lips. It did amazing things to his insides to think that she was remembering their kiss from the other day. Enough so that he almost considered repeating the liberty.

In the end, he didn't kiss her and she didn't answer his statement. His mother and her father exited the breakfast room and she explained to them that she was going out. Moments later, the maid returned with her coat. Rupert could do nothing but take a passive role, donning his own coat when Mr. Stewart brought it and following her out to the street, like the puppy he was.

CECE HATED THE WAY HER INSIDES FELT AS THOUGH they were filled with scrambling caterpillars every time Rupert turned what he considered his charm on her. Or perhaps the strong emotion she felt in response was the opposite of hatred. He was horrid to say the sort of things he'd been saying to her in the past week, and yet, the shivery, tingly way his shocking statements made her feel and the things she wanted to do as a result were certainly diverting. Though they were making it hard for her to sleep. And to take a bath without engaging in shocking liberties with her own person. She'd taken far more baths in the last week than she wanted to admit to.

"Oh, dear. It looks like quite the event is afoot."

Rupert's teasing comment as they approached Henrietta's front door was just the thing she needed to push her out of thoughts that had turned her cheeks red with heat. He was right. Three other ladies she recognized as May Flowers were rushing up the front steps to the open door. Henrietta's stalwart butler stood guard, nodding to each woman as they crossed the threshold.

"I don't suppose I'm allowed in," Rupert said, pausing near the foot of the stairs.

"Certainly not," Cece said.

"I'll just wait here for you, then."

Cece sighed. "You don't have to. Go home."

"You are my home, my dear, sweet—"

She growled in frustration, turning away from his meaningless platitude and rushing into the house along with two other women.

A swell of chattering greeted her as she followed the line of ladies heading to the ballroom at the far end of Tavistock House. It was one of the larger townhouses in Mayfair, which seemed appropriate, given that Henrietta was a marchioness. What took Cece by surprise, however, was the volume of the din and the tension that crackled in the air. Everyone seemed to be arguing. Unsurprisingly, Lady Claudia seemed to be at the center of the maelstrom.

Cece made her way to the side of the ballroom, where Henrietta was giving orders to harried-looking servants serving refreshments.

"What seems to be the trouble?" she asked as soon as Henrietta noticed her and stepped away from the team of maids.

Henrietta fixed her with a wary look and cupped her elbow, drawing her to the side. "Lady Claudia has been in a snit for the past few days, since the St. James's Park rally. Her kettle boiled over this morning when our newsletter reached her front doorstep."

Cece frowned. She'd received the May Flowers newsletter that morning as well, along with her bouquet of red carnations. She wished that she'd taken the time to read it instead of flirting with Rupert.

She opened her mouth to ask Henrietta what it contained, but was cut off as Lady Claudia took charge of the mass of upset women.

"This is an outrage," she shouted above the chatter, dampening it to silence. She held a crumpled broadside, clutched over her head. "This is an absolute scandal, and it must be stopped at once."

Henrietta sent Cece a significant look before moving closer to Lady Claudia. The ladies present quieted even more, making space for Henrietta as she headed to Lady Claudia's side.

"*Petals* has always contained political articles," she said with a shrug that was far calmer than Cece felt. "What makes it a scandal now when it wasn't last week?"

"You know full well what I am referring to," Lady Claudia said, her voice still raised. "The position you have taken on behalf of us all where the Irish Question is concerned was not sanctioned by this group, nor is it a position we should be taking at all."

"The Irish Question is at the heart of politics today," Henrietta countered her. "If we do not take a stand on the most important political issues of the day, then what is the point of forming a political society?"

"It's not the issue that we object to," another member, Lady Jane Hocksley, said, stepping up to Lady Claudia's side. "It's the assumptions you have dared to make on behalf of us all as to how the issue should be resolved."

"The Prime Minister himself supports Irish Home Rule," one of Henrietta's supporters, Lady Beatrice Lichfield, insisted. "It is the only right and moral side of the argument to take."

A swell of noise from those who supported Irish Home Rule and from those who opposed it rose up so fast that Cece was tempted to cover her ears. She wanted to stand by Henrietta's side, to show her support with her presence and her words, but the members had closed her and Lady Claudia into a space at the center of a thick circle of anger and indignation, and Cece was helpless to do anything but watch from the fringe.

"Is your objection against Home Rule alone, or is your primary concern that an article was printed in our privately circulated newsletter supporting the cause?" Henrietta asked, still maintaining absolute calm and control.

"Both," Lady Claudia snapped, seemingly offended that Henrietta would ask in the first place. She was met with cheers by those who supported her, which was followed by contradiction from those who took Henrietta's side.

"It has long been established that any member who wishes can submit an article for the newsletter," Henrietta said over the chatter. She turned to Lady Claudia. "Have you written an article that supports your point of view?"

Lady Claudia turned a shade of pink that was so alarming Cece almost laughed. Lady Claudia wasn't laughing, however. "You know full well that writing has never been my forte. How dare you throw that back at me in a meeting like this?"

Her vehemence made Cece frown. Perhaps there were more things about Lady Claudia than she knew.

"As I said," Henrietta went on. "Any member may write an article for the newsletter." She turned to the roiling crowd of members. "I believe it would be more effective for us to hold this debate through the civilized medium of writing than to lash out like prize fighters in an arena. I encourage each of you to write a piece reflecting your own point of view."

"That solves nothing," Lady Claudia said, stamping her foot. "The time has come to decide where the May Flowers stand on this issue. Do we stand with the subhuman rabble of farmers and thieves that would assume power in Ireland and overrun God's natural order there, or do we stand for what is right and orderly?"

Shouts from people on both sides of the issue rang out. The strength of emotion from everyone shocked Cece.

At last, Henrietta managed to calm the ladies once more. "This is not an issue any of us will be able to solve in one meeting," she said. "Especially one called without warning and without giving either side a chance to form well thought out arguments." She sent a rare peevish look to Lady Claudia. "Therefore, in addition to writing articles, I propose we schedule a formal meeting to address the issues. I shall send around for everyone's calendar, and a suitable time that works best for the most members will be decided on."

"This is dictatorship," Lady Claudia grumbled, pushing her way through the stirred-up ladies in the direction of the door. "If this is how you propose to continue to run the May Flowers, I foresee trouble down the road."

She didn't stay to say more. She stormed out of the room, half a dozen followers marching in her wake.

A different sort of chatter rose up as the meeting— which wasn't much of a formal gathering to begin with— fell apart. Groups of May Flowers broke off to speak in hushed voices, taking advantage of the tea and biscuits that Henrietta's staff passed around. Several more left a suitable time after Lady Claudia and her cadre, so as not to appear to be following them. The entire encounter left Cece feeling off-balance.

"I worry about what's to come," Henrietta said, making her way through her remaining guests to Cece's side. "This is more than a simple issue affecting a ladies' social club. I'm afraid it has infiltrated the entire Liberal Party."

"It has," Cece agreed. "It makes me fear for the future. If the Liberal Party divides over this issue, it will ensure the Conservatives will regain power and hold it for years to come, and their aims are so contrary to everything we've been fighting for."

Henrietta hummed in agreement. "Would you be

willing to write an article outlining the argument in favor of Irish Home Rule?" she asked.

"Of course," Cece said. "I'll do whatever I can to help." Assuming she could write something that made a shred of sense. She'd grown proficient at letter-writing while Rupert was away, but articles were a different beast.

"I knew there was value in adding you to our ranks," Henrietta said. A moment later, her expression shifted to a curious grin. "And how are matters between you and Lord Stanhope?" she asked.

Cece felt heat flood her face. "He is as much of a menace as ever," she said, unable to fully meet Henrietta's eyes. She would most certainly see all the ways that Rupert was getting under her skin. "In fact, he insisted on loitering outside your home to wait for me."

"Oh?" Henrietta seemed impressed. "I must say hello to him."

Cece winced, but she could do nothing to stop her friend as Henrietta led her across the ballroom and back down the hall to the front door.

The sight that awaited them wasn't what Cece expected, though. Rupert was still there, as he'd promised, but he wasn't alone. Lady Claudia stood by his side, looking adoringly up at him as Rupert told some sort of story. It wasn't until Cece and Henrietta drew near that it became clear he was bragging about his time in Africa.

"And with that," he finished up whatever he'd been

spouting, "the locals were appeased and we were able to continue with our business."

"How thrilling," Lady Claudia said, boldly resting a hand on his arm. "I do so love a tale of daring and heroism. Our soldiers abroad are the first and last defense against the evils of these savage nations. I only hope everyone appreciates your sacrifices as I do." She batted her eyelashes at Rupert, then turned to stare haughtily at Cece.

Cece was tempted to roll her eyes. She wasn't even slightly fooled by the woman's garish act. She seemed to have gotten it into her head that Rupert—one of the few, single earls under the age of forty in Britain—was on the marriage market. The shrew would have to adjust her expectations when she learned that—

"Thank you so much for your kind attentions, Lady Claudia," Rupert said, smiling at the woman the way he used to smile at Cece. "It is truly bolstering to hear that there are those of the fairer sex who support our efforts, at home and abroad." He sent a teasing, sideways glance to Cece that was as good as tweaking her nose.

"You must know that you will always have my support, Lord Stanhope," Lady Claudia said in a disgustingly moony voice.

Rupert grinned, and even though Cece was fairly sure he thought Lady Claudia was as ridiculous as she did and that his grin was mocking, he said, "Lady Claudia, my mother is hosting a ball next week at Campbell

House. I would be thoroughly delighted if you would come."

"I believe I have already received an invitation, my lord," Lady Claudia said, her eyes as round as a cheetah who sensed it had its prey cornered.

"I insist you come as my special guest," Rupert went on. "It is so gratifying to have a special guest, after all."

Again, he peeked at Cece. The beast was teasing her. It was a heartless shift in tactic from his shameless innuendo at breakfast. Of course, Lady Claudia couldn't know any of how he had behaved toward her not more than an hour ago. As much as Cece disliked the woman, Rupert was being cruel to Lady Claudia and impudent to her. She wasn't going to stand for it.

She turned deliberately away from Rupert, facing Henrietta. "I'll prepare that article for you straight away, Lady Tavistock," she said with the brightest smile she could manage. "Now, if you will allow me to take my leave, I have a great many things to accomplish today. As much as I would enjoy a longer visit, I have no time for idling in the street."

"Perfectly understandable, Lady Cecelia," Henrietta said, clearly trying not to laugh. "Allow me to walk you to the end of the street."

"Thank you."

Cece smiled as Henrietta hooked and arm through hers and the two of them marched away from Rupert and Lady Claudia.

"Looks like you have a rival in more ways than one," Henrietta whispered when they were out of earshot.

"I'm not in the least bit worried," Cece said, her head held high.

At least, she wasn't worried about Lady Claudia. Rupert and his newfound, wily ways, however, were on track to spin her inside out and upside down.

*a*s much as Rupert would have liked to spend all his time post-homecoming wooing Cece—or teasing her until she lost her temper, which was just another form of wooing in his mind—the duties of his title couldn't be ignored.

"I feel as though I'm a year behind at university, listening to the debates in Lords," he lamented to Reese as the two of them walked from the Palace of Westminster to their club farther up Parliament Street.

"It must be a baptism by fire," Reese said sympathetically, though his brow was knit in a frown as they stepped around pedestrians heading in the opposite direction and made their way to The Tower Club's door.

Rupert laughed humorlessly. "I did everything I could to keep abreast of the situation while in South Africa, but news travels damnably slow across that sort of distance."

Their conversation paused as the door attendant let them into the club and they strode along the echoing, marble halls to the private sitting room they and their friends had commandeered as their own. Freddy was already there, reading a book, drinking tea, and looking even more threadbare than the last time Rupert had seen him. Fergus had managed to gain entrance as well, although that had taken a colossal effort on Rupert's and Reese's part. The secretaries of the club hadn't been keen on admitting an Irishman, even if he was teetering on the brink of inheriting an earldom. Harrison Manfred, the Marquess of Landsbury, and John Darrow, Viscount Whitlock, were there as well, playing chess in the corner.

"All you really need to know to appear informed in the House of Lords," Reese continued where their conversation had left off once they were seated comfortably in leather armchairs as a footman fetched their tea, "is that nothing at all is getting done at the moment because of The Irish Question."

Fergus glanced up from the letter he was writing at the small table under the window, his green eyes lighting with interest.

"How so?" Rupert asked. He thanked the footman as he was handed his tea, then took a biscuit from a plate on the table between his chair and Reese's to dunk.

Reese took a sip of his tea before answering. "The Home Rulers are so intent on having their case heard and bringing the matter to a vote that they have obstructed

business in Commons time and time again with filibusters."

Rupert grinned. "Irishmen talking until they drop?
I'd like to see that."

"Yes, well, none of them are actually Irish, and it's a
damned nuisance, if you ask me," Reese said.

"I beg your pardon?" Fergus stood from his letters,
walking over to face Reese with his arms crossed
confrontationally.

Freddy lowered his book and looked as though he
might tackle Fergus if he assaulted Reese in any way.

"I don't mean to offend you, O'Shea. Truly, I don't.
But even you must admit that these Home Rulers are
preventing other, important issues from being discussed
in Parliament."

"If Commons wants to get on with things, they
should vote on Gladstone's proposed Home Rule bill and
move on," Fergus insisted.

"If only it were that simple," Reese sighed, rubbing
his face.

"Why isn't it simple?" Fergus pressed on, his posture
tighter.

Rupert glanced between his two friends, feeling as
though he were watching a boxing match. Both were
absolutely the best of men, but each had had entirely
different upbringings and experiences.

Reese looked as though the last thing he wanted to
discuss was his opinion on Home Rule. Even less so
when Harrison and John stopped playing chess and

turned to listen to the debate. But Reese sighed and said, "I'm not one of those who believe the Irish are incapable of governing themselves, you know. Yes, that belief is insidious. I deplore the men who see your fellow countrymen as somehow subhuman. The suffering your people have undergone is staggering, and I wish there were something I could do about it."

"Then do something," Fergus said. "Let us have our own parliament and govern ourselves."

"If only it were possible," Reese went on. "The entire empire is at stake. How can we expect to maintain the respect of our various, far-flung colonies and continue to govern them if we are seen as unable to govern our closest colony of all?"

"Perhaps you should stop thinking of Ireland as your colony and start thinking of us as a sovereign nation," Fergus suggested, anger infiltrating his tone.

Reese looked genuinely alarmed. "Ireland as a sovereign nation?"

He posed the question, but before any of them could answer it, Freddy unceremoniously blurted, "Rupert, how are your efforts to win back Lady Cecelia progressing?"

Rupert was so grateful for the chance to diffuse what was on the brink of turning into a war between two of his closest friends that he felt no guilt at all in answering in an overly loud voice, "Splendidly." He took a last sip of tea, put his cup aside, and sat forward in his chair. "Not only have I turned her head with hints of absolute wickedness, I think I've managed to give her the impression that hers might not be the only attentions I could seek out."

He sounded like the worst sort of cad to brag about those things, but his words had the desired effect. Fergus stepped back, moving to take a biscuit from the side table, and Reese relaxed into his chair. The flush that had come to his face began to subside.

"You can't mean to tell me that you're deliberately making a lovely young woman like Lady Cecelia jealous, can you?" Harrison said, stepping forward to take Fergus's place.

With the initial mission of stopping Fergus and Reese's argument completed, full sheepishness for his declaration slithered down Rupert's spine. "It's all just a bit of fun," he insisted. "Cece knows my true feelings."

John groaned, crossing to sit on the edge of Freddy's sofa. "I have never observed an incident of a man assuming a woman knows he's merely joking turn out in the gentleman's favor."

Freddy made a sound of agreement. "You're playing with fire if you think making Lady Cecelia jealous is going to win her back to your side."

"Maybe," Rupert said, "but you should see the way she flushes and how her whole body quivers with frustration when I get under her skin."

His friends hummed and murmured, making sounds of warning and amusement together. He had the feeling they were amused by his stupidity, though.

"If you really want to win a woman like Lady Cecelia back to your side," Harrison said, "you need to do it with flowers and hearts and poetry. Nothing I have observed of the woman says she's the rougher sort."

"She's lovely," John agreed with a smile. "In fact, if Rupert here hadn't already staked a claim years ago, I might have given it a go myself."

Rupert's grin dropped. "I say," he protested.

"That's a good point," Reese said. "Lady Cecelia is lovely. You'd better be careful, Rupert."

"Didn't you dance with Lady Cecelia at the ball welcoming the soldiers home last week?" Harrison asked Reese, sending a teasing grin Rupert's way.

"I did." Reese nodded.

"I thought you never danced," Freddy said, his grin growing as well.

"I don't," Reese admitted with a shrug. "But Lady Cecelia looked as though she needed rescuing."

"I wasn't at all pleased with the two of you," Rupert told him with a scowl.

Reese didn't appear to be the least concerned. "And why shouldn't I consider the possibility of making her my new marchioness? Harry needs a mother, now that Constance has passed on."

Rupert was convinced his friend was teasing, up until his last statement turned serious. Then a hard knot formed in his gut. Cece would make a brilliant marchioness and she would be an excellent mother to little Harry. Reese might even be able to summon up what was needed to give her a child of her own, although they all knew any bond of an intimate nature would be unlikely to the point of impossible. All the same, the suggestion put the fear of God into Rupert.

"Enough of this sort of talk," he said, clearing his throat. "You all know Cece is mine, and I would thank you to keep it that way."

To his surprise, Harrison burst into laughter and chucked him in the shoulder. "I think you're the one who needs to remember that and take responsibility for it," he said.

"Hear, hear," Fergus seconded, rejoining the more jovial conversation. Rupert thanked heaven that he looked as though he'd shaken off his political and nationalistic fervor.

"I'm doing the best I can," Rupert insisted.

"Are you?" Freddy asked.

"You can all see for yourself," Rupert went on. "Mama is throwing a ball at Campbell House in two days. If you all come, you'll see just how much Lady Cecelia is enjoying this game of ours."

The others groaned in protest. Freddy picked up his book and looked as though he would dive into it and ignore the conversation. Harrison took a long swig of tea as John walked back to study the chessboard. Reese merely squirmed in his seat.

"I thought you all would enjoy a chance to come out and watch me at work," Rupert said, shaking his head at them all.

"Balls are such a nuisance," Harrison sighed. "Fortune-hunting mamas litter the events like mines."

"I have yet to go to a ball where fewer than half a dozen matrons ask me about my intentions to remarry," Reese agreed.

"And I have yet to attend one where my sister doesn't point out two dozen eligible young ladies for me to marry," Freddy lamented.

"Yes, but there will be a heap of first-rate refreshments," Rupert argued, his grin growing. His understanding with Cece had enabled him to avoid many of the pitfalls of balls and the matrimonial games that went with them, but he'd watched for years as his friends were tossed from one hungry young maiden to another.

"What's this I hear about a ball?"

Every bit of mirth in the room died as Lord Charles Denbigh stepped into the doorway, his ever-present stooge, Lord Montgomery Conrad, half a step behind him. It was as if someone had struck a match and lit the long fuse of a bomb. Rupert could practically hear the sizzle in the air as they waited for the explosion.

"My mother is hosting a ball at Campbell House next week," he said, rising. It was always better to face men like Denbigh on one's feet.

"I know," Denbigh said with a superior smirk. "My sister and I received invitations days ago."

"Then why bother asking?" Harrison muttered, moving to stand with Rupert.

"I heard your talk just now and thought I should

come investigate what sort of ball this occasion will be," Denbigh said.

Rupert could see the ambush, but short of making a rude gesture and showing Denbigh the door, there was nothing he could do about it. "Who knows why my mother throws her balls and events. She likes to entertain, I believe."

"I assume she'll be barring undesirable sorts from entering?" Denbigh asked with a pointed look to Fergus. "It's disgusting how lax some people and institutions have gotten lately when it comes to inviting chattel through the door."

There it was. Another excuse to throw Fergus into a temper.

"I beg your pardon?" Fergus asked, the new argument beginning exactly the way the last one had. Only this time, Rupert had no faith in Fergus's adversary to keep things above board.

"You heard me," Denbigh said with a sneer, looking down his nose at Fergus. "I've complained to the secretaries about allowing a dirty Irishman within these walls, you know."

"Thankfully, they have no intention of going back on their decision to admit him as a gentleman," Rupert said.

"Have they?" Denbigh asked, arching one brow.

"No." Rupert stood his ground. Denbigh was nothing more than an obstacle, in life and in the House of Lords, just like his father had been before him.

Denbigh looked as though he didn't believe him. "I

have half a mind to forbid my sister from attending any sort of ball where dogs are present," he went on.

Rupert's nerves bristled, and he longed to punch Denbigh in his patrician nose. There was no need at all to ask what he meant by dogs being present at a ball, which was horrible in itself.

"What is the point of this interruption?" Rupert asked instead.

"Nothing," Denbigh answered, exchanging a grin with Conrad. "We just popped in to see what sort of mess you all were making of things."

"The only mess I see is the one standing in the doorway," Fergus said, his Irish lilt sounding more like a growl.

Denbigh's face pinched into a deadly glare. "Watch your tongue," he snapped.

"Watch your tongue, *my lord*," Fergus corrected him.

Denbigh laughed bitterly. "You think some miserable patch of land in that festering hellhole of an island makes you my equal?"

"No." Fergus crossed his arms. "It makes me your better."

Denbigh flinched forward, his fist raised. Fergus braced himself, but Rupert and Harrison stepped between the men as Reese leapt to his feet to defend Fergus as well and Conrad held Denbigh's arm. The whole rush of activity happened in one, startling instant, followed by complete stillness and silence. The tableau rippled with hatred and tension.

A moment later, Denbigh stepped back, lowering his arm, though his face and neck remained bright red. "You'll pay for that," he warned Fergus in a hiss.

"Will I?" Fergus arched a brow at him, the personification of defiance.

Denbigh stared at him as though contemplating spitting on him. Thankfully, he turned and marched out of the room instead. There would have been a fight that would have ended with them all being expelled from the club if he hadn't.

It took a few more seconds for the air to clear and tempers to settle.

"All the more reason for the lot of you to attend my mother's ball," Rupert said, attempting to joke in spite of the anger still pulsing through him. When the others glanced at him in question, he said, "We need to stick together and make a public show of what we believe in so that men like him aren't taken seriously."

"And you think we'll all take a stand at a ball?" Freddy asked.

Rupert stared at the doorway where Denbigh had been. "We need to take a stand everywhere, balls included."

CHAPTER 9

*E*ven though it was currently Rupert's haunt, on the day of the ball at Campbell House, the entire family decamped to their second home, abandoning Marlowe House for the night. Campbell House was certainly large enough for the lot of them, as well as a few of Lady Katya's and Cece's father's friends who weren't already staying in London. As loath as Cece was to get too comfortable under the same roof as Rupert, considering the way just the sight of him sent tremors through her of late, it certainly was easier to dress for a ball in the same house as the party.

"You look outstanding," Bianca commented as she, Cece, and Natalia gathered at the top of the grand staircase, ready to make their entrance. "My poor brother isn't going to know what to do with himself with you in a gown like that."

"Are you certain it's not too revealing?" Cece asked.

Ball gowns that season exposed a shocking amount of shoulder and were cut lower than she was used to wearing. Red was a daring color to wear in the best of times, but seeing as the May Flower uniform for the week involved white roses, Cece had commissioned the gown at the last minute to set them off. The true rose pinned above her heart was complimented by a garland of white silk roses dipping low on her chest so that just a hint of her bosom was exposed. They continued across her skirt, highlighting the copious fabric of her bustle. How women were supposed to move, let alone dance, in the styles of the day was a mystery to Cece.

Bianca looked just as glorious and even more scandalous in her peacock blue gown. Her neckline was so daring that Cece was convinced her friend wanted men staring at her chest instead of simply believing she was a delicate beauty. Although, the purpose of Bianca's wild ensemble was obvious as Mr. Jack Craig stepped through the doorway and into the hall below where the ladies stood.

"Does Mama know Mr. Craig was invited?" Natalia asked, peeking through the gap between where Cece and Bianca stood side by side.

"Of course, she does," Bianca said, flicking open her peacock feather fan and fanning herself. Mr. Craig glanced up at that moment. His expression filled with warmth and appreciation of an entirely inappropriate nature. "She's the one who invited him."

"Invited him to tell him off, no doubt," Natalia said.

"The way he's looking at you is decidedly wolfish."

"Yes, it is," Bianca said in a sultry voice.

She bit her lip as she stared down at Mr. Craig. Mr. Craig's eyes narrowed with amusement and his smile widened. He winked at her, then walked on with the rest of the guests making their way to the ballroom.

Cece glanced sideways at Bianca. "How long have the two of you been carrying on now?" she asked with a note of disapproval.

"Jack and I aren't 'carrying on' at all," she said, sounding more disappointed than anything else. "We're friends. That's all."

"Friends who kiss behind the bandstand in Regent's Park," Natalia added with a snort.

"No one is kissing anyone tonight," Lady Katya said, marching up behind them and startling them all.

Cece gulped, even though she hadn't done anything untoward at all, and stepped aside for her stepmother. Lady Katya wore a stunning gown of emerald green that set off her dramatic coloring. Even though she was the hostess and a matron, her gown was cut as daringly as Bianca's, giving the impression that she was still in her prime. Cece only wished she would look as beautiful and fresh and be as commanding, when she reached Lady Katya's age.

"Come, girls," Lady Katya said, walking past and leading them down the stairs. "We're late for our guests' arrivals. We should be in the ballroom already, welcoming them to our home."

"It isn't really our home, though, is it?" Natalia asked as the four of them paraded down the stairs, turning the heads of the guests in the hall below.

"Of course, it's our home," Cece said. "And tonight, it's our palace."

Her comment brought smiles to all of their faces. Cece rather liked the effect. She held her head high and her shoulders square, and didn't even flinch at the way it exposed the creamy expanse of her chest above her neckline. In that moment, as they entered the ballroom and turned every head there, she felt as powerful as a princess surveying her court. She felt as powerful as Henrietta must when she stood at the front of a crowd, speaking about things their mothers' generation could never have dreamed of speaking about. It left her with a surge of energy and the hope that things were advancing for womankind.

That feeling of potency took on a sultry feeling as Rupert and his friends dropped their conversation to stare at them. Mr. Craig had joined their group, and he leaned over to whisper something in Lord O'Shea's ear that made him laugh and nod. Beside Cece, Bianca stood taller, a haughty grin making her look so much like Lady Katya that Cece almost laughed.

Within seconds, Mr. Craig broke away from Lord O'Shea and approached them.

"Lady Bianca, may I have the first dance?" he asked, extending his hand.

"The orchestra hasn't finished setting up yet," Lady Katya informed him with an arch look.

"Then we shall simply have to make our own music," Bianca said, slipping her hand into Mr. Craig's and allowing him to lead her off. As they headed toward the French doors leading to the courtyard at the back of the ballroom, he whispered something to Bianca that made her laugh indecorously.

"I fear we're heading for trouble with those two," Lady Katya said with a sigh.

"Can't you stop them?" Natalia asked.

Lady Katya pursed her lips for a moment, studying the couple as they paused to say hello to one of Bianca's friends. "No," she said at last. "I don't think I can. The time to nip that unholy alliance in the bud was four years ago, when they first met. Bianca has grown too headstrong now. She'll have to learn the hard way that there is too great a class difference for them to marry."

"I'm not sure whether to express my admiration or my alarm at your willingness to let her learn her lessons on her own," Cece confessed.

"Neither am I," Lady Katya told her with a pointed look.

Their conversation ended there. Cece's father approached them to let them all know how beautiful they looked, but his eyes were for Lady Katya alone. Natalia spotted some of her friends and flitted off to gossip with them. That left Cece free to cross the ballroom to join Henrietta and some of the other May Flowers, who were,

of course, talking politics. In making the move, she deliberately avoided rushing straight to Rupert, who looked as
though he expected her to run to him and beg for compli-
ments. The result of that was to draw Rupert instantly
across the room, like a moth to her flame.

"Lady Cecelia, you look like a vision tonight," he said,
eyes glittering with appreciation, particularly for her
neckline.

"Thank you, Lord Stanhope," she said with cool
formality, knowing full well that her true feelings were
painted vividly on her face.

"I don't believe I've seen you wear that shade of red
before," he went on.

"I don't believe you've seen me wear a great many
things before, my lord," she fired back, snapping her fan
open to cool her growing heat.

Rupert's lips twitched and a sensual tension rippled
off of him. Clearly, he wanted to make the same sort of
inappropriate comment to her that he'd been teasing her
with for a week, but with Henrietta and a few of the
other May Flowers standing right there—not to mention
Lord O'Shea, Lord Herrington, and Lord Howsden
catching up to Rupert and greeting the ladies as was more
usual for a ball—he couldn't. Cece grinned at his discomfort and counted it as a point in her favor.

"I imagine that the conversation on this side of the
room is far more interesting than anything we could have
on our own," Lord O'Shea said, smiling at Henrietta.

"I suppose it's all Irish Home Rule with you lot,"

Rupert said teasingly.

"Actually, in this instance, you are wrong," Cece said happily. She had only just joined the conversation herself, but she delighted in setting him straight. "We were discussing women's suffrage."

"A fine and noble topic," Lord Howsden said.

"Do you really think so, my lord?" Lady Diana Pickwick, one of Henrietta's companions, asked.

"The matter should at least be discussed," Lord Howsden answered, careful not to state an actual opinion.

"The May Flowers are very much in favor of women's suffrage, as you would imagine," Cece said, glancing to Rupert and daring him to contradict her.

"I can imagine," was all he said.

"Suffrage is one issue we can all agree on," Henrietta said with a quick, sideways glance.

Cece followed her look to find Lady Claudia and her brother, Lord Denbigh, inching casually toward them as they chatted with various guests standing beside Cece's group. She exchanged a knowing glance with Henrietta. The battle was coming to them. Lady Claudia hadn't passed up a single chance to pick a fight in public since the chaotic May Flowers meeting several days before. But Cece welcomed her approach for an entirely different reason.

"Well then, Lord Stanhope," she said in clipped tones. "It looks as though your special guest has arrived."

Rupert twisted to look at the ballroom's wide doorway. His brow furrowed in confusion. "There's no one who—" He must have caught Cece's meaning a second later when Lady Claudia laughed loudly at something Lord Waltham must have said in the group standing directly next to them. "Oh," he said. "Her."

Cece fought not to smile, which probably made her look as though she'd swallowed a fly. It appeared Rupert wasn't up to continuing his silly efforts to make her jealous after all. She made a note not to be as weak, if the opportunity arose.

"Several women's clubs throughout London and in major cities in the north have already been talking about forming women's suffrage societies," Henrietta went on, maintaining a calm demeanor, even as she saw what was about to happen. "I have no doubt that before the decade is out, there will be formal organizations to promote a woman's right to vote."

Sure enough, the storm broke exactly as predicted.

"A woman's right to vote?" Lord Denbigh said with a derisive snort, wedging his and Lady Claudia's way into the private conversation. "That makes about as much sense as allowing Irish dogs to rule themselves."

The wave of tension that crashed over the small assembly made Cece want to both roll her eyes and ball her fists to fight back.

"Let's keep the conversation civil, if you please," Lord O'Shea said in a tight voice.

"Civil?" Lord Denbigh said, his face coloring. He opened his mouth, but seemed to think better of speaking. That may have had something to do with Lady Claudia tugging his arm and scowling at him. He cleared his throat and said, "Everyone knows that a woman's place is in the domestic sphere," instead of whatever he had been about to say.

"No one is saying a woman shouldn't be in the home, Lord Denbigh," Henrietta replied with a smile that was astoundingly pleasant for someone who was in the middle of being attacked. "But we are skilled in that we can handle both running a household and becoming involved in politics. Even voting."

Lord Denbigh snorted a second time, sounding even more odious than before.

Cece couldn't be silent. "After all," she said, trying to be as smooth as Henrietta, "if a man can be employed outside the home and still find time for political involvement, so can a woman."

"Nonsense," Lord Denbigh scoffed. "Women are feeble. Their constitutions cannot handle the strain of conflict. It damages their reproductive capacity. Any fool knows that."

"Funny," Rupert began in a grinding voice. "I wasn't aware that you knew the first thing about a woman's reproductive capacity."

Lord Denbigh glared at him. Cece had the feeling they would all be caught in the middle of the sort of male debate that was as pointless as it was embarrassing. Why men couldn't simply stick to the issues at hand instead of lowering themselves to personal insults of a delicate nature was beyond her. She glanced subtly around, looking for a way out.

"I'm surprised that you would believe that," Henrietta went on, blinking at Lord Denbigh. "Your own sister is a member of a political organization, is she not?" She nodded to the white rose pinned to Lady Claudia's conservative bodice.

Cece unexpectedly caught Lord Howsden's eye just as Lord Denbigh sputtered, "If she does so it is only with my permission. Your little tea club is nothing and has no importance in the grander scheme of things. If it did, I would never allow Claudia to participate."

Lady Claudia's mouth dropped open and she stared up at her brother. She snapped her mouth closed without saying anything, though.

"Men like you, men who stifle the women in their lives, may just become a thing of the past," Rupert insisted. He sent a sideways glance to Cece, as though he'd said the words only as a way of scoring points with her.

Cece was almost beyond noticing, though. Lord Howsden must have seen the desperation in her eyes. "It sounds as though the orchestra is ready," he said, stepping around Rupert to face Cece. "Lady Cecelia, would you care to dance?"

"Of course she wouldn't," Rupert spoke for her.

Cece ignored him, sliding her hand into Lord Howsden's offered one. "Thank you, Lord Howsden, I would love to."

She grinned like a cat with a canary and held her chin up as Lord Howsden escorted her away from the bubble of tension that had surrounded their group and out to the relatively fresh air of the dance floor.

"You looked as though you needed an escape," Lord Howsden said as he took her into his arms for a waltz.

"You are an astute observer of the human condition, Lord Howsden," she said, relaxing in his arms as they began the first steps. "It's not as though I do not enjoy a good debate now and then, but one must choose one's sparring partners wisely."

"Oh?" Lord Howsden asked. "Do tell."

Cece glanced back to the group as they turned in the dance. Henrietta and the other ladies had found dance partners as well, leaving Rupert, Lord O'Shea, and Lord Denbigh looking as though they might tear each other's throats out.

Cece sighed as she returned her attentions to Lord Howsden. "Debate is one thing, but if two people with no intention of changing their minds whatsoever lock horns, it is no longer a debate, it is war. And I have no wish whatsoever to go to war."

"Neither do I," Lord Howsden chuckled. "And you're right. Denbigh only uses words as cudgels to beat those he feels superior to."

Cece hummed. "I'm beginning to see that his sister is the same way."

Lord Howsden made a sound of agreement. They twirled from one end of the dance floor to the other in silence before he said, "I do not like conflict. If there were a way to send everyone to their corners to cool off for a while, a way to ease tensions for just a short period, I would jump on it."

"I agree wholeheartedly," Cece said. "But there's nothing like the heat of a London summer to keep tempers high."

"I have half a mind to retreat to Albany Court and to leave it all behind, if not for certain draws in the city." He glanced back to Rupert and the others, although Cece had the distinct impression that the object of his observation was Lord Herrington above the others.

She put the ensuing questions his look of longing raised in her instantly out of her mind and instead said, "Why not retreat to Albany Court? It's only a short train ride to the north, if I remember correctly."

"It is and you do," he said.

"Then why not invite us all for a bit of rest and relaxation?" As soon as the idea parted her lips, Cece was excited by it. "A house party would be just the thing right now."

Lord Howsden's face lit up as well. "Do you know, that would be perfect." His smile widened. "I knew there was a reason I liked you, Lady Cecelia."

"Please, call me Cece," she said, returning his smile. "Even though it is wildly inappropriate."

"And you may call me Reese, as all my friends do." He then added mischievously, "Tongues will wag when people see how close we have become."

"Let them wag," Cece laughed, his comment making her aware that a large number of people were already watching them. "Certain people could do with a bit of gossip to keep them on the straight and narrow."

She sent a glance off to Rupert, who was watching them as intently as his friends were arguing with Denbigh. And as shameless as it made her, she liked it.

"Only an ignorant Irishman would support a cause as ridiculous as woman's suffrage," Denbigh bellowed, his face red, beads of sweat forming around his brow.

"And only a dolt would think that women are incapable when they've raised every one of us," Fergus argued in return, just as worked up.

Rupert barely heard either of them, although a huge part of him knew he needed to be involved in the argument. He couldn't drag his eyes away from Cece and Reese, though. They were getting along. A little too well. He'd said something to make her laugh, and she was being far too charming in return. He hadn't seen Reese smile like that since their days in university. Maybe the queer bastard *did* have his sights set on Cece as the next Marchioness of Albany.

"I refuse to be insulted by an Irishman," Denbigh growled, swaying intimidatingly closer to Fergus.

The man was so bullying and vile that it forced Rupert to remind himself that Reese was actually his friend and that there were bigger things to be concerned about than fabricated jealousies.

"Denbigh, I respectfully request that you keep your voice down and your anger in check. This is my mother's ball and her husband's house. Show some respect," he said.

Denbigh turned his anger on Rupert. "Anyone who fancies themselves as a friend of the Irish isn't worthy of my respect."

"Would you like to say that again?" Freddy asked, looking surprisingly fierce as he too faced Denbigh down.

"I'll say it as many times as I like because it's true," Denbigh said, looking as though he was willing to take on all of them.

"All the same," Rupert said, holding up his hands, "this is not the time or the place. If you want to resort to brawling in the street to make yourself feel big, kindly do it in the actual street."

Denbigh looked thoroughly disgusted for a half second before an eerie light of inspiration shone in his eyes. He stood straighter. "You want to solve this like men?" he asked.

"I hardly think resorting to fisticuffs is solving anything like men," Freddy said.

"Who said anything about fisticuffs?" Denbigh asked, jerking back with mock offense. "I am suggesting we resolve this like gentlemen." He paused, narrowing his eyes at Fergus. "At least, those of us who are capable of being gentlemen."

"I'll rise to any challenge you set me," Fergus said, which was the best possible response at a time when Rupert himself would have eviscerated the man with insults.

Denbigh continued to look down his nose at Fergus. "Fine. I challenge you to a cricket match."

Rupert blinked. "A cricket match?" It seemed like such a benign way to settle a vicious debate that he instantly distrusted it.

"You form your team and I'll form mine," Denbigh said, shifting his focus to Rupert as though declaring him captain of the opposition. "We'll play in three weeks' time. At Lord's Cricket Grounds. I have connections there." He grinned gloatingly.

"As do I," Rupert said, standing just as tall and staring Denbigh straight in the eyes. "You're on."

Denbigh laughed, the sound both scoffing and proud. "I'd like to see that red-headed dog figure out which end of a cricket bat is up."

"I hate to inform you, sir," Fergus growled, "but I was an opening batsman and all-arounder on our university team. Our *undefeated* university team."

Denbigh looked taken aback for a moment before recovering himself. "We shall see," he said, then promptly walked off.

It was as though he took a cloud of bad air with him. Once Denbigh was gone, Rupert finally breathed easy, letting his back and neck unclench.

"Cricket," Freddy said with an uncertain shrug. "We're good at that."

"Which means there has to be more to the challenge than that," Rupert voiced his concern aloud.

"Does there?" Fergus asked. "An idjit like that might just be daft enough to think I really can't play and that losing on the cricket pitch is the darkest blight against a man's honor that there is."

Rupert rubbed his neck uneasily. "He might just be that dumb."

A peel of laughter nearby snagged his attention. Cece and Reese twirled past them, enjoying their waltz a little too much. Rupert clenched his jaw. Wasn't it bloody well time for the song to be over?

He caught sight of several sets of matronly, match-making women watching his Cece and Reese. They all seemed to think a coup was taking place. Rupert turned his attention to Cece once more. She certainly was enjoying herself. And on paper, Reese was a good match for her. Lord Malcolm was a Marquess himself, after all. It could be argued that marrying him would be a step down for Cece. She'd never been interested in rank, but she'd never been interested in a lot of things up until now.

There was only one thing Rupert could do to stop the disaster that had the potential to take place right under his nose. He would have to step up his efforts and win Cece in a way that even she couldn't refute.

CHAPTER 10

*R*upert had to wait until the wee hours of the morning, when the last of the ball guests were saying their goodbyes to his mother and Lord Malcolm, for a moment alone with Cece.

"I don't know why people stay so long at balls," he said, striding up to Cece's side as she helped direct the servants to clear up the last of the punch glasses and serviettes that had been left in various corners of the ballroom.

Cece stifled a yawn and turned to him. She smiled, appearing too tired to put on haughty airs or tease him. It was a good sign, as far as Rupert was concerned.

"People stay late at balls because they enjoy the company and the diversion," she said, handing a glass off to a maid, then stepping over to Rupert's side. "Or because they don't want to go home."

"I can't imagine why anyone wouldn't want to go

home," he said with a seriousness he hadn't displayed for days. "When I was in the Transvaal, all I could think about was going home."

Cece blinked in surprise, her expression lightening. "Truly?"

Rupert looked surprised in turn. "Yes, of course. Why would you think otherwise?"

She shrugged as they made their way slowly across the ballroom toward the hall. "Your letters were always filled with stories of fun and excitement. And you've barely been able to talk about anything else since you returned home." She sent him a look that was surprisingly withering for three in the morning. "I thought you loved being in the army."

"I did, I did," Rupert rushed to say, although his true thoughts on the matter were far more complicated.

Their conversation paused as they reached the hall and Natalia burst out of the parlor across the way.

"Have you seen Bianca?" she asked, her eyes glassy with exhaustion, even as she wrung her hands with anxious excitement.

A knot formed in Rupert's stomach. "No," he said. If Jack Craig had importuned his sister, he would wring the man's neck, Scotland Yard inspector or not.

"When was the last time you saw her?" Cece asked as they continued down the hall together.

"I don't know," Natalia fretted. "I can't remember. I danced with so many amiable young men this evening, and I'm afraid I lost track of her sometime after midnight." She gasped and grasped Cece's arm. "What if she's done something foolish with Mr. Craig?"

"I'm sure Bianca has more sense than that," Cece reassured her.

Rupert had no such certainty. His sister was headed for a heap of trouble, and they all knew it.

"I just wish I knew where she was, even if the answer is scandalous," Natalia continued to fret as they reached the front hall, where their mama and Lord Malcolm were just shooing the last of their guests.

Their mother must have heard Natalia's comments. She turned to them, pursed her lips for a moment, then said, "Bianca has gone to bed. I sent her there over an hour ago."

"Right about the time I suggested Jack Craig might want to go home for the night," Lord Malcolm added in a menacing grumble.

Rupert let out a breath of relief, but it felt as though they'd only had a reprieve from disaster instead of avoiding it entirely.

"You should be in bed as well, young lady," their mother said.

Natalia huffed. "Really, Mama. I'm twenty years old now. I'm not a child."

"Then stop behaving like one," their mother said, pointing toward the stairs.

Natalia looked as though she would argue, but in the end, she let out an exhausted sigh and headed up the stairs. Their mother followed behind as though she would make certain Natalia made it to her room, and Lord Malcolm followed her as though he had the same intention but entirely different designs.

Rupert and Cece exchanged amused looks, starting up the stairs at a slower pace.

"After all that," Rupert said, "I consider the evening a grand success."

Cece raised her brows at him. "And what defines the success of a ball in your mind?"

Rupert let out a laughing breath and grinned. "I did not punch Charles Denbigh in the face in front of everyone and cause a scene."

Cece laughed abruptly, then slapped a hand over her mouth as her shoulders continued to shake. It was the most beautiful sight Rupert had seen in years. Whether it was a change in their relationship or just the exhaustion of the night, for a change, it felt as though they were on the same side.

"Mind you," he continued, slowing his pace even more as they reached the top of the stairs, "I might get another chance to thrash Denbigh to within an inch of his life."

"Oh?" Cece managed to look both curious and wary.

Rupert's grin widened. "The bast—the bloke challenged us to a cricket match."

"A cricket match? Whatever for?"

"To play for honor, I suppose." Rupert shrugged.

"Men and honor," Cece said with a shake of her

head. A moment later, her eyes widened. "Perhaps you could play at Reese's house party."

"Denbigh wants to play at Lord's," Rupert began, but stopped dead when the rest of her sentence struck him. "Hang on. *Reese?*"

Cece smiled mysteriously. "Yes, that's what he asked me to call him."

Rupert's mouth dropped open as jealousy reached up and nipped at his backside. He shifted his weight, crossing his arms, then asked, "House party?"

"I convinced him it would be a good time to invite all of his friends to stay at Albany Court for a while," she said, her smile growing. She must have known full well how irritated he was.

"His friends?" Rupert shifted his weight again. "And are you his *friend?*"

Cece answered with a laugh, swatting his crossed arms playfully.

Rupert caught her hand and held it tight. He met her eyes just as she sucked in a breath. The breath did glorious things to her chest, but it was the fire in her eyes that lured him into a mad sort of boldness.

Without a word, he twined his fingers with hers and tugged her off to the left, to the hallway where his bedroom was located. She and the rest of the family were currently staying in rooms in the other wing. Cece wasn't dense enough not to know what his move signaled, but instead of yanking her hand away or digging in her heels and pulling back, she dashed silently down the hall with him.

Neither said a word or made so much as a sound until they had reached his room at the end of the hall, slipped through the door, and shut it behind them. Rupert turned the lock for good measure before sweeping Cece into his arms and pressing her back against the door. Before he could think of anything beyond the sweet, salty smell of her skin and the way her cheeks were flushed with anticipation, he slanted his mouth over hers.

She responded with a gasp of surprise that opened her mouth to him, allowing him to take all sorts of liberties. He kissed her with a deeper intensity, sliding his tongue along hers and tasting her fully. She made a sound deep in her throat that echoed through him, making his cock stiffen and his blood run hot.

He knew what he wanted beyond a shadow of a doubt, and he was certain from the way Cece's body relaxed and molded against his as he leaned into her that she wanted the same thing. He slipped his hands down her arms to her wrists, grabbing them and pinning them to the door behind her, over her head. With the massive expanse of her bustle wedged between her and the door, the effect was to bend her backwards until she was at his mercy. But she didn't seem to mind.

He teased her lips with his and with his teeth and tongue until they grew plump and red. Then he broke away to whisper, "I want you, Cece. I've always wanted you."

"Dear heavens," she replied, her breath coming in shallow gulps that pressed the limit of her bodice's ability to contain her shapely breasts.

He slid his hands back down her arms to brush her neckline, trying to work out how he could get her out of her ball gown as quickly as possible. He rained kisses across her shoulders as he thought—or rather, as he failed to think—dropping lower and lower until he reached the line of white silk roses that kept him from what he wanted. He curled his fingers around the edge of the garment and tried to nudge it down, but the blasted thing was fastened too tightly for him to do more than expose a few extra millimeters of her skin.

He pulled back and frowned disapprovingly at her gown. "We're going to have to do something about this," he said.

For a moment, Cece was the perfect picture of wanton abandon. She leaned against the door, her eyes heavy-lidded, her kiss-swollen lips parted as she panted for breath. The sight made Rupert harder, so much so that he debated unfastening his trousers then and there. But he wasn't so much of a cad that he would take what he wanted from her without giving her the experience she deserved in return.

A modicum of sense must have returned to her as well. She lowered her arms, pushing away from the door enough to stand straight. "We can't do this, Rupert," she whispered, sucked in a breath, blinked, glanced from side to side as though someone were hidden in the curtains, then went on with, "Can we?"

"We can do whatever we want," he said, slipping his arm around her waist and pulling her flush against him.

He pressed his growing erection against her, or at least tried to, as he closed his mouth over hers once more. There were simply too many layers of fabric and frills to her gown for her to feel his hardness. She made up for that minor disappointment by sliding her arms over his shoulders and kissing him back with as much vigor as he could have asked for.

What she lacked in experience, she made up for in enthusiasm. She hummed with desire as she teased his tongue with hers and raked her fingers through his hair. Desire pulsed through him so demandingly that he genuinely worried he would go off half-cocked. He'd waited for years for this moment and he wanted to enjoy it.

"This won't do," he said, breaking partially away from her, his breath coming in short gasps.

"It's doing quite nicely," she argued, then tried to kiss him again.

He indulged in a brief peck before inching back again and shaking his head. "We need to get out of these clothes. If I'm going to ravish you to within an inch of insanity, I want you fully naked while I do it."

She blinked, her eyes shining with passion and her chest heaving more than ever. "Oh. Oh, my."

Her complete lack of fear in the face of what he was

suggesting resulted in a twist of humor that made Rupert restless. "So if you would be so kind as to instruct me in how to get you out of this extravagance, I would be grateful," he said.

She laughed, reaching behind her to where her bustle met her back. "If I had known we were going to end up like this, I would have worn something much simpler."

Rupert made a sound that started out as a laugh but turned to a strangled groan of desire when the entire bottom half of her gown jerked as she pulled something free behind her.

"You're going to need to help me," she whispered, turning her back to him.

It was ludicrous that such a banal statement and such an ordinary gesture should drive him wild with desire, but it did. He surged toward her, ready to help in any way he could to get her out of her clothes as fast as possible.

CECE'S MIND REFUSED TO FUNCTION IN ANY rational way as Rupert's hands worked at her back, untying the fastenings of her skirt and bustle at first, then working on the row of buttons down her back. Fashionable ball gowns were definitely not designed for madcapped, early-morning escapades. It was likely that they were designed to stop a woman in her tracks if she so much as thought about doing anything silly with a man.

But somewhere between the sheer exhaustion that

lent an air of unreality to everything swirling around her and the wild, relentless ache growing in her core, she wasn't about to stop. It didn't matter that Rupert drove her mad with his bullheaded ways. It didn't matter that it would mean social ruin if they were caught. Her blood was pumping, her curiosity was bristling, and dammit, modern, progressive women had just as much of a right to explore their sexuality as men did.

"There," Rupert said at last with a sigh of satisfaction. "That's the last of it."

He slid his hands into the newly unfastened bodice and helped her shrug it from her shoulders and to push the whole ensemble down over her hips to the floor. Her skin tingled in expectation and her breasts felt heavy and desperate to be touched.

But when she climbed out of the mountain of red and white silk and stepped to the side, turning to face Rupert, he blurted, "Bloody hell, there's more?"

She shouldn't have laughed. Not when she was standing there in her underthings only, facing a man with whom she had a history and an understanding, especially when his trousers were conspicuously tented. But the dismay in his eyes as he surveyed her corset, chemise, stockings and drawers was truly comical.

"Yes," she answered, moving to him and stroking the lapels of his jacket before setting to work on the buttons. "They keep us trussed up tightly to prevent spontaneous outbreaks of sensuality."

He might have laughed at her joke, but before he

could, she pushed his jacket over his shoulders and went to work on the buttons of his waistcoat. Rupert spent half a second helping her by twisting and shrugging out of his things before snaking his arms around her and pulling her in for another searing kiss. He was devilishly good at kissing and always had been. He knew just how wicked she wanted him to be and exactly how to make her feel alive.

His hands interested her more than his lips, though. He stroked her sides, cupping her breasts as best he could through the stiff boning of her corset. He even attempted to work a few of the top hooks loose before losing patience and shifting his hands down to her backside. She sighed loudly at the possessive way he squeezed her, then gasped as he ground his erection against her hips.

Her insides ached to feel more of him that way. He reached for her thigh, lifting her leg over his hip so that he could rub against her, even though too many layers of fabric still separated them. His intensity was vastly different than the coy, teasing games they had played with each other before he'd gone away. They'd fumbled innocently with each other's parts a few times all those years ago, but never undressed and never in a way that produced any results other than longing.

Everything was different now, and Cece knew it.

"I can't wait," she panted against his ear as he rubbed against her in a particularly effective way. "If I don't have you inside me soon, I think I might die."

"God, I hope not," Rupert growled. He dropped her

leg and used both hands to work on the hooks of her corset. "I'd have to die right along with you." He paused, concentrating on undressing her with sharp, pink-cheeked focus. As soon as her corset came loose, he met her eyes and said, "Of course, there is what the French call *la petite mort.*"

Cece was educated enough to know exactly what he meant. She'd had Lady Katya for a step-mother for the past four years, after all. She wriggled out of her corset, not caring where it dropped, then pulled her chemise up over her head to expose everything from the waist up.

Rupert groaned in carnal appreciation at the sight of her breasts. He reached for them, fitting them expertly in his hands and brushing his thumbs over her nipples until her core ached so desperately she thought she might scream.

"They're gorgeous," he moaned, squeezing and fondling them. "I want to...I want...." He bent to bring his mouth to one of her nipples, suckling and raking his tongue over her tip.

"Good heavens, Rupert," she gasped. "If you keep doing that, I won't be able to stand."

"Good," he said, straightening and grabbing at the last of his clothes as though they were on fire and his life depended on removing them at once. "I don't want you to stand. I want you on your back, legs spread. I want to see your cunny glistening right before I bury my cock so deep inside of you that you come hard enough to cause an earthquake."

A shiver shot straight through Cece, helping along what he wanted by causing her to drip with desire. She didn't have any more patience than he did. She tugged at the drawstring of her drawers and kicked them aside, then peeled off her stockings. It was only as she moved to the bed and twisted to flop on her back that she realized that she'd completely forgotten to remove her long, kid gloves.

She started to peel them off before Rupert said in a wolfish voice, "Keep them on."

The strangeness of his demand coupled with the fact that she was thoroughly naked and on her back on his bed was one thing, but he'd undressed entirely as well and stood between her knees at the edge of the bed.

He was glorious, a perfect specimen of male beauty. His mustache might have been atrocious, but his broad, well-defined chest with its masculine hair was scintillating. His stomach was flat and his abdomen muscled. She would have enjoyed the clear strength in his thighs as well if her gaze hadn't stopped dead at the long, thick length of his penis. It didn't matter how many artistic depictions she'd seen and giggled over with Bianca and Natalia, the real thing was stunning. Rupert's cock was large and stood erect, the flared tip already glistening. And where Cece was certain the vast majority of the young ladies she knew would shudder in terror and weep over the thought of attempting to fit something so big into such a delicate space, all she wanted was to feel him lodged firmly inside of her.

"Is this what you had in mind?" she panted, resting her arms submissively on the bed above her head and parting her legs as wide as she could, knees bent.

She knew she looked like a perfect whore offering herself up that way, but it had exactly the effect she was going for. Rupert groaned with desire, hunger that was almost predatory filling his expression. He surged onto the bed with her, covering her body with his so suddenly that she gasped and sighed at the sensation. She braced herself to lose her virginity, but the expected thrust didn't come.

Instead, Rupert kissed her again. It was a savage kiss, far from the sweet and gentle pecks they had shared at the dawn of their relationship. His hands stroked and kneaded her flesh, as if he wanted to tease and explore every part of her at once.

"If this is just a joke and you aren't really ready for me to make love to you, tell me now," he whispered, tension rippling through his body and his voice.

"It's not a joke," she told him. "I want you, Rupert. And if you don't fuck me soundly and soon, I shall be most displeased."

The sound he made was almost a sob. And still he didn't penetrate her the way she expected and wanted him to. Instead, he shifted a hand between them, cupping her sex possessively. She wondered if that was the sort of thing men usually did, at least until his fingers plunged into her.

She gasped, arching her hips into his exploration, as

he stroked inside of her. The wild feeling of being a clock wound too tightly grew within her. Her body resisted him slightly, but she hardly cared.

"You waited for me," he said, joy glowing in his eyes as he gazed down at her.

"Of course, I did," she said, barely able to form words. "Did you wait for me?"

"I did," he said, his hand shifting to stroke her clitoris. "I haven't been with another woman since the moment I met you."

Whether it was his confession of fidelity or the skill with which he brought her to orgasm, when her body burst into pleasure, it felt so good she nearly shouted. She was utterly exposed and beholden to him as he stroked her into a longer and longer climax, watching her wanton enjoyment of everything she felt.

"I'm never going to forget this sight," he purred before positioning himself at her throbbing entrance at last.

He thrust into her without hesitation. Cece gasped as her innocence was taken. She'd expected the pain, but not how quickly it would pass. She also hadn't expected how perfectly delicious it would feel to have him moving inside her, thrusting and grunting in the most undignified way as he mated with her. It was absolutely divine in every way. She wrapped her arms and legs around him, urging him to take her harder and deeper. The coil of pleasure inside her tightened once more as she moaned in time to his thrusts.

Her body launched into a second orgasm just as he cried out and tensed in her arms. She felt a rush of warmth inside her as his hips convulsed against hers. She didn't even care how dangerous it was that he spilled his seed inside of her. It was bliss beyond description to receive him that way, and to know that she had the power to take him from a strong man, full of needs, to the putty in her embrace that he was quickly becoming. He sagged, spent, on top of her, panting and wrung out, without even the energy to withdraw his marvelous member from her. She'd done that to him. She was the one who held the real power.

And as much as it sealed her fate to be his wife, it gave her the gift of knowledge that she was certain Lady Katya and women like her had known for ages. Society might have dictated that she belonged to Rupert now, but she was the one who now held ultimate sway over him.

CHAPTER 11

orning came with startling suddenness.
After madly making love to Rupert in a
haze of sleepy pleasure, Cece had fallen fast asleep. But
that blissful state of spent slumber didn't last long. By the
time the sun reached an angle where it could stream
through the curtains of Rupert's bedroom, making it
impossible to ignore the new day, reality shook Cece to
full, brutal consciousness.

She lay, naked and disheveled, tangled in Rupert's
sheets and his body. He was still asleep and breathing
steadily as he lay on his back. At some point in the night,
she'd cuddled against him. One of her legs rested over his
hip in such a way that his masculine parts stretched along
her thigh. It was eye-opening to find him already in a
state of partial arousal.

She inched away from him slowly, desperate not to
wake him. He was almost angelic in sleep, though he'd

been the very devil in the way he'd plundered her the night before. A thrill zipped through her at the memory and a grin spread across her still-tender lips. She propped herself on one elbow beside him, carefully lifting up the bedcovers to get a look at his naked body in the morning sunlight.

He was a sight to behold. As irritating and high-handed as he could be, she had to admit that. The army had given him a lean physique with well-defined muscles. The dark hair on his chest was deliciously manly, but it was the trail of hair that extended from his navel to his genitals that had her biting her lip. He was well-proportioned there too. Whether it was the rush of cool air as she pulled the covers back, or his body's innate sense that it was being ogled, his penis seemed to expand before her eyes.

A wild idea seized her. Biting her lip harder and peeking up at Rupert's closed eyes and relaxed face, she reached for his penis. She touched it gently at first, her belly quivering at the mix of soft and hard. Hard increasingly won out as she circled her hand more fully around the shaft and worked it from base to tip. The effect was mesmerizing.

Rupert sucked in a breath and shifted, his body going tense. It was all Cece could do not to giggle or lose her nerve and pull away. She glanced mischievously up to his face to see if he was awake yet. His eyes were still closed, but judging by the flush of his cheeks and the grin that he was failing miserably to hide, he was.

She pushed herself to keep going, to explore this side of him boldly and without turning into a fainting violet. He seemed to be egging her on, daring her to back down, by shifting his hips and opening his legs enough to give her fuller access. If he thought he could intimidate her with his sexuality, he was wrong.

She stroked him harder, until he felt like an iron rod in her grip. Slickness formed on his tip and his breathing turned shallow and rapid. The grin left his face to be replaced by a pinched look of pleasure, and he parted his lips to voice his enjoyment of her teasing, but that was just the beginning.

An electric jolt of excitement coursed through her as a change in the tension in his body signaled his loss of control. The sounds he made turned desperate and he jerked his hips along with her strokes. She had the uncanny feeling as though he were utterly helpless, in spite of the obvious strength in his body, as the pleasure she gave consumed him. She could have asked him for anything in that moment and he would have given it.

A moment later, he gasped and his groin tensed before a stream of pearly liquid shot from him, spilling across his abdomen. Cece watched in fascination as he groaned in acute pleasure as a bit more seed spilled from him, then as his body slowly uncoiled into absolute relaxation as he caught his breath. His penis began to soften and instinct told her to stop stroking. Instead, she gazed down at him, fascinated by the picture of debauchery he made and wondering if she should feel guilty for being so aroused by the sight.

She didn't have time to decide.

"Right," Rupert sighed at last. He reached for a corner of the sheet to wipe the seed from his abdomen, then came fully, scintillatingly awake. He surged toward Cece, flipping her onto her back and kneeling between her legs. "Now it's your turn," he said, gazing down at her with eyes so wicked they made her feel like desire personified.

He hooked his hands under her knees and yanked them unceremoniously apart, exposing her sex fully to him. She shouldn't have liked the aggressive move, but it left her swimming in need. She should have been shocked out of her senses when he bent forward, spreading her intimate flesh with his fingers and closing his mouth over the most private part of her, but all she could manage was a gasp and a moan of pleasure as his tongue went to work.

It was fast and it was heady. She was already aroused from pleasuring him, and her body was primed for orgasm. So much so that she was almost angry when the throbbing, unfettered, divine sensation crashed through her within seconds. Rupert's mouth against her sex was a revelation and she wished she could have held out as long as possible to revel in the sensation of him licking and stroking and suckling her so wickedly for much longer. He certainly was putting his all into the act.

"You wanton little minx," he growled as her pleasure

began to subside, moving to cover her, his stomach sliding against hers. "You wanted that badly."

She wrapped her arms and legs around him, sliding her fingers through his hair, but she refused to give him the satisfaction of thanking him or falling into his image of a weak and wanton woman. All she did was grin as though the whole thing were her idea and to ask, "Where did a humble soldier like you learn to give pleasure like that?"

Unexpectedly, Rupert looked embarrassed. "I wasn't lying to you when I said I've remained faithful to you since the day we met."

Cece wanted to writhe in discomfort at the guilt in his voice. "But?" she asked, loosening her hold on him and letting her legs drop to the side.

Rupert's face reddened. "Before we met…. Mama had quite a few friends that took it upon themselves to give me a proper education, as they called it."

Cece blinked, suddenly feeling as though Rupert's weight above her was oppressive instead of sensual. "You were seventeen when I met you, weren't you?"

"Eighteen," he corrected her. He must have seen the question in her eyes. "Yes, I was inappropriately young," he said. "But I was also willing and eager."

"I see." Cece pushed against him. To his credit, Rupert let her roll out from under him and stand. She bent to retrieve her chemise, fretting at the mass of discarded clothing that she wouldn't be able to put on again without help more skillful than anything Rupert could give her.

"Don't be like that about it," he said, scooting to the edge of the bed and sitting.

Cece whipped back to face him, her eyes round with indignation. "Don't be like what about what?" she demanded, in spite of knowing exactly what he was saying.

Rupert winced and rubbed a hand over his face. "That was all in the past. It will stay there. I don't intend to take any other woman to my bed but you, my wife, for the rest of my life."

Any other morning, his words might have melted her heart. She gaped at him, clutching her chemise to her chest, even though it did little to hide what he'd already thoroughly enjoyed. "I am not your wife," she reminded him.

He shrugged. "We can remedy that soon enough. Especially now. I'll have the banns read starting this Sunday. In three weeks' time—"

"Who said anything about us marrying?" she asked indignantly.

Rupert paused, his mouth hanging open, staring at her in disbelief. Considering the wild state of his hair and his complete nudity as he sat on the bed, the picture he painted was one of absolute bafflement. "Surely," he said at last, glancing over his shoulder at the rumpled bedsheets with a wry grin. "I mean, you could be with child now."

Cece pulled herself to her full height, tilting her chin up. "What difference does that make? I did not go to your bed last night as a way to corner you into a speedy marriage. I went there for pleasure."

He blinked at her. "I never said you bedded me to spring the leg shackles around me, even though some women would."

"I am not that sort of woman." She twisted away from him, bending over to scoop up as much of her clothing from the night before as she could and using it as a shield against his boorishness.

"I can see you're not that sort of woman," he said, standing and attempting to help her but only getting in the way.

She snapped straight, glaring at him. "And what is that supposed to mean? Do you think I am a whore for succumbing to your seduction so easily?"

"What? I—you're not—I never said—"

"Never mind," she huffed, carrying her armful of clothes to a chair that sat near his cold fireplace. "I'm going to need a robe or some such to wear back to my room."

"Of course," he said, tossing the clothes he'd picked up onto the bed and heading to his dressing room. "And I'm not trying to insult you. I love you. I always have."

"In spite of your *education*?" she asked, knowing full well she sounded petty and jealous and hating it. But she'd adored making love with Rupert, and even though she knew the experience would have been vastly different if he hadn't learned how to do it all those years ago, a selfish part of her wished she was his only lover as he was—and would continue to be, whether she was ready to tell him that or not—the only one she would ever have.

Rupert returned from the dressing room and thrust a thick, masculine robe at her. "Do you want to marry me or not?" he asked, frowning.

Cece snatched the robe away from him and shrugged into it. "Not at present," she snapped.

"When then?" he asked, sounding as perturbed as she felt.

"I will let you know," she said, clipping her words and turning away from him.

"Are we going to have other nights like this?" he demanded as she crossed the room to the door.

She reached the door, but turned to him before unlocking it. "Do you mean are we going to fuck again?" She deliberately used the harshest tone and word she could think of. "Probably," she said with a shrug. "I liked it. You're good at it. As a modern woman, I believe wholeheartedly in the concept of free love."

"No, you don't." Rupert called her bluff with a wry laugh. "You're loyal and true, through and through. But if you like fucking so much, my door will always be open to you, as I suspect your legs will always be open to me."

Cece yelped in offense, sending him a look of pure contempt. It didn't help that her insides coiled with arousal and her nipples tightened at the crude suggestion.

It seemed wildly paradoxical that he could be so horrible and that she would want to shed his robe and fall to her back willingly so that he could use her until they were both sated.

The only way she could combat the conflict of feelings within her was by unlocking the door, wrenching it open, stepping into the hall, and slamming it behind her. The loud smack and the effort it took to pull off such a childish gesture actually felt good. That would teach Rupert to think he could control her with her pussy.

The dark cloud of frustration continued to hang over her as she stomped through the house to her own room on the other wing. She had half a mind to slam her own door for good measure, but it wouldn't have done any good. Her frustration had already started to melt away as she crossed from one part of the house to the other, and it was gone entirely by the time she poured water into the porcelain basin to wash.

It wasn't until she was mostly dressed and her maid came in to help with the last of the fastenings and to do her hair that she realized just how unwise everything she'd done in the last eight or so hours was. Betty was unusually silent as she dressed Cece's hair and her expression was disapproving. She glanced at her unslept in bed through the mirror. If one servant knew, they would all know.

That knowledge brought with it a far more sickening thought as she made her way downstairs to the breakfast room. It took a supreme effort of will to keep her expression neutral as she entered the room where her entire family was already seated at the table, eating and gossiping about the ball. It didn't help matters one, tiny bit that Rupert reached the room mere seconds after she did and that the family glanced up from their chatter to see them in the doorway at the same time.

All conversation stopped dead. Five sets of eyes— apparently, Lord O'Shea was still residing in the house too—bored into them. All of them, even Natalia, looked as though they were in no doubt of what had happened after everyone went to bed.

Cece wanted to weep with embarrassment. She couldn't even meet her father's eyes. But she refused to give in like a ninny and flee from the room under the certainty that all of those closest to her knew just how sinful she and Rupert had been the night before. She kept her chin up and did the only thing a self-respecting lady could do at a moment such as that. She ignored every one of them and marched to the sideboard to fix a plate of breakfast meats and eggs worthy of a sailor about to circumnavigate the globe.

By the time she took her seat at the table, nodded to the footman to pour her tea, and took the first bite of her breakfast, the conversation had resumed its normal pace.

"I thought that Lady Helen was paying far too much attention to Lord Beaumont," Natalia said in a superior tone. "He so clearly wanted to dance with me, not her."

"Lord Beaumont was dancing with a variety of ladies

and behaving just as a gentleman should," Lady Katya replied.

There was something censorious in her tone, and when Cece glanced casually her way, she found her staring at Rupert with a harsh frown.

For his part, Rupert looked just as angry as he had when she'd slammed the door on him. He didn't even acknowledge his mother's comment, nor did he look at anything other than the toast he was spreading with marmalade.

"I don't see why women should have to wait for a gentleman to ask them to dance," Bianca said, pushing the last of her eggs around with her fork. "We know who we want to dance with, so it makes much more sense for us to do the asking. Don't you agree, Cece?"

Cece was forced to glance to Bianca. Her friend wore a mischievous look that asked far more than just one question. Beyond Bianca, Lady Katya was studying her with a penetrating gaze. Cece felt her face heat. "I have no opinion on the matter," she said in a rush before returning to her ham.

"Of course you do," Bianca said. "You're a May Flower. They have opinions on everything important these days, Irish Home Rule, women's suffrage, intimate relations, social protocol."

Cece pressed her lips shut, lowering her shoulders and wondering if she would have been better off taking breakfast in her room.

"Bianca, give it a rest," Rupert snapped from the other side of the table.

Cece glared at him. "Don't speak to your sister like that on my behalf. I'm perfectly capable of ignoring her prying on my own."

Rupert raised his hands in defense and leaned back in his chair but said nothing. The two of them stared daggers at each other before returning to their food.

"Look at that," Cece's father said in a gravelly voice that was either amused or furious, Cece couldn't tell. He nodded across the table to Lady Katya. "They've got us beat."

Lady Katya's lips twitched into an unexpected grin that filled Cece with dread even before the woman said, "It took us a year to go from lovers to enemies, but they've managed it in one night."

It was the last straw. Cece shot to her feet, pushing her chair back so fast it would have fallen over, if the footman hadn't caught it, and throwing her fork onto her plate with a loud clatter. "This family is an absolute disgrace," she huffed, staring down each one of them, even her father, with looks of fury. "It's a wonder anyone in polite society cares to acknowledge us at all. Not one of you has any respect for anyone's dignity. You can't just let something go without joking about it at the breakfast table. Well, I won't sit here and be made a laughing stock by the very people who should have the most compassion for the awkward situation we all find ourselves in. I've had enough scandal for one season."

She stepped away from the table, making a speedy retreat into the hall before any one of them summoned up the gall to say something intended to soothe her. Her only consolation as she turned the corner was that Rupert stood and watched her leave. She caught him turning his glare on the rest of their family, as if censuring them on her behalf, before the whole sorry mess was out of sight. If only it could be out of mind as well.

CHAPTER 12

*R*upert scowled and gripped the handle of his cricket bat as though his life depended on it, staring Fergus down as he completed his run-up as though the devil himself were charging at him. As soon as Fergus released the ball, Rupert's instincts took over. He grunted as his muscles worked to swing the bat as hard as he could. The ball hit the bat's blade square in the sweet spot with a satisfying thwack.

"Whoa!" Freddy called from mid off, twisting to watch as the ball sailed high over everyone's head and well beyond the boundary.

Reese stood from his position as keeper behind Rupert's wicket, letting out a long whistle. "Shot!" he called out in congratulations, raising two hands skyward, as though he were the umpire as well as the keeper. As they were just practicing, he might as well have been both.

"That's the third ball you've donated to the urchins of St. John's Woods," Fergus said, shaking his head and marching across the wicket to thump Rupert's back. "And you're not that good of a cricketer."

Rupert straightened in indignation, knocking his bat against his pads to work off more of the restless energy pulsing through him. "What do you mean I'm not that good?" he demanded, far more irritable than he should have been at a friendly practice with his closest friends. "I was one of the regiment's star players in South Africa."

"In your dreams, perhaps," Freddy said, jogging toward the group forming around Rupert. He and Fergus exchanged chummy laughter.

"He was the captain of our team at Cambridge," Harrison said, striding in from square leg.

John joined them as the other men they'd managed to recruit for their impending match against Denbigh and his cronies continued tossing a ball around or practicing batting at the far end of the Lord's Cricket Grounds field.

"Captain or not," Fergus said, resting his forearm playfully on Rupert's shoulder, "something is clearly eating at him."

Rupert shrugged his friend off, heat flooding his face. "Let's forget the idle chit-chat and resume our practice. The last thing we want is for Denbigh to show us up at the match."

"The last thing we want is our star player too distracted to hit a ball straight," John corrected him.

Rupert glowered at him. "Did you not just see the six I hit?"

John smirked. "How many times have we seen a lad hit a ball like that only to be bowled out on the very next ball due to lack of concentration?"

It was true and Rupert had to admit it. He sighed and banged his bat against the dirt of the wicket before turning and walking toward the bench at the side of the field.

"Hold up," Fergus said, chasing after him. The others followed in his wake. "It wasn't an insult. We're just having fun with you. Especially since we all know good and well what's turned your head so thoroughly."

"The fairer sex makes fools of us all," Harrison laughed in agreement.

"How would you know?" John teased him. "You haven't seen the right side of a skirt in months."

"That's because I have my eye on one skirt in particular, and I don't intend to stop until I make it mine," Harrison answered.

John snorted. "Lady Helen Armstrong is never going to give you the time of day. I hear she won't settle for anything less than a duke."

"I'm a bloody marquess," Harrison said indignantly. "That has to count for something."

Rupert ground his teeth and picked up his pace to get away from his friends and their talk. "You'd think we'd all turned into women the way we gossip these days," he muttered as he reached the bench and threw his bat down, then flopped into the seat to remove his pads.

"Come off it," Freddy chided him good-naturedly. "We've always talked about women, our prospects with them, how to marry the right one." He sent a guilty look Reese's way.

Rupert glanced sullenly up at Freddy, risked a sly peek at Reese—who was watching Freddy with a forlorn expression—then scowled harder and returned to unbuckling his pads. "Yes, well, finding the right woman is not my problem. Making sense of her, however...." He let his sentence end with a wary laugh.

"Ah, so it's the lovely Lady Cecelia that poses the problem here," Fergus said, sitting on the bench by Rupert's side and spreading his arms across the back. He looked more like a king on a throne, surveying his domain, than an Irishman freshly discharged from the army who had yet to take up any other responsibility.

Rupert tossed one of his pads aside and frowned at his friend. "I thought I had her," he said, loath to go into more detail, reasonably certain his friends would know all if he said too much. "I thought that after the night of the ball, she would want to rush to the altar and that would be the end of that."

John hummed knowingly, unable to conceal the adolescent grin that tugged at the corners of his mouth. Fergus thumped him on the back again in congratulations. Harrison and Freddy exchanged knowing nods.

But Reese stood where he was, arms crossed in

thought, a serious frown etching lines between his eyes. "So you compromised her, then?" he asked.

Rupert stared at him with irritation at the truth being spoken aloud and sheepishness over the implied censure in his friend's voice. "What transpired between Lady Cecelia and myself is none of any of your business."

The others seemed to take that as an admission of guilt.

Reese let out a breath and shook his head, his arms dropping to his sides. "Did you deliberately seduce her in order to corner her into marriage?"

"What? No!" Rupert threw his other pad aside with far more violence than was necessary and glared at Reese. "If anything, she seduced me."

It wasn't exactly true, but neither was it completely a lie. He would have stopped with a kiss if Cece had told him to. She'd said in as many words that she wanted what had happened between them as much as he did. But knowing she was a willing and eager participant didn't settle his soul or relieve the burden of guilt that pressed damnably down on him, no matter how much he insisted to himself that it shouldn't.

His friends continued to stare at him, so he heaved a sigh and explained what he shouldn't have had to. "It wasn't intentional. One thing led to another. In the morning, I made a casual comment about having the banns read. You would have thought from her reaction that I'd said exactly the opposite, that I'd had my way with her and never wanted to see her again."

"That makes no sense," Harrison said, scratching the back of his neck with a confused look.

"I've never understood women one way or another," Freddy admitted with a shrug.

"What exactly did you say to her?" Reese asked in sharp, distinct tones.

Rupert glanced up at him again, feeling the same way he had his first year at Eton when he'd been dragged into the headmaster's office for cheating on an examination. "All I said was that I would have the banns read so that we could be married as soon as possible. It was the logical, moral, and upright thing to do."

Reese narrowed his eyes slightly as he continued to stare at Rupert. "Did you ask her if that was what she wanted?"

A feeling as though headmaster Reese had taken the switch down from its mount on the wall behind the desk sent cold fingers of dread through him. "Isn't it obvious?" he answered in a mumble.

The rest of his friends seemed to catch on to Reese's line of logic. They hummed and groaned and acted as though Rupert had missed the cricket ball and had his bails blown off the stumps in spectacular fashion.

"What in the devil is wrong with telling the woman I love, whom I have intended to marry for nearly five years, and whose honor I have—arguably—imposed on, that we can be married as soon as possible to keep things above board?" he demanded.

"You have to introduce something like that gently,"

Harrison argued. "Women are delicate and cannot handle direct confrontation like that."

"On the contrary," Reese said, shaking his head. "Women are far stronger than any of us have given them credit for."

The others turned to Reese with looks of shock and bafflement.

"You're the last person I would expect to hear defending the strength of women," John said.

Reese's face turned stony. "Why?" he asked. "Because my wife died in childbirth or because I have always preferred the company of men?"

Dead silence pressed down on their group. Of course, they had all known from the start what Reese was like. But it was never, ever spoken of.

Reese cleared his throat and went on. "The world is changing at a faster pace than it ever has. It's not just the proliferation of technological innovation and medical advancement. Women are slowly but surely taking up places in society that our fathers and grandfathers would never have dreamed of. Perhaps my own, unique view of the positions of the sexes allows me to see things differently, but mark my words, we cannot continue to treat women the way they have been treated. We must genuinely value their opinions and stop referring to them as feeble creatures who do not know their own minds."

As loath as Rupert was to contradict his friend when he acknowledged full well that Reese had a legitimately different experience of such things, he said, "But that is exactly the point. I do not believe for a second that Cece does know her own mind in this matter."

"Then you are a fool," Reese shot back at him. "She deserves to be with a man who will appreciate her strengths."

Rupert's back shot straight and every muscle in his body tensed. "I suppose you're referring to yourself? I've seen the way the two of you have formed a friendship. Do you truly think she would be happier married to a man who is repulsed by the idea of bedding her?"

The air crackled between them. Their friends looked on in tense silence.

"I was referring to you," Reese said at last, each word clipped and distinct.

Deep embarrassment flooded Rupert. Only an ass of the highest order would lash out at a friend who was trying to help him on such a personal level. "I'm sorry," he muttered, lowering his head and slumping his shoulders.

He would have goaded himself into a better apology if their conversation hadn't been interrupted by the sardonic greeting, "Well, well. Isn't this a sorry display," as Charles Denbigh approached. He was dressed in cricket whites and escorted Lady Claudia. "Giving up already, gents?" he asked, adding, "And you," with a sneer for Fergus, implying he wasn't a gentleman.

The mood instantly shifted. Rupert stood when Fergus did, ready to defend his friend with words or even fists if he had to.

"Our practice isn't over," he said, glancing past Denbigh to see a cluster of men gathered at the far edge of the boundary, carrying bats and dressed for practice. "We have the field until noon."

"It's nearly noon," Denbigh said haughtily. "Though I don't see how practice will help you one bit. You can't teach a dog to dance, after all."

Tension crackled around them. The only one who seemed nonplussed was Fergus.

"I've seen plenty of dogs dance," he said, crossing his arms and sending a polite smile to Lady Claudia.

Rupert's gut clenched at Fergus's audacity. Luckily for him, neither Denbigh nor Lady Claudia caught the insult.

"I'm so looking forward to your house party next week, Lord Howsden," Lady Claudia said with a smile for Reese. "How kind of you to invite all of the May Flowers."

Rupert had to hand it to the woman, she knew how to insert herself to stop a male argument from happening. "You'll be there?" he asked, playing along, if only to keep Fergus from ending up on the wrong end of a fistfight.

"Of course, I will, Lord Stanhope," Lady Claudia said with a particularly cloying smile. "I take it you will be there as well?" Her cheeks were a rosy pink as she waited for Rupert's answer, batting her eyes.

"I will," Rupert answered with a friendly nod. It struck him that Lady Claudia wouldn't have balked if he'd proposed having the banns read immediately after bedding her. Then again, he didn't think Lady Claudia was the sort to dance willingly into a man's bed the way Cece had with him. Lady Claudia seemed more the kind to close her eyes and pray for it all to be over quickly.

All the same, Lady Claudia broke away from her brother and wedged herself between Rupert and Fergus, forcing Fergus to take a long step back to accommodate her enormous bustle. "I do so hope we can spend quite a bit of time together in the country," she said, resting her fingertips boldly on his forearm. "I have been informed that the grounds of Albany Court are simply lovely and that there are a variety of gardens and walks in which one can enjoy a bit of privacy."

"It's true," Reese answered with a perfectly straight face and eyes bright with mirth. "There is even a particularly devilish hedge maze that my late wife had planted to enjoy with her companions."

"That sounds positively delightful," Lady Claudia replied, gracing Reese with a smile before turning back to Rupert. "You will come rescue me from the maze if I get lost, won't you?"

"Of course, I will," Rupert said, trying not to burst into laughter at the woman's clumsy flirting. If she thought she had half a chance with him simply because he and Cece had rowed in public, she was a ninny. But that didn't mean he couldn't be civil with her. Perhaps it might even light the fire under Cece's feet that a morning in bed doing devilish things hadn't.

"I shall count the days until the party starts," she said, breathless and starry-eyed.

Denbigh cleared his throat. "Claudia, my dear, could you give us men a moment alone?"

"But of course," she said. She made a demure curtsy to Rupert. "Good day, my lord. Until we meet again."

She turned and walked off, though her steps were somewhat awkward and swaying, enough to make Rupert wonder if she was attempting some sort of seductive walk. If that was the case, the poor woman had a lot to learn.

The amused grin was wiped off his face a second later when Denbigh growled, "If you so much as look at my sister sideways at this ridiculous house party, I'll use your balls for cricket practice. Do I make myself clear?"

Rupert huffed a laugh. "You have no need to worry on my account," he said.

Of all things, Denbigh reeled back, looking mortally offended. "Is my sister not good enough for you?"

Rupert sighed and held up his hands, seeing straight away that he wasn't going to win the argument, no matter which course he took. "We're only here to practice cricket," he said.

Denbigh sniffed and tugged at the bottom of his sweater. "Fat lot of good practice will do you." He shot a condescending look to Fergus. "We'll wipe the floor with you."

"I'd like to see you try," Fergus growled in return.

Rupert wanted to roll his eyes. Just like that, they

were back to the same pissing contest they'd begun with. None of it would be settled until the match was actually played. Truth be told, he wasn't certain things would be settled even then.

"Your team can have the field," he said, no longer in a mood for conflict of any sort. "I think it's time for us to practice lifting pints in the pub." He nodded to Reese and the others, then bent to scoop up his discarded pads.

"Your day is coming, O'Shea," Denbigh growled before turning and stomping back across the field to where his team and his sister were waiting.

"That man is a first-rate ass," John said, watching him go with a scowl. "I hope we humiliate him and his team."

"What we really need to humiliate him is a team full of Irishmen," Fergus said.

Rupert brightened, as did the others.

"Do you have any Irish friends in London who play cricket?" Freddy asked.

Fergus shrugged. "Most likely. I'll ask around and see who I can scrounge up."

"It would be incredibly satisfying to beat Denbigh with a squad filled with Irishmen," Harrison laughed.

They signaled to their teammates still practicing that it was time to yield the field as they headed to the club-house to change into more suitable clothes.

"You aren't really going to pay attention to Lady Claudia at my house party, are you?" Reese asked as they crossed the pitch.

Rupert shrugged. "I'm not going to ignore her."

The others groaned and shook their heads in disapproval.

"I thought your present aim was to convince Lady Cecelia to marry you, not to make her want to slice your cock off and feed it to the swans in Reese's pond," Freddy said.

"I can be amiable to a woman without making promises or crossing boundaries," Rupert argued.

Fergus laughed and slapped a hand on his shoulder. "You're right. You don't understand the first thing about women. You've got a lot to learn if you want to keep your little head intact."

Rupert had the horrified feeling that his friend was exactly right.

CHAPTER 13

*U*nder usual circumstances, Cece loved trains. She'd loved speeding along through the countryside, watching the world whisk by, since she was a child traveling with her father between their ancestral home in Scotland and London. But the relatively short train ride from London to St. Albans, sequestered in a first-class compartment with Rupert, was akin to torture.

Almost a week had passed since the night they'd spent tangled up in passion, and tempers were still high for both of them. They'd managed to be civil to each other in the presence of their family, although that likely had more to do with the fact that they were both far more irritated with their meddling, smirking, unconventional family members than with each other. Which was saying something.

"Mrs. Morris sent biscuits for the trip," Rupert said in

an overly-polite voice, searching through a carpetbag on the seat beside him. "Would you like one?"

"No, thank you," Cece replied with equal politeness. She glanced briefly at him, seated across from her in the rear-facing seat—which he'd taken without comment, knowing she hated riding backwards—then resumed watching the blur of the London suburbs shifting into countryside out the window.

"They're the sort with raspberry jam in the middle," Rupert went on.

Cece's mouth instantly watered, and she dragged her gaze back to him, tempted to lick her lips. The biscuits had been wrapped in a cloth which was now spread open over Rupert's legs. The small mound of raspberry-filled biscuits dusted with powdered sugar roused her with temptation. Almost as much as the shapely hips and masculine curves of his trousers directly behind the biscuits.

She bit her lip, feeling heat rise to her face. The very last thing she should be noticing while enclosed in a train car with Rupert was his body. But now that she knew what that body looked like without clothes, now that she had experienced the wonderful things it could do, her mind simply refused to think of anything else. She'd had more than one restless night in the past week, thanks to the memories of his hands exploring her body and his mouth doing scandalous things to her nether regions. The fact that she would succumb to him in an instant if he were to make the slightest move to renew their carnal dealings was a blow to her pride on so many levels.

"You look like you want it," Rupert said.

Cece blinked and sucked in a breath, drawing her errant gaze up from his crotch to his eyes. "I beg your pardon?"

"You look like you want one," he said, his expression blank but his eyes smoldering.

She pressed her lips together. If he was going to pretend he hadn't goaded her on purpose, then she would respond in kind.

"If I must," she said, keeping her back stiff and leaning forward to take a biscuit. She deliberately chose one from the far side of the pile that allowed her to brush her hand across the center of his trousers.

Rupert sucked in a breath and stiffened, proving to Cece that she did have the upper hand after all. She settled back in her chair, fixing him with a coquettish smile, and licked the edge of her biscuit before biting into it with shocking sensuality.

"Vixen," Rupert growled. He quickly gathered the edges of the cloth, securing it around the biscuits and setting the whole parcel on the seat beside him. That done, he adjusted his hips to what Cece supposed was a more comfortable position, given the sudden change in the energy in the air. Evidently, he wasn't going to settle for her taking the upper hand, though. He looked her dead in the eyes and said, "If this trip wasn't less than half an hour, I would bend you over that seat, bunch your skirts around your waist, and take you from behind so vigorously that you would pray for the whistle to blow so that it drowns out your cries of ecstasy."

Cece swallowed her mouthful of biscuit so awkwardly that she nearly choked on it. Instantly, the vision of Rupert doing exactly as he promised filled her head, making her throb so acutely that she, too, had to squirm to sit more comfortably. She pinned her hopes of keeping the upper hand on saying, "Did you try that with any of your mother's friends?"

"No," he answered firmly and calmly, crossing his arms, his eyes daring her to throw another insult at him.

She had nothing else to say, so she glanced out the window once more, finishing off her biscuit. Her breasts felt heavy with the need to be touched and her tightened nipples rubbed frustratingly against her corset with the train's rocking motion. In fact, that motion was not helping to dispel the cloud of lust that Rupert's continued, hungry stare raised in her.

By the time they arrived at the St. Alban's station ten minutes later, Cece was overheated and her body rippled with restlessness. It was all she could do to wait for the station porter to open their compartment door. As soon as the rush of fresh air hit her, she practically leapt from the train to the platform without waiting for Rupert to do the proper thing and exit first to give her a hand down.

"Cecelia!"

Cece nearly wept in relief as Henrietta called to her from the far end of the platform. She sent a brief look over her shoulder to make sure Rupert had exited the train, then made a beeline straight for her friend.

"Lord, am I happy to see you," she sighed in relief, reaching for Henrietta's hands and squeezing them.

"Oh dear," Henrietta said, studying Cece with a wise look. "Was it that bad?"

Cece twisted to look back at Rupert once more. He was busy dealing with the porter and retrieving their baggage from the compartment. That didn't stop him from glancing her way and winking when he saw her watching him.

She whipped back to Henrietta, certain that her expression was full of dread. "I have so much to tell you," she said.

Henrietta nodded gravely. "I can see you do." She glanced around for a moment, then took Cece's hand. "Come this way. Lord Howsden sent carriages to fetch us all to Albany Court. We'll have more privacy if we talk by them."

They proceeded through the small station and out to the street. St. Albans was a relatively small town, but there was still enough traffic passing by the train station to make enough noise to conceal anything Cece wanted to say. Four carriages bearing the Howsden crest were lined up by the side of the street along with two that looked like hired conveyances. Already, a few of the May Flowers that Cece recognized—some with their husbands and some with only themselves as chaperones—stood beside the carriages chatting.

179

"Are we departing for Albany Court soon?" Lady Jarvis asked Henrietta as she and Cece passed.

"We're waiting for one more train," Henrietta answered. She glanced to the massive timetable on the station's wall, where an attendant was marking the train from London as arrived. "It shouldn't be more than ten minutes."

Lady Jarvis nodded and returned to her conversation. Henrietta walked Cece the rest of the way along the line of the carriages and past them, to the shade of an oak whose leaves were swaying in the gentle, late-spring breeze.

"Now," she said, coming to a stop and turning to face Cece. "Tell me everything."

Twin feelings of embarrassment and relief that she finally had someone to spill her heart to left Cece momentarily speechless. She peeked down the line of carriages to make certain no one was listening to her, and to be sure Rupert hadn't left the station yet. Then she took a deep breath and blurted before she lost her nerve, "Rupert and I spent the night together after the ball last week."

Henrietta's eyebrows shot up, but her surprise was far milder than Cece expected it to be. "I see," she said, paused, then went on to ask, "How was it?"

Cece let out a breath, her shoulders drooping. "It was wonderful," she confessed. She paused, wondering if she should be more explicit with her details. Sense told her not to, so she continued with, "At least until the cold light of day."

Henrietta's expression softened to sympathy and she squeezed Cece's hand. "Regrets?" she asked, as cryptic as Cece had been.

Cece winced and let Henrietta's hand drop. "Not precisely." She bit her lip, praying her friend wouldn't be shocked by her wantonness. "He assumed the whole thing meant the two of us should be married immediately, as if I had lured him into bed to accomplish an engagement."

"But you didn't," Henrietta said, only a hint of a question in her eyes.

Cece shrugged. "I might have agreed to his proposal if he hadn't been so boorish about it. But it infuriates me that men can be so high-handed when it comes to these things, that they can carry out any number of affairs without impunity, but the moment we decide to enjoy ourselves, wedding bells must ring."

Henrietta laughed with far more energy than Cece would have expected. "Yes, it is unfair, isn't it?"

Cece gaped at her, realizing she didn't know her new friend as well as she thought she did. "Are you...." she began, hesitated, cleared her throat and went on, just above a whisper. "Have you had affairs since your husband's death?"

"No," Henrietta answered, still appearing amused. "But if given the opportunity...." Her smile widened as she glanced at the group of Reese's guests waiting to depart for Albany Court. Several were single men, Reese and Rupert's friends. Henrietta hummed appreciatively, then turned back to Cece. "My late husband, Richard, wasn't a terribly passionate man, but we did enjoy our time together. At least until his health made it impossible." A wistful look filled her eyes.

"Do you miss him?" Cece asked, suddenly realizing she knew very little about the late Lord Tavistock.

"I do," Henrietta answered slowly. "Ours was not a love match, but he was a good man. To tell you the truth, I am a bit jealous of the fiery passion you and Lord Stanhope have, even though I know it causes a thousand frustrations for you."

It was Cece's turn to laugh. "And here I've been admiring you for being free of the bonds lust brings with it."

"Oh, I am certainly not free of those bonds," Henrietta said with a mysterious smile, glancing down the line of carriages again. Lord O'Shea, of all people, glanced in their direction as she did. He caught her glance, smiled, and touched the brim of his hat. "I'm not immune to lust at all."

Cece's brow shot up and she instantly began plotting a hundred ways to steer Henrietta and Lord O'Shea into each other's company. But those grand plans were squashed a moment later as a new wave of arrivals poured through the station exit, Lady Claudia Denbigh and—Lord help them—her brother with her.

"This does not bode well," Henrietta said in a wary voice.

She started toward the Denbighs, Cece following. Rupert—who had joined his friends while Cece and Henrietta were talking—furrowed his brow at her curiously, then turned to see what they were marching toward. He scowled at the sight of Lord Denbigh, but it was Lady Claudia whom he should have been wary of.

"Lord Stanhope." Lady Claudia greeted him with an effusion of joy. She sent a pointed look Cece's way before sweeping up to Rupert's side and gripping his arm tightly. "You see? I told you we'd meet again soon. I am so looking forward to traversing the hedge maze of Albany Court with you, just as you promised we would." She sent another, gloating look to Cece.

Cece wasn't fooled for a moment. The split-second of annoyance in Rupert's eyes before he smiled politely at Lady Claudia was all it took for Cece to be convinced she had nothing to worry about. Which was why it was doubly annoying when Rupert said, "I shall be delighted to show you the hedge maze at your earliest convenience, Lady Claudia."

He sent a challenging look in Cece's direction, but Cece refused to give him the satisfaction of tweaking her nose. "Does this mean our group has all arrived and that we are ready to depart for Albany Court?" she asked Henrietta, ignoring Rupert entirely.

"I believe it does," Henrietta said, the cleverness of her smile telling Cece that she wasn't fooled by the display either. "There should be enough room for all of us if we budge up," she said in a loud voice. "Even though more people have arrived than we were expecting." She stared directly at Lord Denbigh as she spoke.

"I am here to protect my sister from some of the more undesirable elements that have somehow been invited to this party," Lord Denbigh answered with only a slight nod. He didn't have to point to Lord O'Shea for everyone to know whom he meant.

Henrietta's smile widened, and she turned to Lord O'Shea and said, "I would be most gratified if you and some of your friends would ride in the lead carriage with me and Lady Cecelia, Lord O'Shea."

Lord Denbigh's superior look hardened into a peevish frown. Lord O'Shea, however, looked delighted. "It would be my pleasure, Lady Tavistock," he said.

"And you must ride with me," Lady Claudia said, gripping Rupert's arm tighter when he attempted to move forward with Lord O'Shea and his other friends. "Wouldn't it be grand if we could have a carriage all to ourselves?"

"I'm not certain your brother would approve," Rupert grumbled.

Indeed, Lord Denbigh looked as though he wanted to wring Rupert's neck. Cece wasn't certain whether she should be alarmed or amused at the turn of events. She headed up the row of carriages by Henrietta's side, peeking over her shoulder to make certain Rupert made it into the carriage nearest him in one piece.

The ride out to Albany Court was snugger than Cece was used to. In addition to her, Henrietta, and Lord O'Shea, Henrietta's brother, Lord Herrington, and Lord Landsbury crowded into the front carriage as well. But as tightly packed as they were—especially the three men, who sat shoulder to shoulder in the rear-facing seat—Cece spent most of the ride trying not to giggle.

"The three of you paint quite the picture, wedged together as you are," Henrietta said as their carriage trundled along the road. Her eyebrow flickered up, and given what she had just said to Cece about lust, there was no mistaking her deeper feelings on the picture in front of her.

"We are yours to command this week, my lady," Lord O'Shea said, his accent particularly lilting as he smiled back at her.

"Are you?" Henrietta's smile reached a level of coquettishness that Cece had never seen from her before.

"Of course," Lord Landsbury said, mischief bright in his eyes.

"Beware of my sister," Lord Herrington said. "She'll have us all standing on our heads if we're not careful."

"I would ask no such thing, Freddy, and you know it," she said, kicking her brother's shin lightly. "But I do have a mission for you."

"Oh? Do tell," Lord O'Shea said, his green eyes dancing.

Cece bristled with excitement as well, filled with the feeling that she was about to be on the inside of a joke.

To her surprise, Henrietta glanced briefly at her before saying, "I'm sure as friends of Lord Stanhope you have all observed his recent, unforgivable behavior to my friend here, Lady Cecelia."

The three men instantly looked so guilty that Cece had no doubt Rupert had failed to be circumspect with his friends when it came to their relationship. The heat of embarrassment made her squirm in her seat.

"We are aware of the situation, yes," Lord O'Shea answered, sending Cece a reassuring glance. "You must know, Lady Cecelia, we do not necessarily condone Rupert's behavior toward you."

The other two nodded in agreement.

Cece's brow shot up. "Oh?"

They seemed reluctant to answer that ambiguous question, so Henrietta went on with, "Lady Claudia appears to want to get her claws in Rupert."

The three men laughed.

"Rupert has eyes only for you, Lady Cecelia," Lord Landsbury said with a gracious nod.

"I know," Cece answered uncertainly.

"We all know," Henrietta added. "All of England knows."

"Except Lady Claudia," Lord Herrington muttered.

"Lord Stanhope seems to be intent on pretending to have an interest in Lady Claudia," Henrietta went on.

She didn't need to say more.

"We told him not to," Lord O'Shea said with a sigh and a roll of his eyes. "We told him he was a damned fool for being crafty like that, begging your pardon." He nodded to Cece.

"No offense taken," Cece said. She wished she had the freedom to swear herself.

"Keeping that in mind," Henrietta went on, her smile growing, "I would be exceptionally grateful if you would take it upon yourselves to lavish attention on Lady Cecelia this week."

A shiver of dread went down Cece's spine. "Oh, I'm not certain that—"

"We'd love to," Lord O'Shea said, smiling broadly at her.

"Rupert is already half convinced Reese—that is, Lord Howsden—has designs on you," Lord Herrington said in a stilted voice.

"Feeding his worst fears for a bit might be fun," Lord Landsbury said with a broad smile. "If you wouldn't mind, my lady."

"But what good would it do to attempt to make Rupert jealous?" Cece sighed. "He knows how I feel about him, and vice versa."

"It would be fun." Lord O'Shea shrugged, or at least tried to. He sat in the middle of the three, broad-shouldered gentlemen, and the gesture rubbed up against both of them. "It's always fun to play tricks on a mate."

"If you say so," Cece said warily.

"It will be a reminder for him to not take things for granted," Henrietta said, touching Cece's hand in solidarity. "Every man needs a reminder not to take the women in his life for granted." She sent her brother a look before turning her smile to Lord O'Shea.

"Agreed, my lady," Lord O'Shea said with a smile and a nod.

The carriages turned a corner and headed through a large gate and onto the grounds of Albany Court moments later. Cece knew the estate was vast, but seeing it for herself—the wide, green fields stretching in all directions, the ancient woods to the north, a flicker of sunlight dancing on the river to the east, and the shining, white stones that lined the drive and several walking paths—left her with a feeling of awe. The house itself was just as impressive, rising up in several stories of Jacobean excellence. A row of servants were ready and waiting at the foot of the small terrace that led to the front door, and Reese himself stood by, ready to greet them all with a smile.

"Welcome to my humble home," he said, stepping forward to offer Cece a hand down as soon as the carriages had stopped.

"It's hardly humble," Lord Herrington said, hopping down from the carriage first and greeting Reese with an eager smile.

For a moment, Cece thought the two men would embrace, but Lord Landsbury and Lord O'Shea clambered out of the carriage before they could.

"We've a plan to rub Rupert's nose in it a bit," Lord O'Shea said in a quiet voice as Reese offered his hand to

Cece. "We're all going to pretend to be in love with Lady Cecelia in order to show Rupert up. Are you in?"

Cece sent Reese a guilty look as he helped her down, her feet crunching on the gravel. "It's a silly idea," she murmured. "You don't have to."

An unusual hint of mischief sparkled in Reese's eyes. "Oh, but of course I do," he said, leading her a few steps away from the carriage and into an open space before bowing decorously and kissing her hand with lingering intensity. When he was done, he glanced up at her and winked.

Cece wanted to roll her eyes. Rupert's friends were all a bunch of grubby boys dressed as full-grown men. But she had to admit to a certain degree of satisfaction when she caught sight of Rupert looking forlornly in her direction as Reese took her arm and stood scandalously close to her as he escorted her up the steps and into his house. Perhaps there was fun to be had in reminding him that he wasn't the only eligible gentleman of her acquaintance after all. The house party was shaping up to be far more interesting than she'd expected it to be, and it had only just begun.

CHAPTER 14

*A*lbany Court was the ideal setting for a house party. Reese's family's ancestral estate dated back to the sixteenth century, and everywhere one turned, gorgeous examples of architecture that traced the course of English history abounded. The original house, built during the reign of Henry VIII, stood at the far southern end of the gardens in all its Tudor glory. The main house had been designed and constructed by one of the finest architects of the reign of James I and looked more like a palace than a family home. The estate had been a stronghold for the Cavaliers during the Civil War and had prospered and expanded through the Georgian kingships and into the current era. It was a model of horticultural planning, an idyll in the swiftly-disappearing countryside around London, and at the moment, it was teeming with young and enthusiastic aristocrats, happy to enjoy each other's company just outside of the sharp eye of society.

Rupert glanced around him as he stood by the edge of a spreading lawn that had been set up with a badminton court, croquet wickets, and even archery targets, scowling. The ladies of the May Flowers were beautiful, lively, and giving the gentlemen a run for their money in the various competitions. The gentlemen didn't seem to mind at all and lavished attention on the ladies. A few of the married couples had already disappeared from the group at large, leaving no one in any doubt of what they'd gone off to do. The entire party had a hint of the scandalous about it, as though all present had agreed to turn a blind eye to goings on.

Which was precisely why Rupert was ready to crawl out of his skin in frustration. He paced from the cluster of chairs where Lady Tavistock was holding court to the edge of the badminton net—which no one was using at the moment—his frown fixed on the group of gentlemen crowding around Cece as she took a turn at archery.

"Practice makes perfect," Harrison told her with a dazzling smile. "I'm certain you'll be chasing us all through the woods and knocking arrows into our bums in no time."

Cece and the two other ladies fiddling with bows and arrows—ladies whose names Rupert was too unsettled to recall at the moment, not that he cared when Cece was there—gasped and giggled at the wildly inappropriate comment.

"Your bum would make a fine target indeed," Cece flirted in return.

Rupert clenched his jaw so hard his head began to throb. He glowered as Cece fired an arrow that sailed wide of its mark and Harrison rushed to retrieve it, like a dog given a command.

"Aim higher," Denbigh said with an uncharacteristic smile, standing far too close to Cece for Rupert's liking. "A lady of your caliber can afford to set her sights as high as she'd like."

"Thank you, Lord Denbigh," Cece said, treating the bastard to a gracious smile.

"Anything for you, my lady," Denbigh said, then sent a gloating look in Rupert's direction.

Cece peeked over her shoulder as well, her eyes instantly meeting Rupert's as though she knew full well he was watching her little charade. She smiled coquettishly, then took an arrow from the quiver Fergus was holding and fit it into the bowstring, squared her shoulders, then raised her bow to fire. The arrow flew far above the target, skittering in the grass behind it.

"Allow me to fetch that one, my lady," Fergus said, handing the quiver off to Reese, who, in turn, handed it to Harrison, then dashed off across the lawn to retrieve the arrow.

"Now there's an appropriate job for an Irishman," Denbigh snorted. "They can fetch as well as any dog."

"Lord Denbigh, I would thank you to keep your opinions about the Irish to yourself," Cece said, pivoting to face him with a stern look. For a moment, whatever game she was playing dropped and the light of genuine irritation shone in her eyes.

"Forgive me, Lady Cecelia, but you cannot possibly see anything of worth in a species of man who would not even be able to feed themselves if not for the guidance of their superiors," Denbigh said with so much condescension that Rupert winced in advance of Cece's reply.

Sure enough, Cece looked as though he'd spit on her. "As I recall, it was the mismanagement of land by absentee landlords who had no understanding of or compassion for the horrible effects of the potato blight that caused starvation, not any shortcoming on the part of the Irish themselves."

Denbigh made an impatient noise and only just managed to keep his patronizing smile in place. "It is clear that your delicate, female brain does not fully comprehend the issues involved, my lady. But I shall not insult you further by pushing you into a condition that is unnatural for your sex when there are so many more suitable and pleasant entertainments to be had. Perhaps you would allow me to accompany you on a stroll through—"

He didn't have a chance to finish. Cece turned her back on him as though he were dead to her and reached for another arrow. This time when she nocked it and drew back to fire, the arrow stuck firmly in the side of the target.

Rupert smirked. He knew full well that Cece was competent when it came to archery. The fact that she was putting on a show of helplessness to gain attention rankled him, but not as much as the way she snubbed Denbigh filled him with pride in her.

That pride evaporated seconds later when Reese stepped up behind Cece and said, "Here, Cecelia. Let me demonstrate how it is done."

The bastard whom he mistakenly called his friend circled his arms around Cece, standing with his chest flush against her back as he molded her arms into the right position, then closed his hands over hers. He leaned close to her ear and whispered something that made Cece laugh and blush, and that had Rupert's stomach twisting in acidic knots.

"I wish they would stop goading you like that," Freddy said with an impatient huff, moving to stand by Rupert's side.

Rupert turned to his friend, his brow shooting up. "They're doing it on purpose?"

"Of course, they are," Freddy said, grimacing and rolling his shoulders uncomfortably. "It was my sister's idea. Henny always was a little mischief-maker."

Relief attempted to wash through Rupert, but it was short-lived as he and Freddy watched Reese help Cece draw her bow and fire a perfect shot. While the other ladies watching clapped in congratulations, Cece threw her arms around Reese and hugged him. The sudden, horrific image of Cece and Reese writhing in passion, Reese enjoying it as much as Cece, burst into his mind and wouldn't let go.

What if they'd been wrong about their friend for all these years? What if all it took was the right woman to change the way a man was. Reese had reproduced, after all, which meant he'd done the deed normally at least once.

"It's irritating," Freddy growled, snapping him out of his thoughts. "He shouldn't be putting on a display like that. It isn't like him." He must have sensed Rupert staring at him. He blinked and color splashed his face. "That is to say, I'm aggravated about this whole thing on your behalf. Henny should know better than to stick her oar into other people's love lives."

Rupert was no more fooled by Freddy's short speech than he was by the way Cece laughed too loudly at something Fergus had just said to her. "The only thing we can do is ignore their little games and efforts to make us jealous."

"Us?" Freddy blinked with genuine bafflement. He frowned at Cece and Reese and their group as the bow was handed off to one of the other ladies. "Why would Lady Cecelia attempt to make me jealous?"

"Not Cece," Rupert began before he thought better of finishing his sentence and pointing out what was obvious as day to him. It dawned on him with more than a little shock that Freddy didn't have a clue that Reese was in love with him. Or, perhaps, that the feelings were mutual.

"If not Lady Cecelia, then who?" Freddy asked. "Lady Patience has an understanding with Lord Clifford, and Lady Nora has been staring at John since she arrived."

Rupert cleared his throat and shifted his shoulders, hoping it didn't look like he was squirming. He was saved the embarrassment of having to spell out something he didn't understand and had deliberately avoided thinking about for years by another disaster entirely.

"Lord Stanhope, there you are." Lady Claudia practically skipped across the lawn from where the croquet match she had just taken part in was ending.

"I've been here the whole time," Rupert said under his breath.

If Lady Claudia heard his comment, she didn't let on. She whisked right up to him, slipping her arm through his and hugging it. "Isn't it a beautiful morning? We couldn't have asked for more agreeable weather for this house party. It's as though the fates have conspired to make this the most memorable week possible."

"I believe you're right, Lady Claudia," Rupert said, glancing over to Cece.

She had Reese on one side, Harrison on the other, and Fergus showing off in front of her as he took a turn with the bow. Even Denbigh was still sniffing around in the background, as if he stood a chance. Worse still, if Cece had noticed Lady Claudia sidling up to him and making moon-eyes, she wasn't letting on. She was enjoying herself far too much with her entourage to give a care for him.

"It's a perfect morning for a stroll," Lady Claudia said, batting her eyelashes at him expectantly.

"It is," he replied by rote, not entirely sure he'd heard her question right.

Cece laughed at something one of his so-called friends said to her, and his gut burned with acid. At the same time, a wealth of carnal feelings rippled through him as well. There was something undeniably sensual about a woman who knew the effect she had on men. When he'd left for South Africa, Cece had been more of the traditional English rose type. She'd become something else entirely in his absence, something even more alluring, like a tiger lily. She held her own in a crowd of men and even stepped forward to take up a second bow and challenge Fergus to a competition.

She was powerful. She'd made that speech in St. James's Park. She was more intelligent than he'd given her credit for. And he would never, as long as he lived, forget the way she'd awakened him the other morning by wrapping her hand around his cock and stroking him until he came. He'd have given his eye teeth to have her naked in his arms again.

"...most darling little duck pond with a bench looking out over the water."

Rupert blinked out of his carnal thoughts, dragged his eyes away from Cece, and stared uncomprehendingly at Lady Claudia. She'd been talking the whole time his mind had been wandering through the tangled and sweaty sheets of his memory.

"Wouldn't that be divine?" she asked with an expectant smile.

Freddy was still standing a few feet to the side. He wore a poorly concealed grin of amusement.

"I'm terribly sorry," Rupert said, meeting his friend's eyes with a sly look. "I've promised to help Lord Herrington mingle with the ladies who are present, making introductions and such. He's in want of a wife, you see."

Freddy's teasing look dropped to shock. His shoulders slumped and he let out a sigh of resignation. "Henny keeps telling me that I could solve all my financial problems by marrying well and giving the title the heir it needs."

Lady Claudia frowned in disappointment. Still holding Rupert's arm, she pivoted to allow Freddy into the conversation. "It is a shame that your family has fallen into such financial straits," she said. "Rest assured, no one blames you at all. It is widely known that your father mismanaged your lands."

Rupert was ready to jump to his friend's defense in the wake of the stinging comment, but Freddy took the whole insult with a shrug. "The past cannot be changed. Truthfully, I am happy to be relieved of the responsibility of managing an estate. I would much rather devote myself to the sciences, now that I am returned from service abroad. But money is a concern."

"I shall take it upon myself to find a suitable bride for you," Lady Claudia said, smiling at Rupert as though the offer were designed to impress him above all. "My dear friend, Lady Maude Carmichael, is set to inherit quite a bit. I'm sure there are other women of my acquaintance who would do as well. I shall become your champion."

"What's this about a champion?"

The hair on the back of Rupert's neck stood up as Cece asked the question from only a few yards behind him. He whipped around, letting go of Lady Claudia's arm in the process, to find Cece and her court of admirers heading in their direction. Reese escorted her, but Fergus, Harrison, and even Denbigh looked as though they would gladly carry her train, if she'd been wearing a gown grand enough.

"We were just matchmaking," Rupert said, not wholly above attempting to beat her at her own game. "Lady Claudia has offered to find a wife for Freddy, and I'm certain she'd be willing to do the same for me, if I asked."

"Oh, absolutely," Lady Claudia said breathlessly, her eyes lighting up like the stars. "In fact, I have a few ideas in mind already." She grasped his arm again as though claiming him in the name of England and her loins.

"It's about time Freddy married," Harrison said with a wink, nudging Reese for good measure. "Every gentleman needs his lady wife."

"I couldn't agree more," Cece said, grinning slyly at Rupert.

"Really?" Rupert blurted before he could stop himself. He crossed his arms, which necessitated shaking

Lady Claudia off. "That's not what you said the other day."

Cece shrugged. "Every gentleman needs a wife, because without one he is nothing more than a feckless wanderer, likely to get into every manner of uncivilized trouble."

Several of the group that was beginning to form around them laughed. In addition to all of them who were already standing there, Lady Tavistock and several of the women she'd been talking to got up from their chairs and hurried over to join them, as though the curtain were going up on a particularly entertaining puppet show.

"Women are a great civilizing influence, yes," Denbigh said, drawing attention to himself by raising his voice. "Which is why they are the crowning glory of any British home."

"Not just the home," Cece argued. "Women are a vital force in all of society. See how many wars and famines have been caused because men alone have been given the power to rule?"

It was all Rupert could do not to grin at her boldness as well as her argument. He cleared his throat, put on a disapproving expression in spite of his feelings on the matter, and said, "Are you saying that if women ruled the world there would be no war?"

"That is precisely what I'm saying, Lord Stanhope," Cece said with her most winning look.

"Nonsense," Denbigh said, jumping in to steer the

argument as though sparring with Cece was the way to win her affection. "Women should exert their influence from the home. That is their realm, not the halls of Parliament or throne rooms."

"Do you think our beloved Queen Victoria should be made to step down from her God-given position so that she can take up knitting at Windsor Castle?" Cece asked.

Denbigh laughed. "Ah, but Queen Victoria is no ordinary woman, to be sure. She is a monarch."

"So are butterflies," Cece fired back. "Are you saying they should rule over the insect kingdom because of their title?"

"You prove my point in the frippery of your answer, Lady Cecelia," Denbigh said. "Women's minds are too silly for serious argument."

Rupert let his arms drop, clenching his fists. It was one thing for him to rile Cece with ridiculous arguments but quite another for an ass like Denbigh to say such things and intend them seriously. At the same time, coming to Cece's direct defense was likely to have the opposite effect than he intended.

"Let's put it to the test, then," he said, mind scrambling for a way out.

"A test?" Cece asked, her voice and her color higher than they should have been, hinting at the full extent of her pique. She stepped away from her coterie and came to face Rupert toe-to-toe. "What sort of a test?"

"Badminton," Rupert blurted, nodding to the net beside their group. "I challenge you to a game of badminton to prove once and for all which sex has the greater skill, stamina, and intelligence."

A buzz of excitement went through the friends and acquaintances around them. The ladies of the May Flowers seemed particularly excited about the possibility of a spectacle to enjoy.

"Come now," Denbigh snorted. "It's entirely unfair for a man to challenge a woman to any sort of physical contest. They're simply not built for it."

Cece whipped around to face him. "You've never seen me play badminton then, sir."

In fact, Cece's past experience with the game was precisely the reason he'd challenged her. Before he'd left for South Africa, they'd all played regular badminton games while in the country at Broadclyft Hall, the Stanhope family's country estate. Cece had been as good as he and his sisters back then, and he could only hope she was just as good now.

"It's the perfect challenge," Lady Tavistock said, fetching two racquets and a shuttlecock and bringing them to Cece and Rupert. "Although I think it only fair that Lord Stanhope play with his left hand, since Lady Cecelia will necessarily be hampered by her skirts."

"He can play with whatever hand he likes," Cece said, taking a racquet and the shuttlecock from Lady Tavistock and marching out onto the court. "As with all women, I am used to excelling in spite of the wealth of restrictions placed upon me. Men are so used to taking the easy path that it makes them complacent."

Laughter and whistles of amusement and challenge followed Cece's words. Rupert grabbed the remaining racquet from Lady Tavistock and marched out onto the other side of the court from Cece. Their friends and the other guests took up places around the court, brimming with palpable excitement.

"I'll let you serve first," he called across the net to her.

"That is the one concession I will take," Cece said, then immediately thwacked the shuttlecock in an expert serve.

Rupert wasn't entirely ready, and her shot was placed so perfectly that it was as though the birdie went straight through his racquet and plunked into the grass as he reached for it.

"One-zero," Cece said with a broad grin, holding her hand out and demanding he return the shuttlecock for her to serve again.

"A lucky shot." Rupert smacked the birdie back over the net to her.

She caught it easily in her left hand, then crossed to the left-hand side of the court. "Everything is luck, my lord. But one makes one's own luck."

She served a second time, as expertly as the first. Rupert was ready this time and was able to return the service. He went easy on her, though, hitting the birdie toward her. Cece returned it with a merciless blow that sent it sailing over his head. Rupert wheeled back and was able to make contact, but his return shot fell short of the net.

"Two-zero," Cece said in a mockingly sweet voice, darting forward and bending to retrieve the birdie for herself.

"Do you know, I think she has a chance of winning," Reese said from the sidelines.

The comment from his surprise rival put the iron in Rupert's soul, and he frowned as Cece prepared to serve once more. This time, he went after the shuttlecock with everything he had, smacking it across the net to the opposite side of the court to where Cece stood. She responded admirably, running to return it in spite of the bulk of her skirts. Rupert jerked to the side to hit the shuttlecock once again, sending it to the other side of her court. Try as she did, Cece couldn't change direction and reach it in time with her skirts.

"One-two," he said, imitating the way she had demanded the shuttlecock be returned before.

Cece retrieved the shuttlecock and hit it silently over the net to him. He could see the frustration in her eyes and knew full well what was going through her head as she swatted her skirts with her racquet. At Broadclyft Hall, she and his sisters had worn much lighter, plain skirts instead of the heavier skirt and bustle she wore now. Rupert could practically see her cursing the restrictive garment in her mind, which was why he served her with an easier shot than he might have otherwise.

She managed to return the serve with a mighty thwack and a scowl, as though she knew he hadn't given it his all. The volley that followed was far more competitive than he would have expected. He won the point in the end, but she played so fiercely that cheers and applause sounded from the sidelines when the point was won.

"Bravo, Lady Cecelia," Fergus called out, earning him a broad smile from Lady Tavistock.

The rest of the match proceeded in much the same way. Rupert knew that he and Cece were well-matched and that if she had been wearing something more sensible the playing field would have been much more level. He tried to let her win points throughout the match to make up for her disadvantage, hoping she wouldn't notice. She must have seen what he was doing, though, because every time he purposefully missed a shot or hit the birdie directly to her instead of making her work to return it, she glared at him.

Unsurprisingly, the match came down to one, last volley.

"Twenty-nine all," Rupert announced before dropping the shuttlecock and serving it.

Cece grunted as she scrambled to return it. Something about the sound fired Rupert's blood. He loved the way she wouldn't allow herself to lose, and even if she did, she wouldn't take it lying down. He smacked the birdie back to her. If she took anything lying down, it would be him, fast and hard and to the hilt. She scrambled back, managing not to trod on the hem of her skirt and fall, and clobbered the shuttlecock to return his hit. Dark circles of sweat had formed under the arms of her dress. He would make her sweat just as hard as he teased her and stroked her and drove her right up to the edge of orgasm so that she begged for it.

The image was so potent that he almost missed the shuttlecock as it dropped just on the other side of the net. He only barely managed to knock it back over to her side. Cece was already rushing the net, though, and just in the nick of time, she smashed the birdie straight over the net, only barely managing not to crash into it herself with the force of her momentum. Rupert reached for the birdie but missed it entirely. It whizzed past him, landing well within bounds.

A cry of victory went up from the women watching, and from most of the men as well. Cece had won, and she'd done it fair and square.

"Well done," Rupert said, panting, blood pulsing, desire rushing through him as he approached the last few steps to the net.

Cece walked to meet him, until they were mere inches apart, with just a flimsy stretch of net separating them. Her breath came in deep gasps that pushed her breasts tantalizingly against the thin fabric of her gown. Sweat dripped down her face, but her eyes shone with excitement and triumph.

"Who bent who over a seat and took them so vigorously they cried out for release this time?" she asked, eyes alive with lust.

She'd mangled the words of his threat from the train, but he didn't care. He understood her meaning, and his cock strained against his trousers so suddenly that he was certain he was embarrassing himself. He didn't much care about that either. All he knew was that if he didn't get between her legs again, and soon, he'd go mad.

"Victory to women," Lady Tavistock called from the sidelines.

"Victory to the May Flowers," one of the other ladies echoed.

"Hear, hear." Reese joined in with the cheers.

Rupert didn't bother considering whether it was part of the plot to tweak his nose. He continued to stare at Cece through the net, oblivious to anything but the way she was mastering him with a look.

"You'll pay for this," he said in a low rumble.

"Pay?" she asked, still panting. "For winning? I hardly think—"

"Tonight," he cut her off leaning closer still to the net. "I'll have you crying out my name in such a frenzy that you'll want to bite on a pillow to keep from waking every other guest in the house."

Her already flushed face burned redder, and her panting increased instead of easing up. She backed away from the net, her eyes still locked on his, neither denying his wicked words nor shying away from them. The only thing that turned her away from him in the end was the mob of her friends rushing to congratulate her, just as his were flooding the court to console him. He didn't need consolation, though. He'd won a far bigger game than badminton, and that night, he would claim his prize.

$\mathcal{A}$ deep sense of satisfaction at having beaten Rupert at badminton stayed with Cece for the rest of the day. She thoroughly enjoyed the attention it brought her as well, even though she was completely exhausted from the effort it took to win the match. After being carried around on the shoulders of her faux admirers and crowned with a wreath of hastily-picked flowers from the garden, she excused herself to return to her room to bathe and change out of her sweat-soaked morning dress. And, though she would never admit it to Rupert, or anyone else, she collapsed into a nap while the maid drew the bath in order to recover.

The afternoon was far more subdued as clouds rolled in and rain threatened to douse any outdoor activity. That didn't stop Reese and Rupert's other friends from showering her with pretend affection as they treated her like the queen of the house party for her victory, decorating a chair in the main drawing room for her and amusing themselves by jaunting off on every ridiculous errand she sent them on. Fergus even insisted on feeding her grapes, like the ancient Greeks supposedly did.

She was seated at the head of the table at supper as well, an honor that had Rupert scowling all through the meal. Although, the more Cece studied him while pretending to hold court like Henry VIII, the more she wondered if his scowl wasn't more of a smolder. The intensity in the way he stared back at her every time their eyes met sent shivers down her spine. She couldn't shake the deliciousness of the words he'd whispered to her across the badminton net at the end of their game. He wasn't bluffing. Rupert never bluffed.

That meant that from the moment she retired to her room after a night of amateur musical performances in which she was once again made to reign as mistress of ceremonies, she was on alert. She was aware of every slip of fabric against her heated body as the maid helped her undress and take her hair down for the night. She considered having another bath, but that seemed like a ridiculous extravagance.

In the end, all she could do was don her nightgown, thank the maid and send her on her way, then climb into the well-appointed bed in the luxurious guest room to wait. The rain that had spit down throughout the afternoon had turned into a steady downpour that drummed against the windows, but that only irritated Cece's already restless soul. She sat up, staring at the door, straining her ears to catch any sign of Rupert's approach. She picked at the coverlet, feeling that if she didn't do something with her hands she'd go mad. She reached for the book on her bedside table, then changed her mind and sat upright again. There was no chance she'd have the patience to read when she knew what was coming. Just thinking about doing all the erotic things she and Rupert had done the night of the ball at Campbell House again sent her blood racing through her veins, priming her body for what would happen.

She almost wept in relief when the handle of her door turned. Without so much as a knock, Rupert whisked into the room, turned, and locked the door behind him. Cece had just enough time to rest back against the pillows and put on a superior look before he turned to face her.

"You're late," she said, trying her best to sound as though she would punish him for his sins.

"So you've been anticipating my arrival then?" he asked, undiluted wickedness in his eyes.

Cece broke out in gooseflesh, especially when Rupert tugged at the sash of the dark red robe he wore as he stalked toward the bed. The robe loosened and he shrugged out of it, tossing it commandingly aside. He wore nothing at all underneath. His naked body was like that of a god in the warm, flickering light of the fire in her grate and the single lamp on her bedside table. The broad muscles of his shoulders and chest stood out in firm relief. His trim waist drew her eyes straight to his hips and his growing erection. His cock was already rising to the occasion, and when he saw how hungrily she devoured the sight, he grasped it and stroked himself boldly.

"I should allow the Queen of the House Party to stroke me to fullness herself," he said, stopping by the side of the bed and caressing himself with such slow eroticism that Cece was writhing with need in no time. She could have watched him toy with himself all day, but he moved his hand away, holding his arms wide at his sides and shifting his hips to present his now substantially stiffer cock to her. "Behold, your prize."

Cece wanted to laugh, but only because the whirlwind of emotions inside of her was too overwhelming to contain. Rupert hadn't been in her bedroom for a full minute, and already he was a picture of carnality. Her body throbbed for him, her core squeezing at the idea of having him inside of her. She wanted to wrap her limbs around him and mate with him until they were both as loud and desperate as he had threatened they would be.

A surprise rumble of thunder brought her back to the moment at hand. She sat straighter, tilting her chin up, and tossed the bedcovers aside invitingly. "You may undress me now," she said, imitating Queen Victoria's regal manner.

"Yes, my queen," Rupert replied, as much in character as she was.

He climbed onto the bed, pushing the covers farther to the side. The way the mattress dipped with his weight sent a thrill through her, but that was nothing to the way he grabbed her ankles and thrust them apart, kneeling between them. She gasped, gripping the mountain of pillows on either side of her, then held her breath as he took hold of the hem of her nightgown and drew it up toward her hips with painful slowness.

"Are you trying to torture me?" she asked breathlessly as he paused just short of exposing her curls to tease her inner thighs with feather-light strokes.

"Yes," he answered frankly. "I intend to torture you the way you tempt me on a daily basis." He gripped her knees and parted them as far as they would go, still not moving her nightgown to expose her center.

"I never teased you like this," she panted, willing herself not to tremble at the way he brushed his fingertips up to her inner thighs.

"You drive me to distraction on an hourly basis," he insisted, meeting and holding her eyes with fiery intensity. "Every smile sends blood throbbing through me. Every look makes my heart race. Every word you speak makes my cock hard." His hands reached so close to her sex that she couldn't think, and then he tightened his hold on her thighs so much she gasped. He leaned forward and whispered in her ear, "How does it make you feel to know that I stroke myself until I come every night while imagining you doing the same?"

She let out a breath that was half moan, trembling with the intensity of her need for him. It was madness for him to admit such thing to her. "You are a wicked man," she managed to say, leaving out how desperately she loved it.

"I know," he said, then shifted to close his mouth over hers in a punishing kiss.

Her body blossomed with pleasure as his lips molded to hers and his tongue invaded her mouth. He was aggressive in his ardor, groaning in triumph as she succumbed to whatever he wanted to take from her. She kissed him back, letting go of her pillows to rake her fingers through his hair.

Without her arms to steady her, she slipped down, utterly at his mercy. Her shift meant that the fabric bunched just below her hips moved as well, exposing her throbbing sex to him. He seemed to know it without looking and let go of her thighs to bring one hand up to possessively stroke her cunny.

"I knew you'd be wet," he murmured against her lips as his hand went to work, teasing and caressing her primed flesh.

He was relentless, circling her entrance before thrusting two fingers inside of her. There was nothing soft or hesitant about the way he claimed her, stroking her in just the right way. She gasped aloud as he pleasured her, trying not to fulfill his earlier prophecy by crying out loud enough to wake whoever was in the room next to hers. Another clap of thunder and the rain beating furiously against her windows helped conceal her moans of passion, but when he brushed his thumb over her clitoris as his fingers continued to invade her, she was lost.

"Dear God," she cried out as an orgasm as powerful as the thunder outside enveloped her. Pleasure so intense it made her want to weep radiated through her as her inner muscles squeezed his fingers. He groaned in triumph as she convulsed and then went limp as her orgasm subsided. She was left feeling loose and blissfully happy, in spite of the madness of the whole thing.

"You're a devil," she panted as he moved his hand away from her and drew her nightgown up over her head.

"Me?" he asked indignantly, tossing the garment aside. "You're the one who can't keep your hands off me."

In fact, he was right. As soon as her arms were free, she reached for him, sculpting the lines of his chest and abdomen with her palms as he leaned toward her. With a throaty laugh, she reached for his cock and balls, fondling them and watching as his face tensed with pleasure. She loved the way he felt, hard and soft together, and the way he so obviously enjoyed her touch. Not many men would take such enjoyment in their woman behaving so sensually. At least, so she'd been told. With her new experience, she wasn't so sure that the unspoken rules of feminine behavior were actually true behind closed doors.

Rupert made an urgent sound, then pulled his hips away from her, pushing her hands aside. "Too soon," he hissed, then dipped down to kiss her. As his lips caressed hers, more sensual than demanding this time, Cece felt as though someone had lit a match of understanding in her mind. He could bring her to climax as many times as he wanted, or as she wanted, and they could continue with their games. But if he came too soon, the game would be over. At least for a while. She smiled as the realization hit her. Perhaps women had been given an advantage in the game of love after all.

She pushed against his chest, and when he rocked back, he wore a look of surprise. "I want to look at you," she said in sultry tones. "Lie back."

Curiosity and delight lit Rupert's expression, and he sprawled back to give her what she wanted. He rested on his back with his legs spread as wide as hers currently were, propping himself up on his arms. His thick, hard cock stood straight up against his abdomen, its tip flared and slick, looking as though it were a cannon that could fire at any moment.

"Only a minx enjoys looking at a naked man in full arousal," he said, teasing her with a look that dared her to drink in the sight.

"I believe we've already established that I'm a minx," she said, pushing away from her pillows and shifting to kneel between his legs.

"If I had known just how minxish you were, I never would have joined the army."

Cece arched a brow, a spike of anger adding spice to the desire that still pulsed through her. "So if I had spread my legs for you four years ago you would have actually consulted me before leaving?"

Guilt pinched through his aroused expression. "I didn't mean it like that."

"Perhaps not." She leaned forward, planting her hands on the bed on either side of his waist. "But I should punish you for it."

The feeling of power that surged through her as she trapped him beneath her was heady. She could see as clear as day that he was caught between pleasure and guilt, and she would have been lying if she said she didn't enjoy it.

"How on earth do you propose to punish me?" he asked, as though anything she did to him would only give them both heaps of pleasure.

She arched one eyebrow and lowered herself over him, bringing her mouth dangerously close to his straining cock. "Too soon, you said?" she asked. With her heart pounding at how daring she could be, she licked the tip of her tongue along the length of his staff, from balls to tip.

Rupert sucked in a breath and jerked at the sensations her bold move produced. "If you do, it will be your loss as much as mine."

"Is that so?" she asked, planting the lightest possible kiss on the underside of his cock's flared tip. He made a sound of pleasure and frustration. "I've already had one orgasm, and I could easily demand you give me another. And you would."

He might have tried to laugh, but the sound came out as desperate panting as she kissed the head of his penis again, taking it partially into her mouth, though she would need to use her hands to position it correctly for deeper play.

"You wouldn't dare," he gasped, flopping back to lay fully on the bed, his hands behind his head. "You want my cock inside of you too badly to suck me off."

Shivers of wickedness rippled through her at the new words and actions he was inadvertently teaching her. "You think so?"

She lifted herself above him and brushed her fingertips along his length, watching him with a raised eyebrow and a mischievous grin. For a moment, he looked uncertain. That uncertainty intensified when she took hold of his staff and held it up and away from his body. He tensed, alarm in his eyes, as she bent forward, bringing her mouth tauntingly close to his cock as she held it upright.

In the end, he was right. She didn't want to pleasure him with her mouth half so much as she wanted to feel him stretching and filling her. At the last moment, she shifted to straddle him, holding him in just the right position so that she could sink onto him, sheathing him deep inside of her. She gasped as he jerked up, lodging hard within her, and bit her lip as the urge to move on him turned irresistible.

Except that she had no idea what she was doing. She froze where she was, wanting so much more but not knowing how to get it. The movements she was able to make were frustratingly inadequate.

"Like this," Rupert said, his voice rough, gripping her hips.

He guided her to move more boldly, but in her eagerness, she moved too much and he slipped out of her. With lightning quickness, he adjusted her above him, positioning her so that her breasts brushed against his chest, and brought his cock back to her entrance. She bore down on him from a slightly different angle, humming in satisfaction as he slid home. He kept her from moving too erratically and losing him again as she set up a steady, pleasurable rhythm.

Like magic, everything clicked in her mind and she suddenly understood how she needed to move to get the most out of the position they were in. From that point, their joining was bliss, and it progressed swiftly. She set the pace, squeezing and bearing down on him until the first signs of her body about to explode with pleasure radiated from her sex and through her entire body.

"Oh," she panted as she came closer and closer, the rain still sharp on the window and thunder in the distance. "Oh, yes." Rupert grunted and tensed and abandoned himself to the pleasure of it all with her, and within moments, pure pleasure throbbed through her as her body burst once more. "Yes, oh, yes, Rupert!"

He cried out and jerked hard into her a few times before they both lost every last ounce of energy as their passion was spent. The rain continued to pound and the thunder to roll, but they could have been a thousand miles away for all the heady contentment Cece felt post-orgasm.

"You can punish me like that any day," Rupert panted, caressing her and stroking her back as he lay as if helpless under her.

Cece laughed and struggled to prop herself above him, careful to keep his softening cock inside of her. "No, silly. Your punishment is that you must shave that ridiculous moustache."

Rupert raised a hand instinctively to his upper lip. "But I like the moustache. It's manly."

"It's ugly," she laughed, knowing that no part of him could ever truly be ugly to her.

"You'll grow used to it in time," he insisted. "I haven't even shown you the sort of magnificent sensations it can produce in the right regions."

"No." Cece laughed harder, pushing away from him at last and flopping back onto her pillows, the right way around in the bed.

Rupert crawled around to join her, pulling her into his arms and twining his legs with hers as they lay side by side, still too hot to reach for the bedcovers. "A man's facial hair is his birthright," he insisted.

"Then why aren't you born with it?" she giggled. She couldn't stop her giggles now that their game of seduction was over and they were back to being who they were, Cece and Rupert, who had loved each other for years.

"An oversight of nature, I can assure you," he said.

She sighed, shoulders still shaking, and said, "Well, I won't marry you if you keep it."

"Who said I wanted to marry you?" Rupert asked, his eyebrows flying up.

Cece gaped at him. "Isn't that what all of your ridiculous displays are about? Getting me to marry you in spite how angry I am at you?"

"You don't seem very angry to me," he said, closing a hand around her breast and teasing her nipple between his thumb and forefinger.

"I'm furious with you," she insisted, arching into his touch all the same.

"Well, I don't want to marry you," he said.

Cece froze, frowning, then propped herself on one arm beside him. "Why not?" she demanded, certain he was teasing, but anxious all the same.

He shrugged and rolled to his back, resting one arm behind his head. "Men don't fuck their wives like that, only their mistresses. Therefore, I'll keep you as my mistress so that I can have you bouncing on my balls whenever I want."

Twin bursts of relief and irritation shot through Cece. She smacked Rupert's chest, then pivoted to face away from him, curling on her side as if she would go to sleep. "Fine. Don't marry me, then. But don't expect me to beg my way into your bed as your mistress either."

She closed her eyes and pretended to nod off. A moment later, Rupert looped his arm around her and drew her back flush against his chest. More than that, his cock pressed against her backside, and it wasn't nearly as flaccid as she expected it to be.

"You couldn't keep yourself out of my bed if you tried," he whispered against her ear, taunting her. "You like this too much." He flexed his hips against her in a way that brought to mind all sorts of unusual positions for making love. "And as soon as I have a bit of a rest, I'll show you just how much you like it," he said, some of the daring leaving his voice as he relaxed, nuzzling her hair.

"I'm sure you will," Cece said indulgently, reaching back to pat his thigh.

In truth, she looked forward to it. She looked forward to all sorts of things. But if Rupert thought that bending her to his will was that easy, he would soon be proven wrong.

CHAPTER 16

The storm blew itself out during the night, leaving the grounds around Albany Court glittering with raindrops and dew as the sun rose on a new day. Contrary to his promise to make love to Cece again once he'd rested, he slept deeply, well past the first rays of dawn and the chorus of birds twittering happily in the garden. Cece didn't mind at all. She was just as happy to wake up to such an idyllic scene, particularly as it meant waking up naked and content, snuggled against Rupert's side.

She rubbed the sleep from her eyes and propped herself on one elbow, careful not to wake him, so that she could study him in the fresh, morning sunlight. He truly was a handsome man, even with the dreadful moustache. He had the same high cheekbones and commanding brow that his mother had, and though she'd only seen a single portrait of his long-dead father on a visit to Broadclyft Hall, Lord Richard Marlowe had been a handsome man too. She traced his expressive lips with her fingertips, her heart thumping within her as she remembered all the things those lips had done to her. Maybe she should thank his string of nameless, past lovers for teaching him instead of resenting him.

A smile danced across her lips. She did thank them, but she would never let Rupert know that. She loved him with all her heart, but his head did have an unfortunate tendency to swell. Though, if she were honest with herself, she liked that arrogance too. Mostly because it was infrequent and couldn't hold a candle to the kind, generous, and intelligent man Rupert was at heart.

She scooted closer to him, leaning forward to kiss him, like Sleeping Beauty in reverse. Sure enough, he stirred and sucked in a breath as she nibbled on his lower lip. His mouth curved into a lazy smile as he circled his arms around her and rocked to his side, pressing their bodies together.

"Good morning," he rumbled in a sleepy voice.

"It is a good morning," she said in reply, brushing her fingers through his tousled hair. "Any morning waking up with you is good."

He hummed in agreement and scooped a hand down over her backside and thigh to lift her leg over his hips. The movement brought them into intimate contact, and Cece wasn't at all surprised that he was already half hard.

"Do you think anyone would notice if we stayed in

bed all day?" he asked, grinding against her and growing harder as he did.

"Yes," Cece answered with a laugh, wriggling to help the process along. "I wouldn't be surprised if they were all downstairs at breakfast already, gossiping about how scandalous we are."

"Nonsense," Rupert said, kissing her neck and fondling her breast. "House parties are designed for illicit assignations. I would bet my fortune that half the company is doing exactly what we're doing right now."

"And what are we doing?" Cece asked, breathless.

He shifted and entered her in one swift, firm move. It was the best answer he could have given. She let out a long, low moan of enjoyment as he clamped a hand over her backside, holding her hips perfectly to accept his luxuriously slow thrusts.

Their mating was quick and far simpler than the night before. It was no longer a game of one-upmanship, but rather a deep expression of intimacy. Rupert rolled her to her back so that he could fill her more fully with each delicious movement. She closed her eyes and reveled in the feeling of being one with him, digging her nails into his backside to urge him on. Within no time, pleasure coiled tight within her, then burst into sizzling release. He followed her into orgasm, sighing with joy as his seed poured into her.

It wasn't until afterwards, when the two of them lay in a pile of loose arms and legs, spent and sated, that reality came knocking on the door. Literally. The door handle rattled, and when the maid attempting to enter to light a fire in the grate saw it was locked, she whispered, "My lady?"

Cece tensed and Rupert sucked in a sudden breath, sitting up. The maid must have put two and two together and realized her mistake in saying something. Footsteps skittered down the hall. Rupert laughed, running a hand over his face and climbing out of bed.

"It looks as though Reese forgot to instruct his staff about the true purpose of house parties," he said, heading to the washstand.

Cece propped herself on her elbows and watched him. She would never grow tired of looking at his naked body, his lean muscles, the perfect curve of his backside, his manly bits hanging down in front, looking thoroughly used. The whole thing brought a smile to her face.

"Don't think I don't see you gloating over there," he said as he splashed water on his face and briefly rubbed his important parts with one of the towels on the washstand.

"I have every right to gloat," she said, getting out of bed herself and joining him at the washstand. "I'm going to be the mistress of a handsome and talented man."

Rupert laughed and finished washing, then strode across the room to fetch his robe. They both knew his declaration from the night before was nothing but silliness and that marriage was inevitable for them. The flash of teasing in his eyes as he threw his robe around his shoulders and tied the sash was proof of that. But Cece liked leaving things unspoken and ambiguous for the time being.

He strode back to the washstand before she could do more than wet a sponge. Part of her wanted to call the maid back to have her draw another bath, but the labor and time involved would be too much. Instead, she let Rupert draw her into his arms for one last, powerful kiss.

"If I had thought things through last night, I would have brought a change of clothes with me," he said, then kissed her again before letting her go. "I'm not exactly looking forward to sneaking back through the halls in nothing but a robe."

"It's your own fault," Cece said with a pointed look, turning back to her ablutions. "Don't let Lady Claudia see you or it would break her heart."

Rupert had the good humor to laugh at her quip. He stole one last kiss, then crossed to the door. He unlocked it and peeked out into the hall. Cece assumed it was empty when he glanced briefly back at her, winked, then disappeared, shutting the door behind him.

She turned back to her bath with a happy sigh, almost reluctant to wash away the evidence of their passion. The maid returned a short while later and helped her to dress and put up her hair for the day. Though the young woman didn't say anything outright, the grin she couldn't keep off her face was all the proof Cece needed that Reese's staff knew exactly what was going on in his house.

Rupert was right when it came to predicting the

guests would be slow to wander down to breakfast as well. More than half of the guests were missing from the long breakfast table by the time Cece took a seat across from Henrietta and smiled at the footman who poured her tea and offered her a selection of pastries. Almost all of the married couples were absent, and quite a few of the single men and ladies as well.

"You had a good night," Henrietta said by way of greeting, a knowing glint in her eyes.

"Yes, I did," Cece replied. She sent a brief glance farther down the table, to where Lady Claudia was staring blearily at her plate of eggs and toast. "I slept like the dead after exerting myself so much yesterday." She picked up her tea and flickered one eyebrow at Henrietta before taking a sip.

"That is precisely why ladies should not engage in athletic activity the way you so shamelessly did with Lord Stanhope yesterday," Lady Claudia snapped, proving that she'd been listening in and that Cece had been wise to choose her words with Henrietta. Lady Claudia tilted her chin up imperiously and went on with, "I would think you would want to be more careful, considering how Lord Stanhope's attentions have all but left you."

It was all Cece could do to keep herself from laughing. Her lips twitched in spite of her efforts and she asked, "Whatever do you mean?"

A superior look spread over Lady Claudia's face. "Lord Stanhope wasn't in his room last night."

"He wasn't?" Cece asked, blinking. She was a fair actress when she wanted to be.

"No, he wasn't." Lady Claudia's gloating look deepened. "And you know what that means. House parties are notorious, after all."

"What does it mean?" Cece went on, playing innocent.

Lady Claudia blushed and peeked around the table to be sure that none of the others were listening. She leaned closer to Cece and Henrietta and whispered, "It means that he clearly spent the night in someone else's room, in someone else's bed." The smile she sent Cece was so triumphant that if Cece hadn't known better, she would have thought Lady Claudia was admitting to spending the night with Rupert herself.

Henrietta must have drawn the same conclusion. "How do you know that Lord Stanhope wasn't in his room last night?" she asked with an expression that implied the answer and accused Lady Claudia.

Sure enough, Lady Claudia's cheeks flushed deep pink and her shoulders stiffened. "I—" She glanced around the table with a guilty, hunted look. "I heard one of the maids say," she rushed on, fumbling her words.

"Did you?" Henrietta asked, arching one eyebrow.

"He wasn't there," she snapped. "His bed was made. There was no sign of him." Lady Claudia swallowed. "The maid said so."

"Well, if the maid said so," Cece said with as much innocence as she could muster, which wasn't much. She and Henrietta exchanged a look, and Cece came so close to bursting into laughter that her eyes watered.

Lady Claudia huffed and faced her breakfast with a stiff back and bright red cheeks.

"Honestly," Henrietta went on, her expression stern while her eyes danced with mirth. "I don't understand the shocking laxity of morals in young ladies these days."

Cece hummed in agreement, selecting a croissant from the plate the footman had left near her place. "They never would have gotten away with it in our mothers' time."

"Certainly not," Henrietta agreed. "I think it shows a distinct lack of character. Why, I would be tempted to curtail the involvement of such women in the May Flowers if accusations of impropriety could be proven."

"Really," Lady Claudia huffed, her embarrassment switching to anger. "You act as though you and you alone rule the May Flowers."

The breakfast room was slowly filling. A few of the new arrivals glanced their way with interest.

"I was elected to serve as Head," Henrietta reminded her.

"Well, perhaps it's time for another election," Lady Claudia said in a tight voice. "Some of us aren't at all satisfied with the leadership."

"Are we talking about elections?" Lord O'Shea asked as he strode into the room, Rupert at his side.

"It seems inevitable at this point," Rupert answered. "Gladstone has been having increasing difficulty holding things together, what with all the Irish Home Rule problems."

"Not to mention The Third Reform Act passing last year," Lord O'Shea went on. "I, for one, am desperately interested to see how extending the vote to Irish farmers and extending the franchise in general changes election results."

They passed where Cece and Henrietta were sitting. Rupert sent a rakish grin Cece's way, but beyond that, he pretended not to notice her. "The Conservatives are shaking in their boots, of course," he said as he and Lord O'Shea took seats at the other end of the table.

"Men," Henrietta muttered, though her expression brimmed with good humor. "They assume everything anyone talks about is directly related to them."

Cece hummed in agreement, sipping her tea. "I do think there will be a general election soon, and I am interested in seeing how last year's reforms change things."

The conversation settled into a harmless buzz as more people came down to breakfast. The seats between Cece and Henrietta and Lady Claudia were filled, blocking Lady Claudia from sticking her oar in where it wasn't wanted again. Cece was far happier to talk to Reese about the previous night's rain's effect on his gardens. She noted several looks from Rupert as she and Reese talked, but unlike the day before, there wasn't a hint of jealousy from Rupert.

Cece was just getting around to asking Reese what sort of entertainments he had planned for the day when

Lord Denbigh marched into the room, his face pale with anger, his fists clenched at his sides.

"Claudia," he barked, striding up to her place at the table. "Pack your things. We're leaving at once."

"But...but I didn't do anything," Lady Claudia insisted, cowering.

Cece was too startled to gloat, and as it turned out, she would have been wrong to.

"I've had a telegram from Father," he went on. "We're needed back in London immediately. The steward of his Irish lands, Mr. Murtaugh, has been brutally murdered by those savage tenants of his." He practically spit the words.

A ripple of shock passed over the table. Cece put down her teacup to keep from dropping it. "Dear Lord, I'm so sorry," she said.

Most of the rest of the guests at the table said similar things.

"Terrible luck." Rupert added his condolences to the others'.

"Luck?" Lord Denbigh bellowed, glaring at him. "It's not luck, it's a crime. A crime perpetrated by sub-humans who have been encouraged by your separatist clap-trap."

Reese rose from his chair and stepped to Lord Denbigh's side with a placating gesture. "Let's keep calm heads," he said. "The trouble in Ireland isn't going to resolve itself at the breakfast table."

"Your Mr. Murtaugh is one of too many land managers who have been attacked recently," Harrison added, though whether he was saying it as a concession or to lessen Lord Denbigh's rage was debatable.

"It's the fault of the managers that they're murdered in the first place," Lord O'Shea grumbled at the other end of the table, rising from his seat and glaring at Lord Denbigh.

Cece gulped and pressed a hand to her stomach. It was a blessing that the breakfast table separated Lord O'Shea and Lord Denbigh, but that didn't stop a war of words.

"It doesn't surprise me at all that a dog like you would applaud murderers," Lord Denbigh growled.

"And it doesn't surprise me that you would make a hero and a martyr out of a man who probably starved, beat, and raped his way to what he called land management," Lord O'Shea replied.

Several of the ladies at the table gasped. One or two got up from the table and fled the room. Cece's stomach roiled, but she was ready to jump to the defense of the Irish if she had to.

"You support upsetting the natural order of things?" Lord Denbigh shouted. "You champion those who would strike back at their betters and fly in the face of the role in society that God has ordained for them?"

"I doubt the Almighty ever intended for men to be treated like cattle," Lord O'Shea fired back. "I believe He would weep if He saw the oppression that persists in His name."

"The Irish are no better than cattle, and acts of

violence like this only serve to prove it." Before Lord O'Shea or anyone else in the room could contradict him, he snapped. "Come along, Claudia. We're leaving. Now."

He pulled Lady Claudia's chair back so fast she almost spilled to the floor. Without a word, fear in her eyes, Lady Claudia scrambled to her feet and scurried out of the room without a look at anyone.

"We can delay the cricket match, if you'd like," Rupert called from the end of the table as Lord Denbigh marched after her.

Lord Denbigh stopped as though Rupert's words were an arrow that had struck him in the back. He whipped around, glaring at Rupert. "The match is still on," he growled. "I wouldn't pass up the opportunity to crush you all for anything, especially now."

He didn't wait for a reply before charging out of the room, radiating fury.

A long, painful silence followed. Cece sat frozen in her chair, not sure if she should say something to diffuse the situation or if she should simply drink her tea and pretend nothing had happened.

"If you will excuse me," Reese said at last, breaking the tension. "I must speak to my staff about departures."

Reese's exit relieved some of the tension, and a dozen, whispered conversations started up around the table. Cece wished she were sitting next to Rupert so that they could discuss what had just happened.

"I hate to say it," Rupert spoke over the low chatter,

"but perhaps this is not the best time for a house party after all."

"You may be right," Henrietta said, glancing across the table at her brother. "It might be best if we all head back to London."

"Particularly as this unfortunate event will likely have political consequences," Lord Herrington agreed with a nod.

Murmurs of agreement sounded around the table. Cece met Rupert's eyes across the distance and nodded. It would be best for them to be in London if the murder of Lord Denbigh's father's steward led to bigger trouble.

Breakfast was finished in a hurry. Reese had more than just a quick talk with his staff to deal with as the majority of his guests requested their things be packed and brought down for departure right away. Cece packed her own trunk, since she was perfectly capable of doing it and felt the maids could be used elsewhere. She did it with a heavy heart, though, and by the time she gathered with the rest of the guests on Albany Court's front steps, waiting for the carriages to be brought around, she had the distinct feeling as though someone had died.

"Of course, someone has died," Reese told her when she confided as much in him. "We might not have known Mr. Murtaugh, but I fear his death will affect us all."

"I fear you're right," Cece told him, glad that the two of them were friends.

That sense of gloom stayed with her all the way to the station, while Rupert exchanged their return tickets for the next train to depart, and as the two of them settled into a first-class compartment together.

Which was why, when the train rolled forward and Rupert moved to sit on the seat beside her, circling his arm around her shoulders and grinning at her like a schoolboy with a sweet, she recoiled.

"Rupert, what are you doing?" she demanded, pushing away from him and moving to the opposing seat when he tried to kiss her.

Rupert blinked in surprise. "We're alone in a train compartment once again," he said, a hint of offense in his voice. "Since we enjoyed each other's company so much last night, I figured—"

"You figured what?" she snapped. "That I would be in an amorous mood after hearing of the violent death of a man? That I would want to engage in wicked activity when the entire political situation in Ireland may be about to explode?"

Rupert clenched his jaw. "If we held ourselves back from love every time the situation in Ireland was about to explode, there would be no love at all."

"Then perhaps there shouldn't be any," Cece said, louder than she intended to. A porter passing in the train's narrow hall beside them flinched in his steps and frowned at her through the window.

Rupert reached over and drew the shades to give them some privacy. "I didn't mean to offend your delicate political sensibilities," he grumbled. "I withdraw my offer of intimacy."

Cece's eyes snapped wide. "You act as though it were something I requested, not something thrust upon me."

"You didn't complain about things being thrust upon you last night," he said in a quiet, sullen voice.

"Rupert Marlowe, you do beat all," Cece huffed. She crossed her arms, shook her head, and stared out the window at the passing countryside, as irritated with him now as she had been on the way up to Albany Court.

"Forgive me for wanting to take comfort in the arms of the woman I love during times of distress instead of fretting uselessly about it," he said, as put out as she was.

She glared across the compartment at him. "Don't fret about it, then," she said. "Don't behave inappropriately to the moment either. Use the power you have as a lord, as a man, to pass laws that will make the situation right. I only wish that I could do the same."

She settled into her seat, writhing with discomfort in a thousand ways. She was miserable that women were so helpless to address the problems of the world, miserable that Rupert seemed to think the answer to everything was sexual congress, and miserable that anyone had to die, or kill, for what they believed in. If things didn't change soon, she might end up doing something rash and causing an even bigger scandal than she already had.

CHAPTER 17

*E*very time he thought he was taking a step forward, Rupert found himself sliding back to where he started. He tossed the bag containing his cricket kit into a corner of the porch that ran along one side of the pavilion bordering the pitch at Lord's, bending over to draw out his bat as if unsheathing a sword. He would never understand Cece, never in a million years. Just when he thought things were finally perfect between the two of them, she turned into a cold fish once more.

He jerked around, intending to stomp down the porch stairs for a little practice before the momentous game against Denbigh and his friends began, but instead, he nearly thwacked Fergus with his bat.

"Careful, there," Fergus said, laughing and holding up his hands. "It's Denbigh's squad you want to beat to a pulp, not me."

Rupert softened his scowl, shaking his head. "Sorry," he mumbled, heading on down the steps to the grass.

Fergus followed him, his bright, ginger hair shining in the sunlight and contrasting sharply with his cricket whites. Where Rupert was all frustration and darkness, Fergus looked as though he'd been knighted and handed a sack of gold all at once.

"Why are you in such a good mood?" Rupert asked him. The question came out like an accusation, leaving a bad taste in his mouth.

Fergus shrugged and followed him out to the wicket, catching a ball that Jack Craig, a last-minute addition to the team, tossed his way. "The sun is shining, the birds are singing, and I get a chance to show up Denbigh and his lot today."

Rupert glanced sideways at his friend just as a peal of feminine laughter swelled from the edge of the wooden grandstands that started several yards from the pavilion. His heart leapt for a moment as he instantly spotted Cece front and center in the group. She and the rest of the ladies wore stylish, white day dresses with some sort of large purple flower pinned to their chests. Cece's blonde hair was piled atop her head and topped with a tall, brimmed hat decorated with purple ostrich feathers to match her flower. She looked like a fashion plate, but considering the simple lines of her skirt and the lighter fabric, she was also dressed as though she might challenge him to another badminton match.

Cece wasn't the only woman who caught his attention, though. Lady Tavistock was laughing louder than the rest of the women. Not only that, she glanced their way and sent Fergus a smile that was so coquettish it might as well have been an advertisement of availability.

"The sun is shining indeed," Rupert grumbled, shaking his head.

They reached the wicket, but rather than jumping into practice, Fergus clapped a hand on Rupert's shoulder and turned him to face him. "What have you done now?" he asked.

Rupert glared at him. "What makes you think I did anything?"

Fergus answered with a flat stare, crossing his arms.

"Women are a mystery," he said with surprising vehemence. "They say one thing then behave inconsistently. They smile one moment then tell you off the next."

"What did you do?" Fergus repeated in more ominous tones.

Rupert huffed in annoyance. "Why must I be the one at fault?" The heat rising up his neck and face stung of guilt. He answered his own question with, "It's Denbigh's fault. Him and his father and their Irish holdings."

Fergus's brow shot up. "Don't tell me you're blaming the Irish for all your problems too."

"No, of course not," Rupert grumbled. "But things were going so well at the house party." A rush of heat of another kind filled him at the memory of just how well. "Then Denbigh's father's bloody steward had to go and get himself killed, and—"

Fergus held up a hand to stop him. "Never mind. I know why Lady Cecelia is vexed with you."

Rupert let out a hopeless, irritated breath, his shoulders dropping. "All I wanted was to come home from South Africa, leave the army behind, and to take up my duties as Earl of Stanhope with the woman I love at my side. I didn't expect to leave one battle just to enter another."

"Life is full of battles," Fergus told him with a rare streak of seriousness. "You're my friend, Rupert. You're like a brother to me. But the whole purpose of serving our country was to put our youth behind us and to take up the responsibilities of men. That includes swallowing your pride now and then and thinking with something other than your cock."

"I'm not just thinking with my cock," Rupert argued, though an uncomfortable itch spread down his spine even as he spoke the words.

Fergus raised one eyebrow doubtfully. He let his arms drop and shifted his stance. "If you can't learn to take the slings and arrows of life in stride, you're going to find yourself fighting more battles than any sane man should ever get himself into. And if you refuse to listen to the woman you love, listen to the things she doesn't say as well as the things she does, then you won't even give yourself a safe place to retreat to when the rest of the world attacks."

His friend was right, but pride kept Rupert from

admitting it outright. "And you derive all this wisdom from your vast experience with women?"

Fergus grinned impishly, glancing past him to Lady Tavistock and the rest of the ladies, who were moving away from the grandstand toward the pavilion. "I do all right," he said, leaving Rupert to imagine what was going on.

"Wait! Where are you going?" One of the older gentlemen, Mr. Clarke, who had come to watch the match from the pavilion porch called out to the approaching ladies. "You can't come up here."

Rupert's uncomfortable conversation with Fergus and his focus on his own problems instantly dropped. He steeled himself and marched back toward the pavilion, Fergus on his heels.

"What do you mean we can't go up there?" Lady Tavistock asked, looking like a general at the front of an army of white-clad women.

Mr. Clarke flapped his mouth indignantly before forming words. "Ladies are not allowed in the pavilion."

"Why not?" Cece asked. She sent an imperious, side-ways look to Rupert as he and Fergus reached the scene. "Are you afraid we'll damage the place?"

Some of the other May Flowers laughed. Mr. Clarke didn't look remotely amused.

"It simply isn't done," he said dismissively. "Ladies have never been allowed in the pavilion. Ladies should not be wandering free across the grounds at all."

"Are we a flock of sheep that has been set loose to

destroy your grass, then?" Lady Tavistock asked with a look of shock and offense.

Mr. Clarke's face pinched as though she'd said something foul. "I refuse to discuss the matter with a jumped-up female who thinks too much of herself. Where is your husband, madam? Why has he not restrained you?"

Lady Tavistock's expression went stone cold. "My dear, late husband, the Marquess of Tavistock, is in his grave, sir."

Mr. Clarke turned red and stammered, "I'm very sorry, my lady, very sorry." He then straightened and went on with, "But ladies still aren't allowed in the pavilion."

"Never mind," Cece said, catching Rupert's eye with a sideways glance then moving closer to him. She snatched the cricket bat right out of his hand and said, "A lady's place is on the cricket pitch."

A flurry of approval and excitement arose from the dozen or so other May Flowers as Cece rested the bat jauntily over her shoulder and marched out toward the wicket. Lady Tavistock slipped over to take the ball from Fergus's hand before catching up to Cece. Rupert exchanged a glance with Fergus, then both of them rushed to catch up to the ladies.

"You can't possibly propose to play cricket," he said, falling into step by Cece's side.

"And why not?" she asked, one eyebrow raised. "I've handled a bat before."

The look in her eyes that accompanied her words

caused Rupert to miss a step and choke on the reply he was about to make.

Fergus caught the meaning of the comment as well and laughed outright. "I'll show you how to bowl, Lady Tavistock," he said, crossing behind Cece and Lady Tavistock to take the ball from her. "It's all in the action of your swing."

"What's going on here?" Jack asked, jogging to meet the invading group of women, along with several of the other players.

"Since your opponents have yet to arrive, Mr. Craig, the ladies of the May Flowers have decided to take up cricket and challenge you instead," Cece said.

Most of the other players laughed congenially.

"Lady Claudia is going to be devastated to have missed this," Cece's friend, Lady Diana Pickwick, laughed as she stepped away from the group of women to pick up a cricket ball that lay abandoned in the grass. She tossed it to one of the other women, Lady Beatrice Lichfield.

"Lady Claudia would never approve to begin with," Lady Beatrice answered with a laugh.

"Why isn't Claudia here?" Lady Diana asked.

"That lot never approves of anything the rest of us do these days," Cece said, ignoring the question.

Several of the other ladies hummed in agreement. Rupert was surprised to find at least half of them scowling. He'd been under the impression that the May Flowers acted as one.

"We should form a May Flowers cricket team," Lady Tavistock said, her expression lighting with inspiration.

Several of the other ladies, Cece among them, voiced their agreement and delight.

"You know, there are scientists and physicians who are beginning to postulate that women should be physically active," Cece said. "Contrary to the prevailing notions about female fragility."

"Hear, hear," Lady Diana seconded.

Jack grinned. "Have any of you ever played cricket before?"

A chorus of no's and disappointment sounded from the women.

"Never," Lady Tavistock said. "But there's a first time for everything."

"And you condone this?" Jack asked Rupert with a smirk.

"No," Rupert answered. "Not at all."

"Rubbish," Cece huffed, swinging his bat and walking up to the wicket. "How difficult can it be?"

"Far more difficult than you imagine," Rupert said, following her. "This isn't badminton."

"My athletic skills do not end with badminton, Lord Stanhope," she said, positioning herself in front of the stumps and thumping the ground with the toe of the bat before assuming the most dreadful batting form he'd ever seen.

"No, no, you're doing it all wrong," he groaned, walking up behind her. The juxtaposition of irritation at her antics and lust at being able to stand with his arms around her, turning her arms and straightening her back was enough to make him lose his mind. "Your grip is all wrong, for one. Your thumb and forefinger on each hand should form a vee that lines up with the center of the bat's back. Your dominant hand goes on top."

As he positioned her hands correctly, she leaned subtly back into him, pressing her backside against his crotch. Her dress had very little bustle, which meant he took the movement for exactly what it was.

Furious, he took a step back. "Now you've decided to be amorous?" he demanded in a quiet voice, acutely aware of the players and May Flowers scattered around the field. Fergus was giving Lady Tavistock a few pointers about bowling at the other end of the wicket and most of the rest of the ladies had joined up with a fielder to learn how to throw and catch balls, but there were enough people close by that Rupert kept his voice down.

Cece's playful smile vanished as she straightened and turned to him, holding the cricket bat like a cudgel. "Sport is an ideal time for flirtation," she said with stark seriousness. "Death is not. You would do well to learn the difference."

"The difference appears to be whatever you decide it is," he hissed in return.

"And what if it is?" she snapped back, eyes burning with indignation.

Rupert held up his hands and shook his head. "I do not understand the rules of your game, madam, therefore

I refuse to play it." He marched off down the wicket to where Fergus was lining up to bowl.

"Rupert," Cece called after him. She was clearly aggravated with him, but as far as Rupert was concerned, it served her right. "Heaven help us," she followed with an irritated sigh.

"You're treading thin ice, mate," Fergus warned him when Rupert reached his side.

"Just bowl," he growled, veering to the side to take up a position where he'd be most likely to catch the ball if Cece managed to hit it.

"Ready?" Fergus asked Cece, with far too much magnanimity, as far as Rupert was concerned.

Cece resumed her awful batting stance, thumped the bat in the dirt a couple times, then said, "I'm ready, my lord."

Fergus turned to Lady Tavistock and said, "The run-up is important, but so is the bowling action. Observe."

Lady Tavistock watched Fergus with obvious admiration as he charged a few steps forward, then released the ball with what Rupert thought was a pathetic ease. The ball sailed leisurely down the wicket, bounced once, and reached Cece at the perfect height and speed for her to smack it all the way to the border.

Except that she didn't smack it. She missed and missed handily. Her over-exuberant action swung her off balance, and she stumbled inelegantly to the side. Rupert grinned in rude satisfaction and crossed his arms. So his fiendish lady love wasn't an expert in all things after all.

His smirk faltered a moment later when she straightened and looked his way. The raw vulnerability that shone from her at her fumble struck straight at Rupert's heart. It killed him to see her so flummoxed.

"Keep your shoulders square," he called to her. "Remember to follow through. Keep your eye on the ball."

She nodded, her jaw stiff, and resumed her stance in front of the stumps as Freddy threw the ball back to Fergus.

Fergus walked back to Lady Tavistock, said something to her that Rupert couldn't hear, then resumed his spot, ran up, then delivered another ball as though it were floating on a cloud. This time, Rupert held his breath and prayed that Cece would hit it. She managed to make feeble contact with the edge of the bat, sending the ball careening lazily off into the slips.

"Oh," Cece exclaimed, clamped a hand on her hat, and started running toward the opposite stumps. Her smile returned, and by the time she made it inside the crease, she was laughing. "There," she told Rupert as though she'd hit a six. "There's nothing to it."

"You think so?" he asked, sauntering over to her and snatching the bat from her hands. The gesture was curt and he held himself with a cocky air, but the mood had changed between them. They were on the same side again, in spite of the way the air between them bristled with challenge. "We'll see."

He took his time walking to the stumps, grinning to

himself at the oddly swift change in dynamic. He loved Cece. She didn't make the least amount of sense to him. She was proud and shrewish one moment, soft and vulnerable the next, but always brilliant. And if he were honest with himself, he loved her when she was weak, but he adored her when she was strong. He wanted to wrap her in cotton wool and make the world a better place for her when she was helpless, but he wanted to worship at her feet when she set out to boldly conquer the world. That or fuck her until they were both too spent and sated to move.

He reached the far end of the wicket and turned to set up only to find Lady Tavistock holding the ball and practicing her arm swing as Fergus gave her instructions. Sudden dread filled Rupert's gut. Chances were that if Lady Tavistock managed to get the ball across the wicket to begin with, he could hit it so hard it would startle the horses pulling their carriages along Wellington Road. But if he purposely bungled his strike to spare Lady Tavistock's feelings, it was likely she and Cece and every other May Flower there would know and be furious at him for coddling them.

He resigned himself to losing either way and settled into batting stance, eyes narrowed and trained on the ball in Lady Tavistock's hands as she got ready to make her run-up. But a faint commotion near the boundary scattered his focus, and a moment later, Lady Tavistock stepped out of her preparations and raised a hand to her forehead to see what was going on.

Rupert straightened and turned to find a cluster of about eight men in street clothes charging onto the field. At first, he thought they held cricket bats and that they were Denbigh's players, arrived at last but not in uniform. He stepped to the side, prepared to greet the lads and to tell them where they could change, but once the men made it onto the field, they let out what sounded like a battle cry and burst into a run.

"Death to the Irish," one of them shouted, raising his bat above his head.

Except, it wasn't a bat at all. It was nothing more than a fat stick. The other men were armed with similar sticks and boards that looked as though they'd been snatched from a construction site. They stormed the field, charging directly toward Fergus.

"Look out," Rupert called to his friend, eyes wide as he realized what was about to happen.

He lunged forward, ready to defend his friend with his life if he had to, but he was too late. The crowd of toughs slammed into Fergus, wielding their clubs and their fists. Rupert's heart sank to his stomach at the sickening thuds and crunches that followed. He grabbed the first man he could reach and struggled to pull him away from Fergus.

Screams and shouts of terror arose from the women on the field. Lady Tavistock cried out in rage and threw her cricket ball at the swarm of men attacking Fergus, then dashed to the side, pulled one of the stumps from the ground, and began beating the closest of them across his back with it. Cece instantly did the same, attacking the attackers with a stump. Rupert managed to pull one of the toughs away and to smash his fist across the man's face just before the man Cece was hitting twisted and pushed her so hard she sprawled to the ground on her back.

"Cece!" Rupert jumped toward her, scooping her under her arms and pulling her to safety seconds before one of the men attacking Fergus would have stepped back and trod on her.

Another of the attackers shoved Lady Tavistock away. She cried out as she hit the ground, but instantly tried to get back up again. Before she could, Freddy and Jack and Reese and all of the rest of Rupert's friends charged in from the edges of the field to clash with the attackers. The crack of blows being landed led to the sharp scent of blood in the air. Cricket whites were splashed with red as the attackers were pried away from Fergus's now prone body.

A split-second later, as if lightning had struck, the eight attackers bolted. Those in the middle of combat peeled away from the men they were fighting with and sprinted for the edge of the pitch. Not one of them looked back, and several dropped their weapons so that they could run faster. The sudden retreat was so disorienting that Rupert's head spun with amazement at it all.

"Oh my God," Lady Tavistock screamed a moment later, ending Rupert's bafflement.

He twisted to find her scrambling toward Fergus's

sprawled and broken body lying in the grass. Blood oozed from Fergus's obviously broken nose and the corner of his mouth. It dripped from one ear as well, which turned Rupert's stomach with dread. He dashed to Fergus's side, kneeling in the grass and grasping his arm.

Fergus groaned in agony at the simple gesture, but at least he wasn't dead.

"What happened?" Lady Diana asked hysterically.

"Get back," Reese said in a commanding yet calm voice, holding out his arms to shield the ladies from the sight of Fergus writhing weakly and moaning in pain. "If you could all please gather at the edge of the pavilion," he went on, gesturing for some of the other men to help him comfort the ladies.

Cece and Lady Tavistock ignored Reese and everyone else.

"We're here for you, Lord O'Shea," Lady Tavistock gasped, taking his hand gently in hers. "We're here for you."

"Somebody fetch a physician," Cece shouted, standing above them all. "Immediately. Mr. Craig."

"He's not going for a doctor," Harrison called from somewhere far away. "He's chasing after the bastards."

It was a sign of just how much distress they were all in that Harrison would use harsh language with ladies present.

"Jack will catch them," Rupert told Fergus as reassuringly as he could. "Don't worry."

The fact was that Rupert was worried far beyond

anything he'd experienced before. He'd seen men shot and bloody on the field of battle in South Africa. He'd survived an ambush that had killed over half of his regiment in the Transvaal. But he had never seen the kind of brutality that Fergus had been subjected to. His friend could barely move, and any effort he made to try resulted in wrenching cries of agony. A quick assessment on Rupert's part told him Fergus had more broken bones than unbroken ones, and there was no telling what sort of internal injuries he might have. Rupert's mouth went dry at the very real possibility that his friend might die on a cricket pitch in London after surviving the battlefields of Africa, and all because of one man's bitterness and hatred.

Rupert had no doubt at all that Denbigh was behind the attack. He was conspicuously absent, as if already shoring up his alibi for when Rupert inevitably accused him. No wonder the odious Lady Claudia hadn't shown up for the event either.

"Make way, make way. I'm a doctor," an unfamiliar voice called from a short distance away.

Moments later, a middle-aged man in tweed dropped to a crouch beside Rupert. He surveyed Fergus with a quick professional frown.

"They attacked him deliberately," Rupert said, rocking back to give the doctor room to do his work. "Eight men with clubs."

The doctor grunted as two other men jogged up, carrying an empty stretcher between them. "He's been brutalized," the doctor said. "There's an infirmary one street over. We need to get him there fast. He might not make it."

Lady Tavistock gasped in horror. Cece bent over to help her stand and back away so that the men with the stretcher could help Fergus. Rupert stood and moved to Cece's side, wanting to hug her until he was certain she was safe but knowing there was no time. All he could do was watch helplessly as Fergus was loaded onto the stretcher. He cried out in agony, then passed out as the men lifted the stretcher.

"Is he dead?" Lady Tavistock asked shakily.

"Not yet," the doctor said, gesturing for the men to carry the stretcher off the pitch toward the infirmary. "Not on my watch."

$\mathscr{C}$ece's heart beat like a fury against her ribs as she jogged off of the cricket pitch, following the doctor and the men who carried Lord O'Shea on the stretcher. Henrietta hurried along at her side, pale and weeping openly, but silent. As much as Cece hated the drivel about women being too constitutionally weak to bear the sight of violence, she had to admit that she'd never seen anything as brutal as the eight men with clubs beating Lord O'Shea, and she never wanted to see anything like it again.

"He'll be all right," Rupert attempted to reassure her as they crossed through the barrier from Lord's to the street. He reached for her hand, squeezing it as they hurried along. "Fergus is strong. He's survived worse." There was little confidence in his voice.

People on the street, from low to high, leapt out of the way of their macabre procession. A few shouted that they'd seen which way the attackers went, but Cece barely heard them. Her thoughts were only for Lord O'Shea, who had stopped writing on the stretcher and now jostled with every move the bearers made, pale as death.

Blessedly, the infirmary was even closer than the doctor had made it out to be. A man held the door open so that the doctor and stretcher-bearers could race through and into the dim, heavy atmosphere of the building. Cece and Rupert squeezed in behind them, Henrietta bringing up the rear. Lord O'Shea was carried straight through to what must have been an examination room. Rupert tried to follow, but the doctor stopped him.

"He's in critical condition and I cannot have distractions as I work to save his life," the doctor said.

"Understood." Rupert took a grudging step back, deep worry etched in the lines of his face.

The doctor disappeared into the examination room, shutting the door behind him. The thump of the door closing had a morbid finality about it. Rupert stood where he was, staring at the door, his face a mask of fear and uncertainty. Cece had never seen him so distressed in her life.

"If you please," a young woman who looked as though she could be the doctor's daughter said, stepping forward. "You can wait in this room, if you'd like."

Cece blinked and glanced around at their surroundings. The large waiting room where they stood was filled with humble-looking men and women in various states of illness or distress. They watched her, Rupert, and Henrietta with wide, wondering eyes. Several were coughing, and a young child began to cry in the wake of the sudden burst of trauma. The room that the doctor's daughter gestured to appeared to be a second examination room. It had the advantage of being empty and private.

"Thank you," Cece said, sending the young woman the kindest smile she could manage under the circumstances. "We are grateful."

She took Rupert's hand, steering him away from the closed door and into the private room. Henrietta came silently with them, her gaze unfocused as though she were lost in her thoughts.

"Could I bring you some tea?" the doctor's daughter asked in a hushed voice as she saw them into the room.

"No, but thank you for the offer," Cece said.

The woman nodded, then backed out of the room, shutting the door behind her and closing them all in with their thoughts.

A long, anxious silence followed. Rupert paced the room, walking in circles around the long examination table in the middle. Henrietta sank into a chair beside a curtained window, clenching her fists in the fabric of her skirts. It was then that Cece noticed dark flecks of blood standing out against the white of Henrietta's dress and gloves. She had blood and grass stains on her own skirts, but she didn't care.

"He's in the best possible hands," she said, glancing

from Rupert to Henrietta and back again. "We did everything we could."

Henrietta nodded and retreated back into her thoughts, wiping away stray tears with the back of her hand.

Rupert continued pacing, though he, too, nodded in acknowledgement and agreement.

Cece followed him around to the far side of the room from where Henrietta sat, standing in front of him to block his way. "You did everything you could," she repeated.

Rupert stopped and let out a long breath, pushing a hand through his hair. His knuckles were rough with scrapes and bruises from the fighting he'd done. "I just pray it's enough," he said.

Cece leaned toward him, relieved that he accepted her advance and closed his arms around her in a hug. She needed it, and she was certain he needed it as well. They stood in each other's arms for a moment, listening to the dull drone of activity and low voices in the room beside them. They couldn't hear much, but it was enough to know the doctor was doing everything he could to save Lord O'Shea's life.

"I don't know what I'd do if anything happened to him," Rupert said at last in a hollow voice. Cece rocked back, stepping out of his arms to better listen to him. "Fergus saved my life and the lives of so many other men in the war. He thought nothing of himself, only of helping others. He is everything good and noble about this nation, and it enrages me that men like Denbigh denigrate him for his heritage when not one of them has lifted a finger to protect the interests of queen and country."

Cece could only nod, reaching for his hand and holding it as the emotions bubbling inside of him rose into words.

Rupert gazed intently at her. "That is why I joined the military," he said, taking her other hand so that he held both of them. "I know my decision hurt you, and for that I am eternally sorry."

Old pain and wasted anger squeezed Cece's throat closed. Her heartache and resentment felt so far away in that moment that it was almost trivial.

"I didn't know how to explain it to you then," Rupert went on, "and I still don't know how to explain it now. I didn't leave because you weren't important or because I didn't love you. I had to go and serve my country *because* you are important and because I love you with all my heart. I believe in this nation and this life we are so lucky to live, and I would do anything and everything within my power to protect and preserve it for you."

"I know," Cece said, the comfort of realization filling her like a strong, fresh breeze blowing away the fog of confusion. "And I love you for it, more than you can know."

His mouth twitched slightly and a wry grin brought a hint of teasing to his eyes. "But?" he asked.

The simple question made Cece's heart flutter. "But

fighting to protect me and to make a better world for me is not the same thing as valuing and cherishing me as a woman with opinions and emotions in my own right." Before he could reply, she rushed on to say, "Both are necessary."

Instead of speaking, Rupert closed his mouth and studied her. He raised a hand to brush her cheek, rubbing one spot particularly. She realized that she must have had flecks of blood on her face as well as her dress, like any other soldier in the field of battle.

"I love how brave you are," he said at last, his voice rich with emotion. "I love the way you've stood up for yourself these past few weeks, even when you were standing up against me."

"You do?" She blinked.

"Yes, of course I do," he said, a smile spreading across his face and into his eyes. He rested his hands on the sides of her face, studying her with deep affection. "I've been laboring under the mistaken impression that only men are soldiers, fighting for the empire and for what's right. It never dawned on me that there was a war at home that was being fought with equal vigor, and that was experiencing equal casualties." His smile dropped. "It sickens me to watch the way you have been treated, simply for speaking your mind."

"I'm used to it," she told him. "For better or for worse. But that is precisely why it hurt so much for you to rush off to South Africa without consulting me, and for you to send back nothing but platitudes in your letters to me. I could have handled the full truth of your service."

He paused, as if instinct were pushing him to say that no, she couldn't.

"All I want, all any woman wants, is to be respected, especially by those who are dearest to us," she went on, closing her hands over his and bringing them away from her face so that she could hold them. "It has felt so glorious to embrace confidence these last few weeks. I thought the scandal after that first ball would do me in, but I think it has been the making of me. I've never felt so happy or so alive. Freedom from the strictures of society is a glorious thing, but I have only been able to enjoy it because of you." She twined her fingers through his. "Without you, fairly or unfairly, I would have been cast aside after a scandal like that. But because you stood by me—and I never believed for a moment that you were interested in Lady Claudia Denbigh, or any other lady, for that matter—because you remained faithful to me, I was able to rise. That is all I've wanted from the beginning."

"We *are* better when we're together than when we're apart," Rupert agreed, smiling once more.

"In so many ways," Cece agreed, one eyebrow flickering mischievously.

Rupert began to laugh, but the sound caught in his throat as a groan from the other room broke the sweetness of the moment. They both turned to stare at the solid wall, as though they could see through it to where Lord O'Shea was fighting for his life.

"That's a good sound," Cece said, her voice shaking. "It means he's still alive."

"He'll fight," Rupert agreed with a nod. "Fergus will fight with everything he has to stay alive. He'll want to bring the men who did this to justice."

"I want to bring them to justice too," Cece said, a bitter note in her voice.

Rupert shifted to study her. "It won't be an easy fight," he said. "Denbigh is undoubtedly the one behind this."

"Undoubtedly," Cece echoed. "But prejudice and cruelty like that cannot go unanswered. That is the fight that truly matters, not petty disagreements and grudges."

"I'll do what I can with whatever influence my position in the House of Lords affords me," Rupert went on. "But it may very well be that you can accomplish more with your May Flowers to change the hearts and minds of the most important people in the land."

"I'm not sure the high and mighty will every fully listen to us," she said with a sigh.

"They will have to." Rupert smiled. "I'll make sure of it."

His words and the strength behind them filled Cece with confidence. So much so that she was ready to take on the world when the door to their examination room burst open and Jack Craig stepped in, Freddy and Reese right behind him. Lord Herrington rushed to Henrietta, taking his sister in his arms to comfort her.

Mr. Craig's expression was less reassuring. "We caught the bastards," he said, a rough edge of cockney slipping into his otherwise refined accent. "They're being taken to Pentonville for questioning."

"Pentonville?" Cece gaped at him. "Isn't that a bit extreme for questioning about an assault?"

"It's not extreme enough for attempted murder, if you ask me," Rupert growled.

Mr. Craig stepped closer to Cece, removing his hat. "Pentonville is relatively close by, and it'll strike the fear of God into them," he said. "I recognized one or two of the men as soon as they were apprehended. They're known muscle for hire. There's not anyone they wouldn't attack for a few quid, high or low, saint or sinner."

"So Denbigh hired them," Rupert said, rage infusing his words.

Mr. Craig winced. "I would bet my life on it, but not one of them is confessing so far. Which tells me Denbigh paid them well. My men will do their best to extract a confession from them. In the meantime, I'll head back to Scotland Yard and put my network to work ferreting out whatever information I can about any possible connections Denbigh has to those rats or any others." He nodded to Cece and to Henrietta, who had risen from her chair and come to hear what Mr. Craig had to say. "Rest assured, this crime will not go unpunished."

"Thank you, Mr. Craig," Henrietta said in a weary

voice. Lord Herrington stood close by her side, one arm around her waist to support her.

Of all things, the dire moment gave Cece hope. There were men in the world who stood ready to help those who could not help themselves, lovers and brothers, and even men like Reese, who had no immediate connection to either her or Henrietta, but who looked ready to fight until his last breath to advance their cause. With men like those, there was hope for the world.

Mr. Craig turned to go, but he had barely stepped into the large waiting room and no one had time to shut the door to their examination room before the doctor stepped out from the other room. Rupert rushed into the waiting room to hear what he had to say, and Cece and Henrietta followed, Reese and Lord Herrington behind them.

"Well?" Rupert asked, the picture of concern again. "How is he? Will he make it?"

"Lord O'Shea has been grievously injured," the doctor said in a grave voice. "I haven't seen an attack this brutal in ages, perhaps in my entire career."

"But will he live?" Henrietta asked.

The doctor took a deep breath and went on with a frown. "He has suffered several compound fractures of the arms and legs, several broken ribs, and a broken nose. In addition to that, a blow to the side of his head ruptured his eardrum and his left eye has been gouged in such a way that even if it can be saved, he has probably lost sight in it. That is without beginning to take into consideration internal injuries, of which I am certain there are many."

Cece gasped and held a hand to her mouth, her heart racing and her eyes stinging in horror. But there was more.

The doctor went on. "I regret to say it, especially in front of the ladies, but I fear he may never be able to walk normally again, if at all, depending on the extent of the damage to his spine." He turned to Rupert. "Does your friend have someone who could take care of him if he manages to pull through the next few hours? He could have a long convalescence."

"He does," Rupert insisted. "He has friends. We will care for him if necessary."

He glanced to Cece, who nodded vigorously. She would have done anything for Lord O'Shea, knowing how much he'd done for Rupert.

"Fergus can recuperate at Albany Court if he'd like to," Reese said, proving that Rupert wasn't the only one who would step in to help.

"I would offer a home for him as well, if I had one," Lord Herrington added.

"He can stay at Tavistock House or at Tamar Abbey," Henrietta offered, glancing to her brother with a rare show of vulnerability.

"He has friends," Rupert repeated for the doctor.

"Good." The doctor nodded. "Then right now, I suggest you show your friendship by praying for his recovery. I'll do what I can for him, but once he's out of the woods, he should be moved to a proper hospital."

"We'll make preparations," Reese said.

The doctor nodded and returned to the examination room to continue his attempts to save Lord O'Shea. There was nothing more for the rest of them to do but to head out of the infirmary and into the street.

"I'll let you know what else I'm able to discover," Mr. Craig said before nodding to the ladies and hurrying off.

"Denbigh is behind this," Reese said with an ice-cold certainty that hinted to Cece what a powerful man he was behind his calm demeanor.

"He will pay," Freddy agreed, far more agitated.

"If I see the man, I'll give him as good as his goons gave Fergus," Rupert growled.

"Lord Denbigh isn't the only one who should be held accountable for this," Henrietta said with poorly disguised fury. "Others are to blame. Others who knew an attack was imminent and who did nothing to stop it." She met Cece's eyes.

Lady Claudia. There was no doubt in Cece's mind that Henrietta was talking about Lady Claudia and that she was right. Lady Claudia and her closest friends had been suspiciously absent from the cricket match after enough of a fuss had been made of the whole thing that no one wanted to miss it. She must have known, and saying nothing was as much of a betrayal as participating in the attack.

"What can be done?" Cece asked, her own fury growing.

Henrietta stepped away from her brother, standing tall and tilting her chin up. "It's time the May Flowers decided once and for all what they stand for and what they will fight for going forward. And those who are not willing to stand by us will no longer be welcome in our ranks."

Cece swallowed, feeling as though they were standing on the edge of a precipice. "We must call a meeting immediately."

Henrietta nodded. "I'll put the wheels in motion right away. We will all choose which side we stand on by the end of this day, and once the battle lines are drawn, we will advance."

CHAPTER 19

*R*upert took Cece home to Marlowe House so that she could change out of her soiled dress, then dashed over to Campbell House so that he could peel off his dirty cricket clothes, bathe, dress in something appropriate to the grave situation, then run back to Marlowe House. The sun was beginning to set by the time he climbed the stairs to his mother's front door two at a time and burst through into the front hall.

"What are you doing back here so soon?" Cece asked, her eyes going wide at the site of him. She'd dressed in a deep purple gown that hinted at mourning and had pinned a fresh flower to match on her breast. Her face was pale and drawn, though, and tension had her shoulders bunched. She was still the most beautiful woman Rupert had ever seen.

"I'm going with you," he told her. "To Lady Tavistock's house."

Cece gaped at him for another long moment before shaking her head and marching past him out the door. "You can't. The May Flowers is a women's club. You aren't invited to take part in our discussions."

"Maybe not," Rupert said, following after her and catching up to her side as they hit the pavement in front of the house, "but I need to be there for you all the same. I need to be there for all of you."

Cece paused at the corner, turning to study him as they waited for a pair of carriages to pass, no doubt carrying the rich and careless on to some splashy event where they could forget their troubles, forget all troubles. She seemed decades older than the darling young woman he'd left behind when he enlisted. She carried the weight of the world on her shoulders, but she carried it capably. The sight was humbling, and Rupert's heart thudded in his chest at the possibility that he might be able to be a champion to the beautiful, powerful woman beside him and her partner in all things for the rest of his life, if he played his cards right.

The carriages passed, and the two of them crossed the street and continued on.

"I don't know what will happen this evening," she said as they hurried along the street, dodging a young maid on some sort of errand. "I feel as though something momentous will come out of this meeting, but I'm not sure it will be good."

"Whatever it is, I will support you in whatever step you choose to take because of it," he said.

They turned a corner, stepping out of the way of a lamplighter going about his work, and Cece glanced to him with a smile. It was an anxious smile, though, and she didn't have anything to say afterwards.

Tavistock House was close enough that they arrived in good time. It was a blessing that they walked, because a line of carriages was jostling for the best spots to drop off the ladies of the May Flowers. Those ladies were in agitated spirits the moment they stepped down and immediately began chattering to their friends and asking questions. The effect was like carts full of hens crashing together in the market, causing a jumble of noise and feathers and blocked in carriages.

"Do you know what this is all about?" Lady Diana rushed forward to greet Cece with the question.

"It must be about what happened at Lord's this afternoon," Lady Beatrice hurried up beside her, taking Cece's hand, her face pinched with worry. "Do you know how Lord O'Shea is?" she asked tremulously.

Cece tried to answer, but tears shone in her eyes and she swallowed. She turned to Rupert, who answered, "He survived the initial attack. We are still waiting to hear if the doctor was able to repair his internal injuries." It was the best answer he could give.

"We've all been praying for him," Lady Beatrice said, turning to nod at a pale-faced group of ladies who had been at Lord's.

Their fluttering was cut short as a large carriage with the Denbigh crest pushed its way to the front of the line.

A boy hopped down from the back and rushed to open the door. Rupert, Cece, and the ladies clustered around them watched with bated breath as Lady Claudia stepped down, a pair of friends behind her. She was dressed in a festive shade of yellow, her gown of the latest fashion and far too exuberant for the occasion. Most telling of all, though, was that neither Lady Claudia nor her friends wore the purple flower that the rest of the May Flowers wore.

"This cannot be a good sign," Lady Diana said, pressing a hand to her chest.

Lady Claudia shifted slightly to glance in Rupert's direction. She gave him a dismissive look, then glared outright at Cece. Once that message was communicated, she stood stiffer, tilted her chin up, and marched forward and up the stairs into Tavistock House, her friends flanking her.

The energy of the milling crowd of ladies shifted, and they all rushed to follow Lady Claudia into the house. Rupert knew full well that he wasn't invited or allowed, but he marched on at Cece's side all the same. The fact that she didn't try to stop him was a dead giveaway of just how serious the situation was.

A team of servants were waiting in the hall to take the ladies' hats and coats. Rupert managed to slip past them while the ensemble was distracted. He followed the din of voices down the hall and into what was very possibly the grandest sitting room he'd ever seen. Every inch of it was feminine to the core, with sprays of flowers on the wallpaper, vases of flowers placed between windows curtained with pink damask silk, and an array of chairs and sofas that were proportioned for a lady's form. He managed to station himself near the door, beside a concealing potted plant, and to stand as still as possible in the hope that no one would notice him.

His efforts weren't entirely successful, though. Lady Tavistock stood at the front of the room, issuing orders to her staff and friends alike. She was dressed as somberly as Cece and wore her hair in a simple style, far different from the ostentatious way she presented herself to the world. She spotted Rupert at the back of the room right away. Their eyes met, but rather than launching into action to have him thrown out, all she did was nod once before going back to her orders.

It was as close as Rupert was going to get to permission to witness the meeting. He slipped farther behind the plant, loath to upset any of the women by his presence. His concealment was good enough that when Cece swept into the room with Lady Diana and Lady Beatrice by her side, she didn't notice him.

"Ladies, if you would please come to order," Lady Tavistock called from the front of the room.

A dull thunder of ladies taking their seats, or, in the case of Cece, marching to the front of the room to stand near Lady Tavistock's side, followed. Once all the ladies were facing in the opposite direction, Rupert stepped out of his hiding place. A few in the back spotted him, but they were too distracted to do more than blink at him in wonder.

"I've called you all here this evening, taking you away from your balls and soirees, because a terrible thing happened today. Lord Fergus O'Shea was attacked at Lord's Cricket Grounds this afternoon while taking part in a match that the May Flowers were involved in."

A chorus of murmurs rose from the ladies, most of them shocked and dismayed, but some of them far less kind.

"Furthermore," Lady Tavistock went on, "and sadly, we have reason to believe that some of our own numbers were involved in this cruel and brutal attack." Her voice cracked as she spoke.

"How dare you?" Lady Claudia exclaimed, jumping to her feet and putting a stop to any show of tenderness on Lady Tavistock's part. "How dare you make such wicked accusations?"

Rage clenched Rupert's gut for a moment before he could breathe through it. Did Lady Claudia have no sense at all that she accused herself with her words?

"This is outrageous slander and I will not stand for it," Lady Claudia went on, proving that no, she didn't.

It seemed that the rest of the May Flowers were in no mood to pretend either.

"You were suspiciously absent from the cricket match," Lady Diana said. Several of the ladies who had been there nodded and hummed in confirmation.

"I simply could not be bothered to attend," Lady

Claudia said, her nose in the air. "No lady worth her salt would have been caught dead larking about in the presence of rough men and undesirable sorts."

Her friends made sounds of agreement. Rupert was surprised to find that she had so many of them. In fact, the entire room seemed to be separated into halves—those who supported Lady Claudia and those who supported Lady Tavistock.

"Lord's is one of the premier cricket clubs in London," Cece said, stepping forward and narrowing her eyes at Lady Claudia. "Nearly all of the gentlemen present were of the titled class, and those who weren't are highly respected gentlemen."

Rupert wondered if the likes of Lady Claudia would feel that way about Jack Craig. As far as he was concerned, Jack was the very best of men for going out of his way to catch the men who had hurt Fergus and attempting to prove that Denbigh was involved.

Lady Claudia scoffed at Cece's statement. "I shouldn't be surprised that a woman of such low character as you would call the dregs who were involved in that farce of a match gentlemen."

A few of the ladies gasped at the audacity of the statement. Cece stood her ground, her back straight and her expression implacable.

"Every one of us knows the true message of today's attack," she said, taking over the position of authority from Lady Tavistock. "This was a crime of hate and nothing else. Hatred against the Irish. But that hatred is not only misplaced and shameful, it is directly counter to the mission of the May Flowers."

Lady Claudia laughed dismissively. "The mission of the May Flowers is to advance our political causes with the men in our lives who have the power to mold and shape this country. It is a disgrace that any of us should so much as think of supporting those brutish and ignorant Irishmen in any way. They are nothing better than peasants, and all of them should be treated as such."

A flurry of comments and exclamations rose up, both in favor of the Irish and against them, throughout the room. Cece said something to Lady Claudia, but the din was too much for Rupert to hear until the ladies realized the debate was ongoing and quieted themselves.

"...disgrace that such ignorant opinions should be associated with our noble cause at all," Cece finished.

"Disgrace?" Lady Claudia's brow shot up and a look of sharp offense painted her sour face. "The disgrace is the way your lot have torn an otherwise peaceful and productive organization, such as ours, asunder. The disgrace is how you and your ridiculous insistence on Irish Home Rule will tear the entire Liberal Party apart. If we truly want to have the political influence we claim to long for, we need to thrust aside this feckless and ill-advised insistence on any rights at all for the Irish and stick determinedly to the Unionist cause."

Another rush of sound from the assembled ladies gave Rupert the sense that the May Flowers were so much like Parliament in their form of debate that there was virtually no difference. The women had gravitated to their own sides of the room and hurled insults at each other as vehemently as any elected minister or lord did in their own chamber. It filled him with an incongruous sense of pride and confidence in them and their ability to grasp the issues that formed the bedrock of political debate in England. With that pride came the startling thought that perhaps women should be admitted into positions of public power after all. They certainly knew how to debate those issues.

"If this organization or the Liberal Party has been damaged at all," Cece continued the debate, "it is because callous prejudice has outweighed moral rightness and progress. I refuse to stand by any longer and listen to an entire nation be denigrated by ignorance and small-mindedness. The Irish are as capable of ruling themselves and thriving as a nation as any people. We, as women, should be supporting their efforts as they reflect our own. Any class of people that works to suppress a group of men based on their nationality will most assuredly work to stifle the voices of women. We have gained much in recent history, but we have so far to go. Women are permitted to attend university, but not to sit exams or be granted a degree. We may attend medical school and become doctors, but we may not practice in any hospital or on Harley Street. We gained the right to maintain control of our property upon entering marriage, but we are still nothing but glorified children without a husband. If the May

Flowers are to have any chance of changing these circumstances going forward, we must support the rights of all people, Irish, working class, and even the people of the nations far and wide that we have colonized. Their future is our future."

Cece's speech was met by a moment of stunned silence. Even those sitting on her side of the room gaped at her, as though she'd told them all they should run around naked in public. Indeed, her views were some of the most radical Rupert had ever heard, but he had never been so proud of her in his life. He couldn't help but applaud her words, even though it drew attention and was likely to end in him being thrown out.

But rather than sending every eye in the room toward him, his applause was joined by that of a good portion of the other women in the room. The applause grew and swelled, filling the room with noise and Rupert's heart with inspiration. Suddenly, he understood. This was the woman he loved. She demanded respect and power, not for herself, but to serve and protect her home and her empire. Her goals were the same as his, but this was the army she needed to join and this was the battle she was born to fight.

"This is an outrage," Lady Claudia screamed over the applause, effectively silencing it. "Have you all lost your minds? This is not how English womankind should identify ourselves. We are and always have been the moral underpinnings of society, quietly working for the elevation of hearts and minds and advocating for the proper order, established by God. We are not a bunch of slathering revolutionaries."

"Perhaps we should be," Lady Beatrice shouted.

She was met by cheers of "Hear, hear," from the ladies on her side of the room and outraged gasps from the others.

"I refuse to continue to be a part of an organization that has become a walking, breathing scandal," Lady Claudia roared on. "If this is what the May Flowers has become, then I want no part of it."

"No one is keeping you here," Lady Tavistock said, looking like a general or an avenging angel. "Membership in this organization is certainly not mandatory."

"Are you saying you want to banish me, then?" Lady Claudia squeaked, a picture of fury.

"I believe you are saying that you no longer wish to be associated with us," Cece said.

"I do not," Lady Claudia snapped. She stood where she was for a moment, glaring at Cece and Lady Tavistock. A prickly silence filled the room. It was as though Lady Claudia and her friends were waiting to either be dismissed outright or for someone to beg them to stay. Neither happened, and so Lady Claudia huffed and jerked her chin up. "I see how it is, then," she said. "I hereby resign from the May Flowers." She turned to her side of the room. "And I suggest that any of you who wish to avoid scandal and ignominy, any of you who wish to truly uphold the values of English femininity, resign as well."

She waited for only a second before turning her back on Cece and Lady Tavistock and marching through the aisle between chairs toward the door. The two friends who had come in with her did the same, then nearly half of the rest of the ladies stood and followed as well.

As she reached the back of the room, Lady Claudia spotted Rupert. She sent him a look of such loathing that it was hard for Rupert to believe that less than a week ago, she had been flirting with him. He couldn't let the moment pass.

"Have a care, Lady Claudia," he said in a quiet voice. "Your brother will be held responsible for today's attack."

Lady Claudia blanched, but said nothing. She picked up her pace, leading the mass exodus from the room.

The gaping hole left by Lady Claudia and her supporters was instantly filled with noise and anxious chatter as the rest of the ladies stood and spread out, mingling with each other. Rupert stayed where he was, still reluctant to interfere in Cece's affairs, but as soon as she spotted him, she leaned close to Lady Tavistock and said something. A moment later, the two women pushed their way through the roiling crowd of their supporters to meet Rupert at the back of the room.

"She's not wrong," Rupert said as they reached him.

"I beg your pardon?" Cece asked, blinking and looking offended.

"About the split in the Liberal Party," he went on, speaking as he would to any of his male friends. Cece's offense vanished, and determination took its place. "The

Liberal Party is on the verge of fracturing, thanks to this very issue."

"This is the defining moment of our times," Cece agreed. "We must meet the challenge with strength."

"There is strength in numbers," Lady Tavistock said, glancing anxiously over her shoulder at the greatly depleted May Flowers. "I wasn't expecting half of our members to walk out."

"It doesn't matter if they have," Cece told her. "We are firm in our mission, and if each of us has to work harder to accomplish it, then so be it."

"Perhaps you could rally more women to your cause," Rupert suggested. "I'm quite certain there are a wealth of women in London who share your views and who would be willing to stand up for them. Women that, perhaps, were held back before because of the likes of Lady Claudia."

"Do you mean non-aristocratic women?" Lady Tavistock asked, inspiration lighting her eyes.

Rupert shrugged. "And my sisters."

Lady Tavistock smiled. A moment later, Cece smiled as well. "Bianca would be just the rabble-rouser we need," she said, nearly laughing.

"But are we ready for her?" Lady Tavistock asked.

"No one is ever quite ready for Bianca," Rupert said.

Lady Tavistock let out a wry laugh, then turned to Cece. "I cannot do this alone. I need a first mate to help steer the ship."

Cece's face lit up. "I would be honored to lead the May Flowers along with you."

"Thank you." Lady Tavistock reached for her hand and squeezed it. Some of her certainty vanished as she turned to Rupert. "Have you heard anything further about Lord O'Shea?"

Rupert's heart sank and he shook his head. "Not as of yet. But we will let you know as soon as we hear anything." He glanced to Cece for confirmation, and she nodded.

The room was already emptying. Lady Tavistock turned to survey her remaining guests before saying, "I have so much to attend to. Thank you for coming, my dear, and thank you for standing by my side."

"It is an honor," Cece replied.

The two women embraced, then Lady Tavistock headed into the cluster of ladies that remained to reassure them that all would be well.

Cece turned to Rupert. "So now you know exactly what sort of a radical I am."

Rupert couldn't help but smile. "Yes, I do." He offered his arm to her.

Cece took it and they started out of the room. "I suppose you're going to drag me home and lecture me about how I should have more propriety and be less outspoken."

Rupert hummed, pretending to think the matter over as they walked through the hall, and then out into the street after one of the maids handed Cece her hat and gloves. "No, that wasn't what I was thinking I wanted to do with you."

"Oh?" Cece asked, genuinely surprised. "What then?"

Rupert didn't answer. He grinned as mysteriously as he could and whisked Cece down the swiftly darkening street.

"Rupert," she said in a teasing voice. "We're going the wrong way."

"No we aren't," he said. "For the first time in a long time, we're going exactly where we should."

CHAPTER 20

C ece's insides roiled and bubbled and sparked with excess energy from the May Flowers meeting. She should have seen a split coming. She should have guessed that Lady Claudia wouldn't meekly go along with Henrietta's progressive agenda. That didn't stop her from bouncing back and forth between anger and inspiration as Rupert whisked her down the street, dodging men and women of all classes who were on their way either home or out for the night.

Rupert was the other thing that made her buzz as though she'd eaten something exotic and spicy. He'd witnessed the entire meeting, and not only had he not taken her to task, he seemed to embrace the new path she'd just started down.

"Marlowe House is the other way," she said, glancing sideways at him and hoping he would reveal where they were going.

"So it is," he replied with a mischievous grin.

A shiver of excitement zipped through Cece, centering in her heart, which beat wildly as he picked up his pace. She knew Mayfair well and couldn't imagine where they were going. Unless....

"Campbell House," she said, trying not to be disappointed.

"Exactly," Rupert answered, still grinning from ear to ear.

So much for whisking her off to an exotic rendezvous or an illicit evening at a hotel. The house she'd grown up in didn't inspire her with feelings of anticipation, but it did bring with it a certain sense of comfort.

At least, not until Rupert swept her through the front door—which he opened himself as none of the servants seemed to be on hand to open it for them—then drew her into his arms the moment the door clicked shut.

He kissed her with a mad passion that had her wanting to giggle and sigh at the same time. His mouth was demanding against hers, but he also seemed to be worshiping her with his lips and tongue. He pressed the length of his torso against her, sliding one hand up her side to cradle her breast through the stiff fabric of her dress and corset. The sudden, breathless sensation had her feeling dizzy and aroused in a moment. She slipped her arms around his waist, burrowing under his jacket to come as close to touching him as possible, and gave herself to his kiss.

A moment later, he broke their kiss and gazed longingly into her eyes. "You truly were brilliant this evening," he said in a voice like a purring cat about to pounce. "Like a general rousing the troops."

Cece grinned, shifting her arms to his shoulders so that she could run her fingers through his hair. "And you always have been a good soldier."

His grin matched hers, and he tugged her close for another commanding kiss. The swiftly-shifting dynamic of power between them left her pulsing and overheated and willing to do just about anything to get out of her dress, no matter how shocking and ill-advised it would be.

Again, Rupert stopped ravishing her and leaned back, but this time his expression was soberer. "If this is not a good time, I understand. Your May Flowers have just undergone an upheaval, and if you think it inappropriate to—"

She silenced him by lifting to her toes and slanting her mouth over his in a way that brooked no further argument. She had never felt so energized, and even though the situation with the May Flowers was alarming, she had a mountain of excess energy and only one plan for how to burn it.

Rupert sighed deeply and tightened his arms around her. His tongue played with hers, teasing and tasting. Cece could just feel the press of his arousal against her belly through the damnable layers of her dress.

Rupert seemed to share her feelings about the impracticality of fashion. He slid his hand down her back only to encounter an enormous bustle. "Damn these ridiculous things," he said, humor and lust in his eyes as he leaned away from her. "How is a man supposed to enjoy the perfection of a woman's backside with these things?"

Cece sent him a mischievous smile. "We'll just have to remove it."

It was all the encouragement Rupert needed. Bustle and all, he swept her into his arms—which made Cece yelp in surprise—and charged for the stairs. A thrill shot through her at his strength and agility as he took the stairs two at a time, then veered off to the hall where his bedroom was. Just like the night of the ball, she knew exactly what would happen when he shut the door behind them, set her on her feet, and slanted his mouth over hers once more, but this time she welcomed him with the eagerness of experience instead of the determination of innocence.

She fumbled with the buttons of his jacket, and when she undid them, pushed the whole garment off his shoulders. Rupert managed to continue kissing her while shrugging and drawing his arms out of the sleeves, then tossing it aside. He had less success keeping up with kisses as he toed off his shoes and kicked them aside, then unfastened his trousers. Cece giggled at his enthusiasm in spite of the lust pouring through her.

"Clothes truly are a waste of time," she said breathlessly as she went to work on the buttons of his waistcoat.

"We should spend the rest of our lives naked so that

we can be ready to enjoy each other at a moment's notice."

Cece laughed, full of so much joy that it made her dizzy. When Rupert stepped away to shed his waistcoat and shrug out of his suspenders, she reached behind her and did her best to undo the fastenings of her skirt. It was maddening, slow work, though, and long before she could do more than tug a few ties, Rupert had discarded all of his clothes and stood before her, naked and aroused.

She caught her breath at the sight of him and her fingers refused to work at all. She would never grow tired of the lean lines of his torso, the strength in his chest and arms, and especially not of the bold thickness of his erection as it stood straight and tall with desire. Scintillating memories of the way he felt in her hands and the way he moved inside of her left her smoldering and eager to feel it all again.

"I repeat," he said, stalking boldly closer to her. "Clothing is a bloody nuisance."

He tugged her close, but rather than kissing her once more, he lifted her into his arms and carried her a few steps to the desk against one wall. He sat her on the edge of the desk, then reached for the hem of her skirts.

"What are you doing?" she laughed. "The fastenings are in the back and you have to—oh!"

He bunched the mountain of her skirts around her hips and managed to wedge himself between her legs as she spoke. Her words were cut off entirely as he pushed aside the split in her drawers and buried himself deep inside of her. The invasion was so sudden and so glorious that Cece was utterly carried away. Rupert gripped her hips under the pile of her skirts and thrust into her with surprising strength and purpose. The whole thing was so wild and mad and sudden and she was so primed and ready that she burst into throbbing orgasm before she could orient herself.

"Dear god, Rupert," she gasped, moaning as her body radiated with pleasure. She dug her fingers into his shoulders to keep herself from falling over as the surprising burst of pleasure climaxed and began to ebb.

She fully expected Rupert to come as well, but with what must have been a supreme effort of will, he pulled out, still as hard as marble, and balanced above her with his hands braced on the edge of the desk beside her. A look of utter focus pinched his face, as though he were willing his body into control.

At last, he stepped away from her, still erect, the head of his cock slick with moisture, but in command of himself. "What was I saying about clothes?" he asked, panting.

"That they need to go," Cece answered, shivery and panting herself.

She hopped off the desk, her legs wobbling, and turned her back to him. Working out how to undress her from the layers of restrictive clothing was exactly the thing to calm the intensity of his ardor to a smoldering fire ready to blaze again at any moment. As soon as her skirts fell to the floor, she stepped out of them and closer to the bed. When she wriggled out of her bodice, she dropped that to the ground and moved closer still to the bed. Rupert worked the hooks of her corset free and tossed that aside, then lifted her onto the bed itself, laying her back so he could tug off her stockings and drawers while she shimmied out of her chemise.

"You're the most beautiful creature alive," he said at last, drinking in the sight of her naked body splayed across his bed. He dragged his eyes up to meet hers. "All joking aside," he began in serious tones. "Marry me. As soon as possible. I'm ready to forget whatever silly feud that has been keeping us apart. I'll even admit I was wrong in every way and that I'll dedicate the rest of my life to supporting you and making you writhe with pleasure every night if you'll say you'll marry me."

Cece's heart expanded and throbbed in a way that far eclipsed the pleasure of any orgasm he could give her. She loved him. She always had and she always would.

"On one condition," she said, propping herself on her elbows and raising one eyebrow.

"Anything," he said. "Anything at all."

"Shave that ridiculous moustache."

Rupert grinned, then straightened with a look of mock solemnity, like a man condemned. It was a dizzying contrast to the full erection he sported. With a resigned intake of breath, he stepped away from the bed and marched to his washstand, reaching for his shaving things.

"I didn't mean right now," Cece laughed, rolling to

her side to watch him. "We're in the middle of something."

"No," he said solemnly, splashing his face and lathering his upper lip with shaving soap. "A promise is a promise. I must obey at once."

Cece shook her head and laughed, but there was something intriguing about watching him shave off the moustache she'd never liked. It was slow going, since he'd let it grow out so much, but his razor must have been sharp. Bit by bit, the hairy, offensive thing came away. At last, it was gone entirely. He splashed his face a few more times, then wiped it with the towel on the side of the stand. The face she had fallen in love with was back, and she loved it.

"Now," he said, swishing the razor in his washbowl then turning and pointing it at her. "It's your turn."

"I beg your pardon?" Cece sat up, blinking at him.

He picked up the washbasin and shaving soap while still holding the razor and walked over to the bed. "If I have to shave, you have to shave."

A fluttery anticipation prickled her skin as he moved to set the basin on the bedside table. "But I don't have a moustache."

"I know," he said, the light of mischief growing in his eyes. He sat on the edge of the bed and gestured for her to come closer. "That isn't what I'm planning to shave."

"But there isn't anything else for—"

She gasped, both as realization hit her and as he reached for her. He managed to pull her close and roll her to her back, spreading her legs wide, with a few, deft movements. Before she could gather her thoughts, he rubbed the shaving soap in a lather and began to spread it through the curls between her legs.

"You can't," she gasped, tingling and aching at the thought. "It isn't done. It's...it's wicked." She did nothing to close her legs and, in fact, let her knees fall farther to her sides as he covered every bit of her hair with lather and then some. She gasped and wriggled as he stroked her clitoris for good measure. "I'll look like a girl," she complained, or at least tried to. Her breath came in thready gasps that sounded more like mewling than protest as he reached for the razor.

"I'll make a deal with you," he said, his voice deep and sensual. "I'll keep mine shaved off if you do the same."

"How do I even know I'll like the feeling?" she panted.

Pure devilishness filled his eyes. "You will," he said with such certainty that Cece throbbed with desire.

He didn't wait for her to say more. With a deft touch, he set to work with his razor, removing all of the hair that marked her as a grown woman. It was awkward and arousing and slightly terrifying. She'd never dreamed of such a thing. The feel of a shaving razor applied to such tender flesh worried her, but Rupert had a steady hand. The level of concentration in his gaze as he worked made her want to writhe with need, but the fear of being cut kept her frozen. She held her breath as he whisked the razor across the most intimate parts of her, and only when he was completely finished did she let out a breath and relax.

"There," he said in triumph, swishing the razor in the basin, then setting it aside. He rubbed the last of the soap away from her bare pussy with the damp towel, then leaned back to assess his work. A slow, wicked grin spread across his face and fire lit his eyes. "I've never seen a prettier sight."

Cece scooted back toward the center of the bed, lifting to her elbows to peek down at herself. She was as bare as a babe. The whisper of cool air across her skin was undeniably erotic. She couldn't help but shift so that she could reach one hand down to feel what was so familiar and so unfamiliar.

"I stand corrected," Rupert said, his voice rough with lust. "*That's* the prettiest sight I've ever seen."

"This?" she asked, teasing him by teasing herself. It was shocking and dangerous for her to stroke herself with him watching her, but it also filled her with an undeniable sense of power. She could see full well the effect her self-pleasuring had on him. His eyes went dark with desire and his whole body tensed. His erection had never really gone away, but it seemed to stiffen and grow as he watched her.

"I told you that you would like it," he growled, shifting to surge toward her.

She tipped back as he kissed her. With her legs already spread, he fit easily against her. The heightened sensation of his flesh against hers, his hot thickness rubbing against her smooth cunny without entering her, was a revelation. She was too breathless and undone to kiss him back properly. All she wanted was to mate with him, to feel him throbbing inside of her as he strove for his release.

"I need to inspect my handiwork," he said at last, shifting to slide down the length of her body.

He paused along the way to tease her nipples into points with his tongue, but his objective was unmistakable. She gasped when he brushed his mouth over her shaved skin and couldn't even begin to catch her breath as he licked and teased her sensitive folds. The whole thing was amazing and intimate. The sensations were heightened in every way. Within moments, the swooping, tightening feeling of an orgasm about to crash over her began to gather. Sounds that she hadn't known she could make escaped from her, and Rupert groaned in answer.

It was his tongue that undid her in the end as he delved between her bare folds to tease her opening and circle around her clitoris. She arched toward him and cried out as her climax crashed over her. He sucked in a breath and shifted quickly over her, thrusting his thick cock into her and holding himself there for a moment as she squeezed around him.

As her throbbing began to subside, he moved within her, igniting her all over again. She cried out in time to his thrusts, which quickly went from slow and deep to demanding. She loved every moment of it, every mood his desire took on within the short space of time. She moved with him, working to give him as much pleasure as he could take and more while speeding toward another orgasm, hard on the heels of the last one.

She broke apart again with a sigh of triumph, and moments later, his whole body tensed as he spent himself inside of her. It was the most glorious feeling. The two of them were one being, one heart. She wrapped her arms and legs around him as they tumbled from the heights of passion into a much deeper pool of satiety and affection.

"I love you to distraction," she confessed as they lay tangled in each other, trying to catch their breath. "And there was never any doubt in my mind, not for one moment, that I would marry you."

"Thank you," he said, letting out a breath and relaxing into her. He embraced her as if his life and hers depended on it and as if nothing in the world made him happier. "I love you more than you could know."

She giggled, low and deep in her throat. "Good, because you'll have to love me that much when you tell my father why you need to marry me immediately."

Rupert tensed and muscled himself to stare down at her, eyes wide. "You're not with child already, are you?"

Cece shook her head. "Not that I know of."

"Then why do we have to marry immediately?" he asked.

She grinned from ear to ear. "Because nothing and no one will be able to keep me out of your bed on a nightly basis, now that we've made our no moustache pact. And I don't believe I have the power to hide just how well-loved I am when we're out in public together."

"Marriage it is, then," Rupert said, looking as though Christmas had come early.

He dipped down to kiss her. Cece opened herself to him in every way she could, digging her fingertips into his back as their bodies pressed together. He was hers to care for and protect as much as she was his. They might have teetered on the edge of uncertainty in a thousand ways, but together they could face anything.

EPILOGUE

As it turned out, the wedding had to wait slightly longer than either Cece or Rupert wanted to. They were more than ready to rush to the nearest church the morning after the May Flowers meeting, but it took several weeks for the most important guest of all to be in adequate health to attend.

"I only wish I'd been able to stand up with you," Fergus said with a lopsided smile from his wheelchair at the luncheon after the ceremony.

"You'll be on your feet again in no time, old chap," Rupert said, thumping his shoulder.

He instantly regretted the action. Fergus winced sharply through his smile, his mangled face going pale for a moment. Fergus was still swathed in bandages of all descriptions—from the patch of gauze hiding his damaged eye to the splints that held his broken arms still and the bulk of more splits keeping his shattered legs in place under the blanket draped over his lap. Rupert didn't know how his friend had pulled through the first few days or how he managed to keep his smile now. It was as painful for him to see Fergus in a state of near helplessness as it would have been if he'd sustained the injuries himself. But at least his friend was still alive.

"He most certainly will be on his feet soon," Lady Tavistock said, sweeping up to the side of Fergus's chair with a smile that was strained around the edges. "I demand a dance no later than midsummer's eve."

Fergus laughed, though even that seemed to bring him pain. "You might have to wait until Christmas, but I promise that dance will be yours, my lady."

"And there's much you can do to support Lady Tavistock and myself in the meantime," Cece said, returning to Rupert's side after chatting with some of her father's friends.

She looked positively radiant in her white wedding dress, her hair caught up in a crown of curls dressed with orange blossoms. Rupert noted that all of the May Flowers in attendance wore white orange blossoms as well in solidarity. But as far as he was concerned, his beautiful, formidable wife outshone every flower that God had ever invented. Her face shone with joy and her lips were a deep pink from the numerous kisses they'd stolen whenever they could throughout the day.

"I will do whatever you fine ladies need me to do,"

Fergus said, with far more bravado than a severely-wounded man in a wheelchair might have.

"We are hosting a fundraiser for the Irish Widows Society in two weeks," Cece told him, hugging Rupert's arm and glancing up at him with far more adoration than he thought he deserved. "And a week after that, we're staging a march in Hyde Park for better treatment of mothers and children in the workhouses."

"The May Flowers have decided not to hide their radical views any longer," Lady Tavistock said.

"Did somebody say radical views?" Bianca asked, striding over to join their group with an overexcited expression.

Rupert laughed. "Why am I not surprised to see you pop up like a spring daisy when radical views are being expressed?"

Bianca swatted his arm in a playful, sisterly way, but gave most of her attention to Lady Tavistock. "My darling *sister*, Cece, said you wanted to speak to me, Lady Tavistock?" She exchanged a giddy grin with Cece, the way the two of them had been doing for the last several days as their family bonds were strengthened.

"Indeed," Lady Tavistock said, suddenly taking on a more formal air. "Lady Bianca, I would like to formally invite you to become a member of The May Flowers."

Bianca burst into one of the widest smiles Rupert had ever seen from her, but she didn't look surprised. "Cece told me you might ask," she said in a rush. "And yes, of course. I would absolutely adore the chance to be a May

Flower." She clasped her hands in front of her. Rupert waited for her to continue clapping and to jump up and down the way she had as a girl when she'd been given a treat, but miraculously, she restrained herself.

"Perfect," Lady Tavistock said. She reached into the large corsage of orange blossoms pinned to her chest, plucked a few as though she'd intended to do so all along, took a long pin from her reticule, then stepped over to pin them to Bianca's bodice.

"This is such an honor," Bianca said, blinking rapidly to hold back tears.

Rupert gaped at her. "I don't think I've ever seen you cry."

"Nonsense," she said, sniffing. "I cry all the time. I'm rather high-strung, you know," she told Lady Tavistock with a laugh.

Rupert hoped Lady Tavistock knew what she was getting herself into, but the woman was all confidence when she said, "We need high spirits and enthusiasm. We need women who aren't afraid to speak their mind and who can face the enemy boldly."

"She can certainly do that."

Rupert turned to find Jack Craig approaching their group. He looked as distinguished as any of the aristocrats at the party, though his suit was of a simpler cut and he wore it with an air of casualness. Bianca beamed at him as though he were Prince Albert returned from the grave and shoved right past Rupert to stand by his side.

"Look, Jack," she said, standing before him with

shoulders squared and chest thrust out to show off her orange blossoms. At least, that was what Rupert hoped she was showing him.

"Lovely," Jack said with a rake's grin, definitely not staring at the flowers. "I bet they're as fragrant as spring and soft to the touch too."

He started to lean toward Bianca, but Rupert cleared his throat. Jack pulled back, acknowledging the warning in Rupert's eyes with far too cheeky a nod. When Bianca whirled to the side to stand next to him, he placed a hand possessively on her back in a gesture that was far too informal for the setting. Rupert's sense of impending disaster flared to life. The trouble was, he liked Jack immensely, and he owed the man an enormous debt.

"Looking alright, O'Shea," Jack said to Fergus with shocking informality. "You'll be chasing after the bugger with me in no time."

"Remember where you are," Cece whispered as a group of their parent's titled friends walked past.

Jack cleared his throat and stood straighter. He looked every inch the Scotland Yard Chief Inspector as he continued with, "I've done a little more digging, and I think I might have Denbigh cornered." He focused on a frowning Fergus. "Buster Jones might be on the verge of squealing, now that we have proof of his counterfeiting operation. He says he's got all sorts of information he'll offer in exchange for leniency."

"And will you give it to him?" Cece asked. "If he

helps you prove that Lord Denbigh did this to Lord O'Shea, would you actually let him go?"

Jack looked suddenly uncomfortable. "It's a tricky business, my lady. It all depends on whether the information he gives us is useful and if I have enough men at my disposal to track him once we let him go to nab him if he offends again."

"Policing is a delightful game of intrigue," Bianca said, swaying closer to his side and brushing her fingers through his hair as though straightening it.

Again, the feeling of impending dread filled Rupert. Bianca had all the sensuality of their mother, but she had none of the experience and very little of her cunning. He could only hope that his sister had inherited a modicum of their mother's good sense along with everything else.

The orchestra began to play and she practically gasped in excitement and clung to Jack's arm. "A waltz," she declared. "Jack, we simply must dance."

"Anything for you, my lady," Jack replied, looking and sounding as though he'd made a salacious suggestion instead of offering polite platitudes.

He turned to whisk Bianca out to the center of the ballroom, where several couples were preparing to dance. More than a few sets of eyes followed them, and the stodgier of the wedding guests murmured in horror at the pairing. Jack was far from an aristocrat, after all, and Bianca should never have stooped to set her sights so low.

"How do your parents feel about that pairing?" Lady

Tavistock asked, summing the whole thing up with the politest question possible.

"They'll never allow it," Cece answered with a regretful sigh. "Even though they both know how deeply in love Bianca is."

"Love?" Rupert tried not to scoff. "I'm not sure that's what I'd call it."

"It's love," Cece corrected him with absolute certainty. He glanced at her to find her smiling at him. "Believe me, I know what love is."

"And thanks to you, I know now as well." In spite of the crowd around them, he pulled her into his arms and kissed her lightly. He would have kissed her scandalously, but it seemed a shame to do so with poor Fergus looking on, unable to do the same to Lady Tavistock, which Rupert had a feeling he wanted to do. "Would you care to dance, my adorable wife?"

"Absolutely," Cece answered mischievously, glancing past his shoulder. "Is Reese available."

Rupert slapped her hand playfully, then raised it to his lips for a kiss. "Dance with your friend some other time. Right now, it's your husband who wants you."

She laughed and slid easily into his arms. "And I want you," she said. "I have a delicious feeling that I always will."

AUTHOR'S NOTE: IRISH HOME RULE WAS THE

number one political conundrum of the last decades of the nineteenth century. It consumed hours of debate. It polarized opinions. Spoiler alert: It split the Liberal Party right down the middle, leading to the entire party's eventual demise. Proponents of Home Rule would often filibuster Parliament to the point where no other business could be conducted until their cause was heard.

And what was the cause? After the disastrous 1870s, a time that was starkly reminiscent of the catastrophic famine of the 1840s in Ireland, and the pitiful response by the English government, the Irish had had enough. They wanted independence, and in the meantime, they wanted their own parliament and control of their own affairs. The home rule experiment had worked brilliantly in Canada, and the Irish wanted to duplicate it.

But the British fought tooth and nail against the idea. As you may have been able to tell from this story, part of the resistance was a deeply-held belief that if Parliament and the crown showed any sign of "weakness" by giving up control of their closest colony, every other part of the Empire would see and rebel. Loyalists genuinely believed that granting the Irish the right to rule themselves would be the first crack in the complete collapse of everything they held dear. The other major factor in refusing to allow the Irish any independence at all was racism, pure and simple. The Irish were viewed by many as inferior animals, incapable of rational thought of self-governance.

The debate raged for decades and wasn't truly settled until the Irish War of Independence, which ended in

1921. But as you will see in the rest of the May Flowers series, The Irish Question impacted almost every aspect of politics and life in the 1880s and beyond.

I HOPE YOU'VE ENJOYED RUPERT AND CECE'S STORY. Whew! They're together at last! But what kind of trouble will Bianca get into with Jack Craig? There's no way theirs will be a normal love story. In fact, it's impossible for the daughter of an earl and a man born in a brothel to marry at all. But Bianca isn't about to listen to that! Will she and Jack find a way to be together? And will that way spell ruin for both of them? Find out in *It's Only a Scandal if You're Caught*, available for pre-order now!

AND IF YOU'D LIKE TO KNOW MORE ABOUT THE twisted and complicated love story between Cece's father, Lord Malcolm Campbell, and Rupert's mother, Lady Katya, be sure to check out *April Seduction*, part of *The Silver Foxes of Westminster* series!

IF YOU ENJOYED THIS BOOK AND WOULD LIKE TO HEAR more from me, please sign up for my newsletter! When you sign up, you'll get a free, full-length novella, *A Passionate Deception*. Victorian identity theft has never been so exciting in this story of hope, tricks, and starting over. Part of my *West Meets East* series, *A Passionate*

Deception can be read as a stand-alone. Pick up your free copy today by signing up to receive my newsletter (which I only send out when I have a new release)!

Sign up here: http://eepurl.com/cbaVMH

Click here for a complete list of other works by Merry Farmer.

ABOUT THE AUTHOR

I hope you have enjoyed *A Lady's First Scandal*. If you'd like to be the first to learn about when new books in the series come out and more, please sign up for my newsletter here: http://eepurl.com/cbaVMH And remember, Read it, Review it, Share it! For a complete list of works by Merry Farmer with links, please visit http://wp.me/P5ttjb-14F.

Merry Farmer is an award-winning novelist who lives in suburban Philadelphia with her cats, Torpedo, her grumpy old man, and Justine, her hyperactive new baby. She has been writing since she was ten years old and realized one day that she didn't have to wait for the teacher to assign a creative writing project to write something. It was the best day of her life. She then went on to earn not one but two degrees in History so that she would always have something to write about. Her books have reached the Top 100 at Amazon, iBooks, and Barnes & Noble, and have been named finalists in the prestigious RONE and Rom Com Reader's Crown awards.

ACKNOWLEDGMENTS

I owe a huge debt of gratitude to my awesome beta-readers, Caroline Lee and Jolene Stewart, for their suggestions and advice. And double thanks to Julie Tague, for being a truly excellent editor and assistant!

Click here for a complete list of other works by Merry Farmer.

Made in the USA
Monee, IL
13 December 2021